Gorgon Curses

Medusa Memoirs Book 1

Laura Hysell

To my husband and daughters, for all the laughs and adventures, from sun-filled beaches to late-night talks. I love you all and couldn't do any of this without you.

To all my family and friends, I can't express how much your support of my writing journey means to me.

Contents

Night Defender

Tales of Medusa's curse still tell of her hideousness, her stare that turned a man to stone, and her death at the hands of Perseus. Often forgotten were her sisters, also cursed alongside her, suffering in silence. As Medusa died, another took her place. And so it continues, forever. Powerful and beautiful, seductive and deadly, they roam the land hidden amongst the humans. Always three, eternally cursed.

The sun had yet to burn off the early morning fog, but the temperature in the small coastal town had already reached the upper 60's. Today would be a good day. I smiled as I strolled down the bay front, taking in the scents of fish and salty sea air. People milled about, readying fishing vessels for what was bound to be a beautiful day. The dark glasses I wore tinted everything in shades of gray, and I longed to stop and take them off to truly enjoy the beautiful morning, but there were too many people around.

Sighing forlornly, I continued down past the fish market, wrinkling my nose at the overpowering aromas wafting from the building. Holding my breath, I hurried past the business and crossed the street, tapping my cane on the ground in front of me. My business sat nestled on a corner next to an art store and across from one of the many random coastal stores selling clothes, kites and other beach paraphernalia. The large sign for my store had been done in variegated shades of purples and blues, with the words *Night Defender* in yellow script.

"Good morning, Gia," said the woman unlocking the doors of the art store.

I turned toward the voice and smiled. "Good morning. Rachel, right?" I asked, even though I knew exactly who I was addressing. People were always surprised when I remembered them, and she was no different.

"That's right," she said, her voice rising in pitch. "First official day. Do you need help opening up?"

Spinning the keys on my wrist keyring, I easily inserted the correct one into the lock and opened the door. "No, I've got it. Thanks for the offer though," I added.

"Well, if you ever need anything, don't hesitate to ask. I'm just right next door, and we all help each other out around here," she said and I nodded, but the woman still stood there, staring at me.

Turning my back on her, I pushed the door open and stopped. The woman wanted to say more, I knew it, but she held her tongue. I turned toward her and put my warmest smile on my face. "Rachel, did you need something?" I asked as I brushed a strand of my dark green and black hair out of my face.

She pursed her lips and nodded, then realized she was speaking to a woman she thought was blind. "Can you really do what your sign says?" she asked, her bright blue eyes going to the advertisement below the business name.

"I don't advertise things I can't do, Rachel," I said pointedly, smoothing my dress nonchalantly. "What part, exactly, are you referring to?"

"Business protection," she murmured, her eyes shifting back to my face. "You know what happened to the previous business?"

"Yes, I heard before I bought the place," I replied. In fact, I'd gotten a great deal because of the incident. It was nothing new anymore. Vampires targeted anyone they felt was a threat, and a business advertising magical protection was high priority. The problem was most of these places didn't know what they were really selling. The average person still thought a ring of garlic above your door would ward off vampires. "Was your store damaged in the attack?"

She shook her head and said, "No, not really. I wasn't here when it happened, and the attack was pretty targeted. The fire department managed to contain things before it spread. That's part of the reason most of us close up at dark. We know we're losing business, but it's just not worth the danger."

"So you don't try to cater to vampires?" I asked.

"Definitely not!" she affirmed, shaking her hair so vigorously her brown hair slipped out of the neat bun on top of her head. She pushed the stray strands back behind her ear with shaking fingers. "I know there are some that do, but I just can't. No amount of money is worth it. What if they try to control me?"

I nodded in agreement. "You wish for protection against vampires so they can't enter your business?"

"How much?" she asked immediately.

"If you like, I will extend my vampire wards to protect your business as well. No undead creatures will be able to enter. In fact, they will have no desire to come near your store at all."

"How much?" she asked again.

"I take care of my neighbors," I said softly, turning back toward my door. "I'll stop by tonight and put up the wardings. Free of charge, Rachel."

"Thank you," she said thickly, her voice filled with emotion.

"Of course," I murmured as I walked into my store and shut the door behind me. I was surprised at the exchange, because most of the neighbors surrounding my business had avoided me like the plague. The day I had bought the building I had gone door to door introducing myself to everyone on the bay front. Most had treated me like a leper as soon as they heard what my business was, and had summarily dismissed me. The previous business had left a considerably bad taste in most peoples' mouths. The locals quickly assumed I was just like the last - a fake trying to make money off the superstitious and desperate. It was hard to change peoples minds, once they had a set idea. I didn't need them anyway.

As soon as I closed the door behind me, I pulled off the dark glasses. Pretending to be blind was something I had been doing for most of my life, and a long life it was. It didn't make it any easier though. I quickly set up shop, making sure everything was in order. The books were organized around the room, with the vampire books taking up prime real estate front and center. With the books, I had other standard anti-vampire gear, including stakes, crosses, and bottles of holy water. While vampire hunting was strictly taboo unless you had a license, self-defense items were commonplace and even encouraged.

I wandered around, straightening shelves that didn't need it and putting the last touches on the store. My heart pounded with excitement. Today was my grand opening of business. Over the years I had had many businesses, but this was the first one that felt truly a part of who I was at my core. I felt like a mother, cooing over her newborn baby. Doubt crept into mind, but I shook it off. It wasn't like I needed the money; I had a small fortune at my disposal, accumulated and wisely invested over the centuries. This was something I wanted to do.

The clock chimed softly in the corner, and I smiled to myself. I took one last look in the truth mirror I had propped up near the front door and ran my hands through my green-black hair. Bright emerald eyes looked back at me, set against my tanned skin. I had cast the spell on this mirror over a hundred years ago, using it to reveal lies and deceit. I had it in my home before, but this seemed a more appropriate place to determine if someone was truthful.

I stared at my reflection as the clock finished chiming. Anyone who saw me would see a young woman in her mid-twenties, since that's how old I'd been when I stopped aging. That's when my hair had turned from dark brown to this strange black and green color.

Thank goodness for modern hair trends. The last forty years had been infinitely easier to pass as an ordinary human when I didn't have to cover my hair as well as my eyes. Magic and hair dye only got a girl so far.

I turned away from the mirror and put the dark sunglasses back on before opening the blinds and flipping the sign from closed to open. Stepping to the front door, I turned the lock and opened the door, letting in a crisp breeze that swirled my white skirt around my knees. Two women stood outside the door, waiting, with opening-day coupons in hand. Smiling, I ushered them in. The women were human and ordinary, and headed straight to the vampire display. I moved with them, answering their questions as others entered the shop as well. Within the first hour, I had already made over $400, thanks to the fliers and coupons I had sent out.

Just before noon the delivery man arrived with several boxes stacked on his hand truck. I ushered him toward the storage room, where he neatly stacked the boxes of books and supplies I had ordered. He returned to his truck and came back with another man who helped him unload a large, heavy wooden crate, setting it just inside the store room. My skin tingled as I pressed a hand against the unfamiliar box, feeling the sensation of magic within. The shipment had come from New York, but it was not anything I had ordered.

As soon as the delivery men left, I warded the container and returned to the store. Throughout the remainder of the day, my mind returned to the mysterious crate. Periodically, I checked on it, ensuring my ward was properly in place. I needn't worry. After over 500 years, I knew what I was doing.

Most of my clientele was human, and primarily women looking for love potions. I could make them, but they never had the desired effect. Potions always wore off, and then all that remained was anger and hatred, and occasionally a homicide. I couldn't recall a single instance a love potion worked out for everyone involved. Spells, on the other hand, worked extremely well if you knew what you were doing, and I did know what I was doing. They only worked on humans, and could be permanent, but why would anyone want such a thing? After over a dozen girls asked for love spells, I hurriedly made a sign on my computer stating I would absolutely not make any potions or spells designed to attack another human, including love spells. It was rape, so far as I was concerned.

By the time the sun set, I had made over $5000 and felt an air of confidence. Most of the businesses, including Rachel's art store, closed the moment the sun set. I had no fear of vampires, or any creature, for that matter. The wards surrounding my business were almost as extensive as those around my home. Even though I had no fear of vampires, I didn't want them coming around, so I had set vampire deterrents up along with my other wards. During my younger days, I had spent time with a few vampire dens. The stench alone should have been enough of a discouragement, but I was power-hungry back in those days.

No breeze disturbed the tunnels, the musty smell of rot, decay, and old blood permeated the very walls. I followed the vampire into the heart of the den, sniffing my peppermint-scented satchel to damper the overwhelming odors. It didn't help. The vampire turned back to smile at me, flashing his fangs in excitement. Pierre was the first vampire I'd ever met, and he fascinated me as much as I fascinated him. He'd tried to attack me just three weeks prior. Instead of snapping his neck, as Theda had taught me, I decided to speak to him. He was a young and ambitious vampire, proud of the coven he had built. After only thirty years as one of the undead, he had created a coven of over fifty vampires. Most vampires, while ambitious in their own right, did not see past their next meal. Pierre was different, which is why I agreed to help him take over the city.

The den sprawled beneath the city of Naples, utilizing catacombs that had been deserted or walled off to the general public. As we reached the heart of the den, my opinion of Pierre diminished. Despite being young in vampire terms, he seemed to have forgotten the rudimentary aspects of humanity, such as cleanliness. The source of the stench soon became obvious. Pierre had told me of the humans he kept for sustenance, as a way to avoid detection. Men, women, and children had been corralled into a single cage no bigger than a carriage. Buckets of overflowing feces pooled along one wall. Within my first steps into the den I counted three maggot-infested bodies shoved along the edges, their bloated corpses indistinguishable as male or female.

Pierre caught my look, immediately ordering two vampires to take care of the dead. I nodded in approval as I stepped around the vampires. Most were mindless, drunk on blood and little more than animals. These would work well as fodder. The few older ones were more like Pierre, with a mild semblance of cognitive skills. I pointed them out, organizing and sorting the vampires around the room. Pierre jumped to obey my words, fawning over me. I outlined duties for each of them, including food and cleanliness for the humans they kept, and for themselves.

I returned to the den once a week, surveying their work and issuing new tasks. Over time, the vampires became more cognizant, and the stench in the den steadily decreased, although it never fully dissipated. With a modicum of leadership, they had regained a semblance of their humanity. Pierre grew bolder, attacking men in power as a way to impress me. And impress me he did. Men, at that time in my life, held nothing but pleasure of the flesh. Vampires, I decided, were no different.

At the culmination of my plan, we dispersed Pierre's vampires throughout the city, strategically attacking those in control. Pierre and I took a whole family out ourselves. While Pierre painted the walls of the elitist's home red with the blood of the wife, I took the life force of the man of the house, leaving nothing but a stone statue in his place. Satisfied, and full of power, Pierre and I had sex for the first time that night. He was the first man I could be myself around. Too bad he wasn't truly a man.

The tinkling of the bell over the door brought me back to the present. The man who walked in was tall and thin, human, and reeked of fear. I smiled warmly in his direction as he darted directly to the vampire prevention section. "Do you have books on vampires? Like real books?" he asked, even as he thumbed over the vampire books. Sweat dripped down his receding hairline. "Not that stupid made-up crap they sell on every street corner. The good stuff."

"What type of vampire book? Protection?" I asked, moving closer.

He nodded his head vigorously, his attention still on the books before him. "Anything to help me against them." He stopped and held up a cross hanging from a hook. "Do these work?"

"If you are a believer, yes, they work. I have charms and amulets as well, and I do provide magical warding, although vampires can't enter your home unless invited."

"They can't? That's a real thing?"

"Public areas and businesses need special warding, but private residences are protected against vampire entry."

"So at home I'm safe. What about here, or in my car?"

I shook my head. "You're safe here because I have wards in place. Your car is just a car. If you've gotten yourself tangled up with vampires, I suggest you seek help with the police."

He laughed, running his fingers across the books. "They can't help. What else do you know about vampires?"

I reached past him and pulled out a book, placing it in his hands. "Everything you need to know is in here."

"How much?" he asked, his eyes darting back to the cross swinging lightly on the display hook.

"The book is $24.95. I'll throw in the cross for free, but remember, it only works if you believe."

"If I believe," he murmured, snatching the cross and walking toward the register as he slipped the chain over his neck. He handed me cash for the book and immediately began flipping through the pages. "Thanks," he replied as he turned toward the door.

"Wait," I said, reaching under the counter and pulling out a small jar. I stepped toward him and opened the container, pulling on magic through the earth. The faint scent of mint wafted toward me as I dipped a finger into the jar and drew a series of lines across the man's forehead. Magic coursed through me and into the man, settling across him as I muttered the spell of protection. "This won't last long, but it should protect you for a few hours. Long enough to get home."

"Thank you," he said, reaching out to grasp my hand.

"Be safe," I replied as he hurried out of the store and ran to a car parked across the street.

Humans were right to fear vampires. They were evil creatures, with no sense of right and wrong. Life before humans knew about vampires and other supernatural creatures had been relatively easy. While many supernaturals enjoyed the freedom of being themselves now, most of us who had been around for centuries missed the old days. Even many of the vampires longed for the old days, when they weren't arbitrarily hunted. They were nothing more than shadows in the night. I glanced at the clock, thankful to close the store up after such a long day. Most people assumed I was a witch, since I could do magic, and I didn't dissuade them of that idea for the most part. If they knew what I truly was, I'd be hunted to the ends of the earth. Not that they could do anything to me. Death didn't come easy to the Gorgons.

TRUE FORM

AS SOON AS I locked the front door and pulled the blinds, I hurried back to my storage room. The strange box stood in the corner under my wardings. I hesitated, wanting to open it, but moved past it to my cabinet of pre-made potions. Some potions were more stable than others, lasting weeks or even years. Others wouldn't last longer than an hour. My vampire ward was expensive to make, but thankfully it only took a small amount to enact. I took the bottle of gray liquid, along with my chalk, and made my way outside to Rachel's business.

The boundaries of my warding could legally only extended to the edge of my property, but the buffer I enacted helped deter vampires for half a mile. It was unnoticeable to most witches, not that the police force had gotten so far as to hiring many. Prejudice being what it was, witches had, for the most part, decided to stay hidden. Real magic scared people almost as much as vampires did. Still, there were covens in most cities, if you knew where to look. The FBI had even hired witches for their specialty task force, but local police stations usually limited their supernatural hires to werewolves. How they had gotten put on such a pedestal, one could only guess. Werewolves could be just as violent and unpredictable as vampires, but they were living and breathing, and followed orders well.

Rachel stepped outside as soon as she saw me, her eyes darting around worriedly. "Gia, over here," she said.

I turned toward her, letting my ever-present cane click along noisily in front of me. "You didn't need to wait," I said softly.

"You're helping me out! I couldn't just let you take all this risk without me being here to at least watch your back." She bit her tongue, her eyes darting to my cane and then my glasses guiltily. "I mean, it's the least I can do."

"It's fine," I replied, smiling. "In fact, I could use your help. Can you take me to the corners of your property line? I was just going to do the corners of the building, but the edge of your property would be even better."

"Oh, of course," Rachel said, reaching out to take my elbow. "This way."

I let Rachel lead me to the first corner of her property, which butted up next to mine. Kneeling on the sidewalk, I marked a series of lines with the chalk, followed by three drops of the potion, before moving to the next corner. I repeated the process around the property, pulling on magic seated deep within the earth. The marks with the chalk linked the spell, creating a boundary, while the drops sealed the magic. Anything could be used to create the marks, but chalk made for easy cleanup. The ward would last forever, as long as there was no outside magical interference. After placing the three drops on the last corner, I pulled Rachel back and finished the spell. A shiver ran through my body at the passing of the magic, and I smiled at my handiwork. The faint shimmer surrounding the building was testament to my spell taking hold. The magical energy would fade over the next few days, leaving a faint glow only the most talented of witches could sense. The magical residue surrounding a newly enacted spell always left a calling card, and this, though simple to enact, was powerful magic. Anyone with latent magical talents would be able to sense the magic, and anyone practiced with the arts would be able to follow the trail directly back to me. I'd never worried about that sort of thing before. Witches tended to avoid other witches not of their own coven. Now, with laws regarding the regulation of magic, I had to be careful. Most spells, I took the extra time to seal so they couldn't be easily tracked. This one I wanted tracked. After all, I was advertising magical protection. I'd better be able to prove what I could do for anyone looking for proof.

I turned away from Rachel with a loud sigh, as though the magic had greatly cost me. A witch doing such a spell would need to sleep for a week after something that powerful. I was just hungry. "It's done," I said, keeping my voice weak.

"Oh, thank you, Gia," Rachel said, clasping me in a brief hug. "You have no idea what this means to me. May I tell others?"

I smiled and nodded, "Yes, of course, but I need at least a week between casting such wardings as this. They are extremely taxing, and expensive." Rachel's eyes widened and her mouth opened in surprise. I hurriedly patted her arm as I continued back to my store. "Luckily, I still had remaining supplies from warding my own business," I added, shaking the almost empty bottle. "If anyone else wants warding, please send them my way. I'll just need the time and funds to replenish my stock."

"Oh, well, thank you again," Rachel said, continuing to hold my elbow as I walked back to my store. "If you ever need anything, please don't hesitate to ask. I really appreciate this."

We parted at the door and I immediately locked up and hurried to the storage room. The large box towered above me, standing close to 6' high and 3' across. Leaving the wardings in place, I grabbed a hammer and used it to pull the edges of the wooden crate apart, repeating the movement down the face of the crate until I was able to pull off one side. As soon as I saw what it was, I dropped the wards and pulled off the rest of the container.

The stone statue was of a handsome man, preserved for eternity inside his stone casing. I reached out and touched what had once been brown hair, cut in an old style just above the shoulders. His eyes, which had been a deep chocolate, stared at nothing. I moved my hand across his face, feeling the small imperfections in the stone that gave the indication of stubble across his chin. His clothes were simple, but I knew the shirt he wore had been a rich blue with yellow around the trim. His trousers were plain, in the fashion of the day, as were the sandles on his feet. Tears filled my eyes as emotions I had long suppressed pushed to the surface. There was no note inside the box, but I knew exactly who had sent me the statue. It was the same woman who had turned him to stone over five centuries ago. This was a message. She knew where I was.

I sat down, staring up at the man I had loved all those years ago. The magic I had sensed came from within the statue, and I felt an overwhelming hatred for my old mentor spring up. Theda had always had a way with theatrics, but this was going too far. There were two ways for a Gorgon to turn someone to stone. The first, the fast way, was to simply kill them. Their entire body turns to stone as their life force is quickly drained and absorbed. It is a powerful rush of magic, and Theda's preferred format. There is nothing left of the person after that, except a pile of dust. The second way is to drain them slowly. The person still turns to stone, but only on the outside. Their life force is held magically in check, draining slowly over the years into the Gorgon who turned them. Some people die within days, their life force jumping into the Gorgon in a great blast. Others last months or years, slowly trickling away. Their final death is always felt as a blast of energy.

The second way had become my preferred method of feeding. Too long without absorbing someone's life force had a detrimental effect on me. I'd tried it once before. I shivered, suppressing that memory. Theda, on the other hand, preferred to kill outright. She loved the rush, and the power she gained, and only used the slow way when she wanted to make a point. The downside of killing immediately was that she needed to kill more frequently. My vivid green eyes turned once more to the statue. I rarely heard of a person's life force lasting longer than 80 years, but here he was, over 500 years later. How was it possible? I stood up and ran my hands across the statue, feeling the magic residing within. Perhaps it was a trick. Still, I couldn't risk it. Placing an elaborate protection spell around the statue, I ensured it wouldn't break by ordinary means. It was time to do some research.

After securing my deposit money, I locked up the store and walked back down the bay front, sad I had missed the beautiful day outside. Perhaps I could hire someone to help in the shop, if my days continued as profitably as they had today. I couldn't hire just anyone though. I didn't really need to work, but life was boring without some sort of human interaction, and eventually money would run out, especially when I had to liquidize holdings every few decades.

The walk back to my coastal house took a little under fifteen minutes, which was partly why I had bought it. Elevated and overlooking a breathtaking view of the ocean, the house had two floors visible and a hidden underground cellar. The previous owner had used it for wine, and I carried on the tradition, with a few modifications. I stepped away from the bay front, which was quiet at this hour, and turned onto the winding road that would lead to my home. Keeping up appearances, I stepped carefully, using my cane. The appearance of a blind woman was both good and bad. I was frequently helped out by strangers carrying my bags, holding doors for me, giving me discounts, and more. The major disadvantage was that I was frequently targeted by the seedy side of society. Tonight, I suspected, was no different.

The man had been following me since shortly after I locked up the shop. Unable to gain entry into the store, thanks to a large number of magical wards, I suspected he planned to rob me outright instead. Or, perhaps, force me to give him access to my store. Either way, it was a bad idea for him. I continued onward as he closed in on me, matching his footsteps to my own. I faltered, stumbling over nothing, and he stopped his steps as well. Using the cane with more emphasis than needed, I slowed my steps, wanting to deal with the man on my own terms. He was apparently tired of waiting though.

His footsteps increased, and I turned around to face him head on. The man was large, dressed in all black, barreling toward me. He skidded to a halt when I stopped before him. "Give me all your money," he said as he pulled out a gun.

"I have no money," I replied, holding my arms out to my sides to show I carried nothing with me except my cane. My dress, like most women's clothing, didn't even have pockets.

"You own that shop, and you live in that big gated house up on the hill. I know you have money, bitch."

I raised my eyebrows, but I doubted he could see it behind my overly large dark glasses. "You've been watching me?"

"Money, bitch."

"Don't call me that."

"Give me your money, *bitch.*"

I sighed and lowered the cane. "As you can see, I carry nothing with me."

"Your keys," he said, pointing to the keys I kept on my wrist.

"They will do you no good," I retorted.

"Where do you keep your money? House or store, bitch? Let's go now." He cocked the gun for dramatic effect. "You can hear well enough, bitch. That's a gun, and it's loaded and ready. I will kill you."

"This way," I said, walking back toward my house.

"No funny business," the man muttered as he pressed the gun into my back.

I sighed loudly and slowed my steps, clicking the cane against the ground. "You are trying to rob a blind woman. What do you think is going to happen?"

"You think you're gonna get sympathy from me? Blind or not, I know what you are. A witch killed my brother."

"Oh, such a sad tale. A so-called witch killed your brother and now you seek anyone of the same ilk, searching for vengeance. I think I may vomit."

The cold metal of the gun hit me in the head. "You sure are a cold cunt. Maybe after I rob you, I'll warm that cold pussy of yours right up. How would you like that?"

The gate to my driveway came into view, softly lit by lights, but right now I wanted darkness. I stepped off the path and snapped my fingers, eliminating the light and submerging us both in darkness as I hurried into the shelter of the surrounding trees. The man followed me, his gun held in front of him. I snapped my fingers again, and the gun slipped from his grasp. He dropped to his knees, fumbling around in the grass.

Using my cane, I hit the gun, pulling it toward me. He followed on his hands and knees, mumbling curses at me. "You really don't want to do that," I said softly as I hit the gun again, sending it cascading behind me. The man sneered at me and stood up, anger making his face look older although I guessed he was in his early thirties. "You've had a hard life, and I'm sure your grief is great, but it does not give you the right to attack me or threaten me."

"I'm gonna fucking make you pay, bitch. You will squeal like a pig when I fuck you."

"As a thief, I might have let you live. Rapists, though, have no place in this world."

"Fuck you."

I held no hatred toward this man as I removed my glasses. Hunting was not on my agenda, and I rarely killed for pleasure anymore, but this man had pushed all my buttons. Anger I had long held in check bubbled to the surface and I relished in the sensation. "I will give you one last chance to flee. You will not get another warning. You will simply cease to exist."

He laughed, but I heard the hesitation in it. "What are you gonna do, bitch? You think you're gonna cast a spell on me? I'm protected."

I cocked my head, looking at the silver teardrop charm around his neck. Had I been a very new witch, that charm might have kept him safe. Since I was neither a witch nor inexperienced, it did nothing to me. "You are not fleeing, human. You really should," I added, holding myself in check as I stared at his chest.

His feet moved toward me and I reacted, facing him straight on. He froze as my eyes captured his. For a moment, he saw me in all my glory. My eyes, a vibrant green no mortal lived to speak of, glowed with power. Scales, unseen until now, etched across my skin in green and black rippling waves. My hair swirled and parted, making way for writhing snakes that matched the emerald of my eyes and the black of my heart. For one brief moment, I gloried in the power. The would-be thief and rapist was held in rapture of my magic, his eyes seeing me as I truly was. Fear replaced the anger and excitement he had held before. It was short-lived though. I pulled on the magic, letting his life force drain from his body, killing him quickly and without remorse. Energy coursed through me, energizing me, strengthening me, even as it severed all ties this man had to his body. Within seconds, all that remained was a hardened stone replica. Pulling further, I drained him completely until even the statue was gone, leaving nothing but a pile of dust, and consequently destroying all evidence. I put my glasses on and walked back to my house, flicking the lights on as I neared the gate. The gate slid open with a flick of my wrist and a small burst of power. Recharged and refreshed, I slammed the gate closed behind me and headed straight for the cellar. A glass of wine and a good book were just the way to finish out this night.

New Friends

FOUR WEEKS OF RESEARCH had yielded no new info regarding the statue that had been mailed to my shop, not that I had expected to learn anything new since I had already read all the books in my collection several times over. I even attempted to search on the Internet, but technology was not my strong suit. I ended up ordering several thousand dollars worth of books, spanning several centuries dealing with everything from Greek mythology to witchcraft to modern tales of the Fae. I didn't hold out hope of learning anything new, but my library could always use expansion.

Business had been steady, increasing on the weekends, and I finally put up a help wanted sign in my window. Early morning I made my way into the shop to go through the stack of applications I had collected. I had sorted them as they'd been turned in, putting them into two piles: human and other. The human pile was large, filled with young teenage girls wanting to dabble in magic. These, I ignored. The second, much smaller pile held those who were not entirely human, or who held some sort of magical affinity.

Margaret Thurber, age 31, housewife looking for part-time work was at the top of the pile. She was a short woman with curly brown hair and a slight talent for magic. While she wasn't a full-fledged witch, she definitely held that spark of magic waiting to be kindled. Her application stated she had dabbled in small spells and was well-versed in vampire lore. It didn't say why she was so versed in vampire lore though, and that bothered me. Still, she was worth an interview.

The second applicant was a skinny young warlock named Fred. He was 22 years old and had an aptitude for fire. That could be dangerous in a store full of expensive books. He was apprenticed to the local warlock, William Dervish, but needed a job. That Dervish had suggested he apply here put him on the interview list, for pure curiosity, if nothing else. I had yet to meet the known warlock, and he was probably sending Fred here to feel me out, but Fred was still worth a closer look. Not being a part of any coven, since I wasn't really a witch, tended to make me stand out.

The third applicant in my pile was Jess. She was a young and pretty single mom, who knew her way around a shop. She had seemed surprised when I told her she had an affinity for magic, saying she'd never so much as dabbled in anything supernatural. She was just looking for a job and stumbled in my door. She bought five books the first time in the store, and five more a week later, already having devoured the first five. These were large, detailed books, too. Her love of books along with her magical affinity, put her as my last interview candidate.

The fourth and final applicant, Ian Smith, I stared at for several minutes before shuffling into the no-interview pile. The man was a warlock of decent strength, but he had been arrogant and downright condescending to me. While he was probably the most able candidate, I had no room in my life for egotistical men.

I filed the rest of the applications in my cabinet and called the three candidates in for interviews later that day. I wanted to see them work, but I scheduled them during the slower intervals of the day when I had time to chat with them as well. Just before noon, Jessica arrived. She wore a dress similar to my own, loose and flowing, matched with sandals. Her thick, brown hair was pulled partially back with a braid. She greeted customers with enthusiasm, eagerly leading them around the store and recommending books to them. The customers liked her immediately, but the smell of ozone surrounding her put me on edge. At the end of the half hour, I seated her with her back to my truth mirror.

"Jess, what did you think about working here?"

"Oh, this is just what I was looking for. I love helping people and this gets me access to so much knowledge. I mean, you know so much, I feel like it's a great learning experience."

Hmm, I hadn't said much in the time she had been here, letting her chat with customers and only correcting inaccurate information. "What are your thoughts on magic? You said you don't have any experience?"

She shook her head and I watched the mirror behind her as she replied. "I think it's fascinating, but I've never cast a spell or done a potion, or whatever it is real witches do. Sometimes, I get that feeling, you know, when your hair stands on end. Someone told me that's when you're feeling magic. Like, I'm a sensitive, or something."

The truth mirror glowed to my eyes as she spoke, highlighting lie after lie. Not a word she said was true, except the part about her being sensitive, or something. She was definitely something. "So, Jess, you're telling me you've never done magic?" I asked directly.

Her eyes widened as my face turned toward her. "Uh, no, never."

The mirror glowed again, and I sighed loudly. "Why do you smell like ozone then? That is a telltale sign of magic, and my senses are greatly heightened."

She blushed and darted her eyes around the room. Only one other customer was present, a man who very carefully averted his eyes. Magic lingered strongly around him, but I had been too busy with Jess to notice him. Now, I paid him much more attention. "I'm sorry, I just really want this job. I thought you'd be mad if you knew I was a witch."

"You think I want an ordinary human working in my store?" I asked, shaking my head. "I don't know what your plan is, but it doesn't matter. I don't take in liars, Jess. Good day."

She stood, casting a glance at the man before turning and walking away. I stood and walked toward the man, sizing him up. He was tall and handsome, with broad shoulders. The suit he wore fit him well, accentuating his physique. He appeared to be in his early thirties and the power he harnessed was held tightly in check, disguised and muted. To an average witch, his muted power would show up as someone who merely dabbled, but I was no witch, and I certainly wasn't average.

"May I help you?" I asked, plastering my customer service smile on my face.

He smiled back, his eyes taking in my appearance. He lingered a touch long on my breasts before his eyes made their way back up to my face. His magic flickered, as though he were tasting the power in the air. I added a few years to his age as I took in the dark hair and a goatee touched with silver. He would look right at home with a brandy in one hand, a cigar in the other, and piles of money at his feet. His steel gray eyes were sharp, taking in every detail of the room, and me. "You must be the owner, Gia," he said smoothly. "My name is William."

I held my hand out, letting him take mine and shaking it nicely. His grip was strong, but there was no trickle of power, magical or otherwise, from him. It was simply a nice, manly handshake. He dropped my hand and stood back, hands clasped behind his back. "Just William?" I asked, putting an emphasis on his name.

He grinned and added, "William Dervish."

"Of course," I replied. "How many of my applicants did you send here, Mr. Dervish?"

He laughed, real mirth coming through his businessman facade. "Just five, although you only called two for interviews."

"Jess and Fred."

He nodded and said, "Forgive me, but I wanted to get a feel for you before meeting you officially."

"Hmm, who else did you send?"

"Ian, Meagan, and Tom. Meagan and Tom had no magical ability, but they are both very charismatic, and very good looking. I was surprised you didn't invite Ian back, actually. He was at the top of my list."

"Ian was the top of your list? It's obvious we have different ideas of top candidates. He was at the bottom of my list."

"I figured you'd be looking for either some eye candy or someone powerful. Ian was the perfect mix. What exactly are you looking for?"

"Eye candy? What on earth would I have need of eye candy for?" I asked, laughing loudly and walking back toward the front door. He wasn't wrong, though. Ian was a tall, handsome man.

"Well, you're a beautiful, vibrant woman, and not actually blind, so why not?" I stopped walking and turned back toward him, arms crossed. "Is there a reason you pretend to be blind?"

"I don't pretend anything."

"You simply let people believe what they will, and carry that cane around for fun?"

I shrugged and said, "I have an extremely rare eye condition where any bit of light, real or artificial, is blinding to me. My eyesight is compromised, but no, I am not completely blind. Now, I am being very forthcoming. I suggest you do the same."

"My apologies," William said, nodding his head. "I wanted to meet you, and test your meddle. You aren't the first person to sell potions, spells, and various defenses against vampires. People pray on the weak and the scared."

I laughed and peered outside, wondering why I had no customers coming into peak hours of the day. Jess stood outside, along with Fred and Ian. Irritation stirred as I moved to my desk and sat down, crossing my legs casually and letting the dress slide up ever so slightly. "You're cramping my business, Dervish, and I don't believe you're a bleeding heart."

"No," he laughed, shaking his head. "I'm definitely not that. I'm a businessman though, and I protect my own interests."

"I wasn't under the impression we had any business conflicts," I replied. My knowledge of William Dervish was limited to the fact that he was a warlock of considerable power and ran the only coven in the area. I mentally added research of this man to my to-do list.

"No, no business conflicts. Not yet."

I sat up and pointed out the front door. "You are obviously in a different line of work than I am, Dervish. This store is exactly what it looks like. I'm not looking for trouble. I just want to live my life, quietly, and maybe help a few people along the way. Isn't that what most people want?"

"Help people along the way? Now you sound like the bleeding heart, and I don't buy it." He stepped forward and leaned across the desk, pressing his hands into the wood. "You have a darkness surrounding you, deeper and darker than any human I've ever met. Your aura is as dark as a vampire, miss Gia, and I don't trust you."

"You can sense auras?" I asked, surprised. It was a skill limited to very few, and he was only the third person I'd met who could do it. It made me wonder what else he was capable of. "You don't need to trust me, Dervish, you just need to stay out of my business."

"Is that a threat?" he asked, his eyes narrowing and the hint of ozone wafting from him. My skin tingled as he began to slowly pull magic into him, and it pissed me off.

Instead of standing, I leaned back in my chair and cocked my head to one side as I looked at him. "You can sense the blackness surrounding me. Have you asked yourself what it took for me to get this way? I know more than you could ever dream. I have done things you can't even fathom. Yet, you want to argue with me? Fight me? Ruin my business? Threaten me? I'm unsure here. What exactly do you want?"

"Point taken," William said, stepping back, yet still not answering my questions or releasing his hold on magic. "My apologies."

"Get out and take your men with you, Dervish."

He nodded and moved toward the door, straightening his expensive suit as he walked. "Fred really would be an asset here," he said suddenly, surprising me.

"I thought the same thing when I met him. Too bad he won't get an interview now because of you."

He shrugged, casting a glance out the door before looking back at me. "I guess I can't blame you there. We have an understanding?"

"You stay out of my business and I stay out of yours," I stated, still clueless as to what his business actually was, other than as an annoying warlock. William nodded once and stepped out of my store. I let out a breath and relaxed as my shop returned to normal. I hadn't heard much about William Dervish before, but he certainly had my curiosity piqued now. He could be a problem. As my next customers entered the store, I stood and greeted them, pushing thoughts of the strange warlock from my mind.

An hour later, Margaret arrived for her interview. She wasn't exactly what I was looking for, and I found myself regretting the interactions I had with William Dervish. Fred probably would have been the perfect employee. It was probably for the best. Margaret did indeed know quite a bit about vampire lore, but her magic knowledge was utterly lacking. She could be taught though, and really I just needed someone to help run the store. Someone I trusted. As the store emptied, I pulled Margaret to the side to ask her questions.

She was dressed simply in tan slacks and a crisp blouse. Her chestnut hair was pulled up in a ponytail, making her look closer to 21 than 31. She smiled widely, showing straight teeth, while she fidgeted with the edge of her shirt.

"Margaret, what did you think of your trial run?" I asked.

"I haven't had that much fun in years," she replied, leaning forward. "And it's Maggie, please."

"Well, that's good to hear, Maggie. You certainly know quite a bit about vampires. May I ask how you became so versed?" I asked, jumping right to the heart of the matter. It was my main reservation with hiring her.

"I dated one," she said softly, a flush marring her cheeks. "Well, I don't know if that's the right word for it. We were together for a while and he started telling me all about vampires. I met a couple others, but they weren't like him. He was normal, I guess." She shrugged her thin shoulders while the truth mirror stayed blank. "Well, as normal as any vampire can be."

"How long were you together?"

She shrugged again and said, "About six months. I was young and stupid, fascinated by the danger he exuded. I guess I have a type.""What do you mean by that?"

"Oh, uh, my husband is a werewolf."

"And he's okay with you coming to work here?" I asked. Werewolves were notoriously territorial and protective.

"Well, he's a werewolf and I'm human. He won't turn me, not that I really want to be furry once a month, but we can't have kids. He doesn't like me working, says I don't need it, but after five years as a housewife, I just can't do it anymore. I told him he can either let me get a job of my choosing or he can kiss this marriage goodbye. So, here I am. I don't need a full-time job or anything, but I need something to get me out of the house. I'm not worried about working here, either. One of his pack members owns the bar at the end of the bay front. If we have any trouble, they'll come running."

I stared at her, rethinking my initial reaction to hire her. She was a hard worker and friendly, but I avoided entanglements with certain supernaturals. Werewolves were close to the top of my list to avoid. They banded together and if you wronged one, you wronged the entire pack. While I could take on an entire pack, I didn't want to. Werewolves weren't inherently evil, like vampires, but they could be violent. If I didn't hire Maggie, I might have just a few werewolves mad at me, but it would be a minor thing. If I hired her and it didn't work out, I could potentially have an entire pack of werewolves at my door. That wasn't something I wanted.

"You're worried about my husband," she said softly, breaking the silence.

I had been quiet too long, lost in thought, and she caught me off guard. "Maggie, I've known a few werewolves."

"I'd tell you he's not overly protective, but that'd be a lie. Please, I really want this job. How about a trial run? If it doesn't work out after two weeks, I walk away. No guarantees, no repercussions. Please, just give me a chance." She sat forward in her seat, wringing her hands. My magical mirror had stayed quiet through her entire interview, which was a plus after the day I'd had so far.

"If you weren't married to a werewolf, I would have hired you on the spot," I said. The smile left her face and I leaned back, taking a deep breath. "That shouldn't change my decision. When can you start?"

"Really? Oh, you won't regret this. Thank you! I can start right now. Anytime."

"Right now?" I asked, standing up and stretching. "I'll need to show you the register first."

"I've worked one before," she said, jumping up and hurrying over to the till. "It's been a while, but it was similar to this."

I gave her the basics of the till, which she caught on to faster than I had. After an hour, I felt comfortable and left Maggie to walk next door and check in with Rachel. She had called the night before, asking me to stop by sometime today. The sun would be setting soon, and I didn't want to leave Maggie alone for long, even if she was married to a werewolf. Perhaps even more so because she was married to a werewolf. My shop was warded strongly, but that didn't mean it was free of all danger.

Rachel was starting to close down her art store when I stepped inside. She smiled when I walked in and hurried over to me, grasping my elbow and leading me around the expensive vases just inside the door. "I'm so glad you stopped by. I had the strangest painting arrive the other day and I wanted to talk to you about it."

"A painting?" I asked as Rachel left my side and hurried to the back of her store. She came back a minute later with a large painting covered in brown paper.

"Yes, I didn't order it. I figured it was shipped here by mistake. I think it was meant for you," she added, setting the painting carefully down on a table.

"Why would you think that?"

She pulled the paper off the painting, glancing from it to me and back again. "Because it's a painting of you," she said. "Or, perhaps a relative. Although... that's weird."

"What is it?" I asked, moving closer.

"This painting is old. I know art, Gia, and this painting looks hundreds of years old. I suppose it could be a very good fake, but, I don't think so. It's just... this doesn't make sense."

"What do you see?" I asked, stepping up beside Rachel and casting a glance at the painting. Rachel thought I was blind, and I needed her to continue thinking that, but I couldn't help looking at the painting. It was indeed a painting of me, with my hair up and powdered in the latest fashion of the time. The artist had even picked up the subtle greens and blacks that peeked past the blue and white powder that frequented hair in that day. In the painting my head was bowed, as though I were looking at my hands. My hands held a large gold cross, covered in blood.

"It looks like you," Rachel was saying, her words barely above a whisper. "The woman's head is turned down so it's hard to really see her face. She's holding a cross on a chain in her hands, but there's blood everywhere. Even her dress is covered in blood. I've had a few days to look at it, and if I had to guess, I'd say this was painted in the 1700s. France, most likely, based on the hair and clothing. These things can be recreated, but everything I see looks real. Even the frame is old." She flipped the painting over, running her hand across the back. "There's a little water damage visible here on the back, and if you pull the frame away, you can tell the frame protected that area partially. I'm an art dealer, not an appraiser, but I've handled enough to know what I'm seeing. This is unlike anything I've ever seen before."

"What do you think?"

"I think... I'm not sure. I think someone sent this here for a reason."

I nodded, thinking the same thing as I held out my hand. "I think you're right."

"Let me just close up. I'll carry it for you."

I let Rachel close up and carry the painting for me, setting it behind the front counter. Later, I'd move it into the store room along with the stone statue. That the painting had been sent here was no mistake. Theda was playing games with me, and I didn't like it. I closed up shop early, sending Maggie home while I moved the painting into the store room and placed extra wards around the room. So much for a normal day at work.

Werewolves

HAVING AN EMPLOYEE MEANT someone else having access to my store room. The morning after the painting arrived, I hired a moving company to take both the painting and statue back to my home. I placed them in the hidden back room I had forged behind the cellar where they would be safe with my other statues. I only hoped no more surprises would arrive. So far, they were unsettling to say the least.

The next morning, Maggie met me at the shop for opening. A man- werewolf, actually- stood beside her, whom I could only assume was her husband. He stood protectively next to her, dressed impeccably in a tailored suit. The tie around his neck was loosened and he held his hands at his sides, as though ready for a fight. I suppressed the grin that tried to creep onto my face as I thought of facing the werewolf head to head. He was handsome, with dark brown hair and deep-set golden wolf eyes. He exuded confidence, cockiness, actually.

"Gia, this is my husband, Mike," Maggie said. She stepped forward and took my elbow, leading me to her husband.

I held my hand out and stared straight ahead, which put my line of sight somewhere near his right shoulder. He took my hand, shaking it politely before quickly letting go. "Nice to meet you,

Gia. My wife speaks very highly of you," he said, leaning back on his heels. "She said you were blind."

Damn werewolves. I cocked my head to the side and turned toward him. "What do you do, Mike?" I asked.

"Real estate," he replied, but at the frown on Maggie's face, I knew he was lying. "So, why do you pretend to be blind? I can see your eyes behind those glasses."

"Don't look too carefully, wolf," I snapped. Maggie's frown deepened as she looked from her husband to me. "Not fully blind, no, but I do have an eye condition slowly making me go blind. My eyes are extremely light-sensitive and between my already failing eyesight and the need for extremely dark sunglasses to block out all light, I am very nearly blind. I still see shapes, though, and I have learned to use my other senses."

"Including magic," he stated softly.

"Considering your wife has an aptitude for magic, you seem awfully prejudiced."

"I don't like witches," he muttered.

"Good thing I'm not a witch," I replied, pushing past him to the front door. He drew himself taller, trying to be imposing, but I ignored him as I unlocked the shop and lowered my nighttime wardings. He shivered behind me, feeling the echo of my magic. "Nice to meet you, Mike."

"If any harm comes to my wife," he began, but I turned and placed a hand on his chest. He stopped talking and frowned at my hand.

I plastered a smile on my face and pushed him backward with a gentle nudge of magic. He stumbled a few feet before regaining his footing. "Your wife will be perfectly safe here. My establishment is heavily warded against violence of any kind. More than that, I have vampire repellents in place. If one managed to get within fifty feet of this place, I'd be very surprised."

"And what about other witches?"

I shrugged and glanced at Maggie, who was staring at me with wide eyes. "All are welcome here, except vampires. I can't stand the bastards."

The hint of a smile tugged at the corner of his lips. "Well, at least we have that in common."

I shrugged again. "They smell," I replied simply.

Mike cracked a smile, a small one, before nodding his head once. "Eddie runs the bar down the street. If there are any problems..." he left the rest unsaid.

"Enough of the postulating, Mike. If you didn't want your wife working here, you shouldn't have *allowed* her to apply." I glanced at Maggie as I spoke, letting my words sink in. "Maybe you should just go back home."

"I chose to apply here," she stated, putting her hands on her hips and turning toward her husband. "I want to work here. We spoke about this, Mike. Besides, Gia can teach me so much."

I raised my eyebrows at that, wondering what she thought I was going to teach her. How to sell vampire-repelling charms? How to balance a till? I wasn't a witch, despite the similarities in magic, and I hadn't planned on starting magic classes. If I was going to be truthful with myself, I had to admit I had planned on teaching Maggie a little. Enough for her to get by, and protect herself. Maybe more.

Maggie had walked over to Mike and was speaking with him softly. I'd had enough of werewolves for one day. Leaving them to work out their issues, I began opening the store for the day. Only a few minutes later, Maggie joined me inside, a small smile on her lips. Obviously, she'd won the argument. I peered out the window, watching Mike walk away shaking his head. Werewolves were annoying, but loyal to a fault. He'd made a promise to his wife, and he'd keep it. It didn't mean he wouldn't keep an eye on me, because he most definitely would. He was quick too. Most people, supernaturals included, simply accepted that I was blind and went with that assumption. Two days in a row now, I'd been called out on it. Maybe I was losing my touch.

Shrugging it off, I showed Maggie how to open the store. Mornings were the slowest and figuring I needed to give her something to tell her over protective husband, I took out a book on earth magic. "I want you to read this book," I said, handing it to her. "It'll give you a lot of basic information regarding the mechanics surrounding spells and potions. Don't try anything without me, though. At all."

"I won't. Thank you," she said, immediately tucking the book into her bag behind the counter.

"Come here and sit down," I said, clearing a spot in the middle of the floor. I sat down on the floor, legs crossed, with my hands held outward. Maggie hurried to mimic me, pressing her palms against mine. We didn't need to sit down, but it was safer this way. "I'm going to do a basic energy push. This is similar to what I did with your husband, but when I push out with energy, you're going to accept it. Think of it like playing catch, only with energy. You'll catch first, then try to push the magic back to me."

"How?" she whispered, her brown eyes sparkling with eagerness.

I gathered energy into me and felt Maggie shiver in response. "Do you feel that?" I asked, and she nodded her head. "It's energy, pure and simple. Everyone and everything has energy, just in different forms. Some people can manipulate that energy, like you and me. I'm going to gather a very small amount of that force, that energy, into my hands. Pay attention to what I'm doing. When it reaches my hands, I'm going to push it into you. When that happens, you can do two things. You can accept it, drawing that energy in and holding it. Or, you don't accept it. If you don't, you'll likely be knocked on your butt. I suggest you accept it."

"Okay," she whispered, her breath coming faster in anticipation.

"You're not going to be used to holding energy like that. Accept it, take it, keep it in your hands, then push it back to me. Don't draw it further into yourself than your hands, and don't hold it too long. Don't worry about being gentle, either. You can't hurt me."

"Okay," she said again, nodding her head.

"Get ready," I said as I pooled energy into my hands. My fingers tingled with the warmth, but I held it in check. Carefully, I formed what I imagined was a small ball of energy and pushed it slowly toward Maggie. She fell backward as the energy hit her, knocking her onto her back. "Are you alright?"

She nodded her head and sat up, brushing her hair out of her face. "That was faster than I expected," she said.

"It's not good to try and hold onto loose energy too long. Plus, I didn't want to use too much. It can hurt," I added, shrugging. "Ready to try again?"

Maggie sat straight and held her hands out to me. We tried again and this time when I pushed the energy at her, I felt her respond. She still wasn't fast enough, but it was an improvement. By the fifth try, she managed to catch and hold the energy before it knocked her backward. She groaned as she rolled onto her back.

"Sorry about that. I told you not to hold the energy. That was much better, though. Next time, hold it for a second, then push it back out. Just shove it back at me."

"Okay, I'll try," she said.

"You won't hurt me," I said again.

She nodded and stared at me as I pulled energy into me. Already, I could see the improvement in her. She was visibly tracking the energy as I brought it into my hands and formed a small ball. With a nod, I pushed the energy into Maggie's waiting hands. She caught it and smiled, the energy gathering quickly in her hands. "Push it back, Maggie," I urged. Magic and energy continued to grow, forming a large ball in her hands that slowly spread down her arms. Sweat broke out on her forehead, but she still didn't let go. "Maggie, let go!"

"I can't... it's so strong."

"Push it out!" I urged, rising to my feet. She shook her head. Hands spread wide, I drew on the magic of the earth, enveloping us in a bubble of magic. The last thing I wanted was for Maggie to inadvertently ruin my store. "Damn it, Maggie, you need to let go of it now. Don't make me take it out of you."

"You can do that?" she asked. Tears streamed down her face as she turned her face up toward me.

"It's not a good idea, and it'll hurt like hell. Just give me the energy. Waiting will only make it worse." Someone was standing inside the front door of the shop. I didn't have time for whoever it was. "Maggie, now."

She nodded once and pushed the magic back out. I caught it, gasping at the weight of it. It was like catching a 500 pound cloud. With as much finesse as I could muster, I sucked the energy back into me, letting it flow across my skin. I took several deep breaths before releasing the energy shield I'd made. I held out a hand, pulling Maggie to her feet, before turning toward the door. The man standing in the doorway had dark hair, piercing blue eyes, and a perfect smile. He stepped forward cautiously, his eyes assessing not just me, but the entire store. The man was close to my five feet, six inches of height, just a few inches taller. He walked forward oozing confidence, but he was just a little too observant for a human.

"Good morning," I said in my best customer service voice.

"Morning," he replied. "Are you the owner?"

"Gia Marchesi," I replied, holding out my hand. He took it, shaking my hand with a firm grip. His palms were callused and strong, but there was no magic. Human.

"Pleasure to meet you. I'm Detective McNeill. Do you mind if I ask you a few questions?" he asked briefly without waiting for a response as he held a piece of paper out toward me. "Is this a receipt from your establishment?"

Maggie stepped forward and took the paper, looking at it carefully. "It appears to be," Maggie said.

He glanced from me to Maggie to the piece of paper, clearing his throat. A slight blush of embarrassment colored his neck. "It's dated August 9th at 7:28pm for $24.95 for a book," he stated.

"Was there a question in there?" I asked.

"Do you remember the purchase?"

"That was over a month ago," I stated simply. "And not much to go on. If you tell me what you're looking for, maybe I can help you."

"We're trying to track a time line. I believe you may have been the last person to see this man alive. Time of death was sometime between 10 and 11pm. We found this receipt in his pocket."

I sighed, trying to think back. "That was the date of my official grand opening. It was a busy day, but I didn't have many customers after the sun went down." I closed my eyes, trying to remember all the faces from that first busy day. "Was he wearing a metal cross on a simple chain?"

"Yes, as a matter of fact, he was. How would you know?"

I moved toward the vampire protection display and held up a similar cross. The detective swore under his breath. I pulled a vampire book off the shelf and handed it to him. "$24.95," I said.

"He bought the book and the cross?" he asked.

"No, he bought the book and I gave him the cross. He was worried about vampires. I told him to go to the police, but he stated they couldn't protect him." I looked at him, watching his facial reactions behind my glasses. He swore again, silently. "I put a minor protection spell on him before he left and told him his best place was at home. Vampires can't enter a home uninvited. I assumed he was on his way there after he left."

"What sort of protection spell?"

I shrugged and moved around the counter, pulling out the small jar and motioning for Maggie to move toward me. She stepped in close as I dipped my finger in the thick mixture, breathing in the faint scent of mint. I quietly murmured the incantation as I marked her forehead, placing the same spell of protection on Maggie that I had on that man. The detective watched me silently as I finished the spell and stepped back. "For the next three hours or so, Maggie will be protected from harm."

"Any harm?"

I shrugged and said, "Care to test it out?"

"No!" Maggie said, her hand going to her throat. I smiled and the detective chuckled in response.

"No, ma'am, but does this protect against vampires?"

"It protects against attacks. Maggie could trip and fall, but if you tried to push her down, she might stumble but wouldn't get hurt. It's more a source of protection against attacks, I'd say, and very temporary."

"Why haven't I ever heard of this?"

This time I laughed, shaking my head. "For starters, this tiny bottle costs about $10,000 to make, assuming you can find all the ingredients. Plus, you need someone of exceptional magical skill to enact such a spell."

"It didn't look like it took much for you."

"That's because I have exceptional magical skill," I stated. He grinned, but I wasn't boasting. Perhaps William Dervish would be able to cast the spell, but even he'd be hard pressed to make the spell last longer than thirty minutes. "Just because the spell only took a moment to cast, doesn't mean it was easy."

"Guess I'll have to take your word for it," he muttered in response.

"Since you are a human with no magical affinity, yes, you will."

He nodded his head and flipped open the vampire book I'd handed him. "So, he would have been safe for a couple hours after leaving here, which would have put his time of death around the time the protection spell wore off."

"Unfortunately, that sounds about right."

"We didn't see this book on him, or any book for that matter. You're sure this is what he bought?"

"Yes, I am sure. It is a basic guide to vampires."

He pulled out his wallet and handed me two twenty-dollar bills. "Keep the change," he said, holding the book under his arm as he turned to leave.

"Thank you."

He nodded, took two steps, then stopped. "Why didn't the cross work?" he asked suddenly. "I've heard of crosses burning up vamps, and even leaving burns on humans holding them. He didn't have a mark on him, except for the nice bite on his neck."

"Are you sure a vampire killed him?"

"He was drained of blood and those holes…"

I shrugged in response before answering him. Just because it looked like a vampire attack, didn't mean it was one. "A cross only works if you're a believer. To a non-believer, it is simply a piece of metal. To a believer, it is a powerful weapon against the forces of evil. Vampires are the closest thing we have to demons walking the earth. Crosses and other holy objects work very well, most of the time. Sometimes it's enough that the vampire believes the cross will repel him."

"Hmm, other holy objects work too? Like holy water."

"Holy water has been sanctified by a true believer; a priest. That is why it works, even for nonbelievers, all the time. Crosses can be blessed, which would cause injury to a vampire who touches it, but only a true believer can *repel* a vampire with a cross. If you ever go up against a vampire, take a priest with you," I added.

"I'll keep that in mind," he said, stopping once more in the doorway. "I know you said it's expensive, but…"

"You want me to place the protection spell on you?"

"Is that possible? I probably shouldn't ask, but this case has me on edge. It's my first… supernatural case."

I motioned for him to move toward me and opened the jar, drawing faint markings on his forehead. The mixture accentuated my magic, helping the spell take hold over precisely what or who I wanted. Repeating the incantation, I drew magic through me and centered it within the detective. As the magic left me, I knew it was one of my best spells yet. "I'd give this five hours, maybe six," I added softly.

"Six? I thought you said it only lasted about two or three?"

Putting the lid on the jar, I stepped back and admired my handiwork. "Magic likes you," I said softly, watching the golden swirls of magic cascade over him. "You must be a good man."

He laughed at that and walked toward the door. "I don't know about that."

"I do," I replied.

He stopped in the doorway, running a hand through his hair and seeming to contemplate his next move. "What are you doing tonight?" he asked, turning to face me.

"I'm closing up at seven."

"Dinner?"

I smiled, truly pleased. I hadn't had a date in years, and he was just what I needed. Besides, I was full of magic and energy after my replenishment off the would-be thief. "Dinner would be great."

Undead

I KEPT A COUPLE changes of clothes in my shop, just in case of accidents, or the random date with a cop. I'd sent Maggie home early while I closed up and got ready. Evenings were slowing down as the weather began to cool, and I decided to close up thirty minutes early. Detective McNeill had called the shop a little after six o'clock to confirm our date and ask what sort of food I liked, whether I drank, if I liked dancing, and a range of questions before finally telling me he was taking me somewhere nice.

The shop had a small bathroom in the back, which I used to get ready while I waited for my date. I highlighted my already defined cheekbones and applied a deep, red lipstick. There was no point in applying eye makeup. I did trade my day to day glasses for a smaller pair. These glasses wrapped tight to my eyes and were even darker than my daily glasses. If I was pretending to be blind, the other glasses added to the effect. If I simply wanted to ensure I didn't turn everyone around me to stone, I preferred these glasses. They were small and stylish, plus they didn't fall off easily. Perfect for date night, especially with a cop.

After the last few interactions, I decided to stick with the mostly blind story. Easier to play off being able to see movement, adding in the important element regarding never removing my glasses for fear of the tiniest bit of light causing pain and further damage to my cornea. Easier to wear dark glasses than a head scarf, hat, or tying cloth over my eyes liked I'd used to. Better, too, than simply turning everyone to stone. At least the glasses helped contain my curse.

I had two extra dresses in my shop, plus the one I was already wearing. Deciding to go with classic black, I paired the dress with a pair of low red heels. My jewelry was simple silver, since I didn't have time to go back to my house. At just before seven o'clock, there was a distinct knock on the front door of the shop. Smiling at his timeliness, I finished styling my hair, secured my glasses, and grabbed my cane.

There was a second knock at the door before I reached it, pulling it open with a smile. The smile died on my lips as a man pushed into the store, his skin gray and drawn. My eyes went to his neck and the two distinct puncture holes. My heartbeat sped up as I backed away, a true sense of terror enveloping me. The man moved forward, his black eyes wide and staring. Frantic, I stumbled backwards, not sure what I was seeing.

The man continued moving, turning toward me as I moved back and forth, but he didn't seem to be watching me. It was more like magic. The thought was enough to stop me in my tracks. Drawing energy up through me, I cast a bubble around the man, similar to what I'd done with Maggie and me. As he reached the edge, the man bounced off. Several minutes I stood there, getting my heart back in a normal rhythm as I watched the man bounce around in my bubble, growing angrier with each passing minute.

"Gia?"

I stood at the back of my store, cornered between a bookcase and a rack of common spelling items. "Detective?" I said hesitantly.

The detective moved forward until I could just make out his form beyond the sphere holding the man. He wore a suit and tie, but held the gun before him trained on the strange form bouncing off the walls of my magical sphere. "Are you alright?" he asked, his eyes never leaving the man, if that's what he was.

"I am unharmed," I said slowly.

"Is this your doing?"

"The containment sphere is, but that creature most definitely is not," I replied, squeezing my way past the trapped dead man. I shifted my magic so I could walk by, pressing it tighter as I analyzed the form in the center of the circle.

"That's the dead man I was asking you about," he said softly, his eyes flicking to mine as I moved up beside him. "Well, he's supposed to be dead."

"He is dead," I said bluntly.

"But..."

"This is necromancy, Detective. Someone is controlling him."

"Who? Why?"

I was staring at the dead man, trying to figure out the same thing. The last time I'd seen a necromancer was during the vampire rise of the Great Depression. I'd hoped to never see another. "I do not know, Detective," I replied softly.

"You sure you don't know this man? He was just a customer?"

"Just a customer," I replied softly, choosing to ignore the unsaid questions. He was a detective, after all, and it was in his nature to investigate. "You said this was your first paranormal case?"

He lowered his gun finally and nodded. "Just got... promoted," he said, spitting out the last word as though it left a bad taste in his mouth.

"I hope you know what you're getting into, Detective," I said, waving my hand toward the dead man who was now trying to bash his way through the shield. "What do you want to do with him?"

"No clue," he muttered. "This wasn't in the handbook."

I smiled and shook my head. "A necromancer could deal with this, or you can burn the body."

"If we burn the body there goes our evidence."

"Did you have a vampire in mind for this case? Perhaps you were getting close to answers." He was shrugging his shoulders, but I couldn't help but notice the way the dead man kept trying to go after me. Why? I didn't know anything. "I don't particularly want a zombie in my shop."

"Oh, right, I should probably call this in."

"I don't want a bunch of police in my shop either."

"This is a crime scene now," he muttered.

"The hell it is," I replied, gathering magic into me. Turning to the sphere, I picked it up and moved it out my front door. The detective followed, cursing as the circle of magic plopped down in the vacant lot across the street with the angry zombie inside. Snagging my purse and the bottle of protection solution, I followed the detective outside, slamming the door behind me. He had a phone to his ear and turned to glare at me as I stomped outside.

"Don't go anywhere," he said angrily.

There was nowhere to go. I was a supposedly visually-impaired woman who lived a few blocks away. Sirens were already playing through the early evening air. As I looked around, I noticed a sheen of dark magic in the air leading straight to my front door. I could easily follow the trail, but it would only show me where the zombie had been, not necessarily who had conjured it. Necromancy was different than what I did. It left a mark, and a smell, I thought, wrinkling my nose. Perhaps I could find a way to follow the source?

"Gia?" the detective had been speaking to me, but I was lost in thought. I turned toward him as the first police car's lights came into view. "I think dinner will be a little later."

I blinked, trying to figure out if he was joking. He smiled slightly and shrugged his shoulders.

"What?" I asked.

"Dinner... if you still want to have dinner with me, that is."

I took a breath and walked toward him, watching him as he watched me. He was still turned toward the zombie, but his gun was lowered. His eyes watched me, lingering on my breasts, as I walked toward him. It made me smile. "I'm starving," I said as I moved up beside him.

Two police cars swung down the road and parked, blocking the road in either direction, followed by several more cars. "Steven," a man called, getting out of an unmarked car.

"It's contained," the detective called back.

The man who had called to him walked forward. He was tall, somewhere close to 6'5, with broad shoulders, a strong jaw, and sandy blond hair almost as rumpled as his suit. The suit in question was navy blue and looked as though he'd been wearing it for the past several days. His bright blue eyes flicked around, taking in every feature and detail, cataloging and assessing. He flicked a glance to the name of my shop, then me, before settling on the dead man. "Isn't that our John Doe?" he asked, stopping on the other side of detective McNeill.

"Sure is," he replied. "This is Gia Marchesi, owner of *Night Defender*. She put the containment spell around him...it... the creature. Gia, this is my partner, Detective Hunter Daniels."

Detective Daniels glanced at me, grunted, then turned back to the zombie. Other police swarmed onto the scene, their guns trained on the dead man, not that it would do them any good. Bullets wouldn't penetrate my shield, and even if I lowered it, bullets wouldn't stop the undead. "Do you have any contacts with necromancers?" I asked.

"Do you?" Detective Daniels asked pointedly.

Ignoring the remark, I placed a hand on Detective McNeill's arm. "As I mentioned before, the only way to get rid of a zombie is either with a necromancer or to burn it."

"We don't consult with anyone dealing in black magic, like necromancy," Detective Daniels snarled. He pulled out a stick of gum and began chewing it while staring at the zombie in question. "What's that thing doing here?"

"Not sure," Steven replied. "But we need to do something with it."

"I'll call the chief," he replied, stepping away and pulling out a phone. He stopped and turned back. "Can you take care of that thing?"

"I am not a necromancer and I do not deal in black magic," I replied icily. "I can contain it, move it, or burn it. I cannot get it to talk though, and I cannot return it to its natural state. I cannot lead it back to its controller either."

There was a simple bench outside my building, which I sat on to wait. After thirty minutes, a new car appeared on the scene. William Dervish stepped out, with Ian on the other side. The taller man glared at me before taking up a bodyguard position behind William, arms crossed over his black shirt as they moved toward the detectives. Steven shook both their hands, while Detective Daniels stood back with his arms crossed looking intimidating, and mimicking Ian. They spoke briefly before William turned and walked toward the enclosed zombie, brushing invisible dirt off the sleeve of his impeccable suit.

"Is the shield your handiwork?" William asked, his voice carrying easily.

Sighing, I stood and joined him, letting my cane click loudly in front of me. Between the dark glasses and the lack of natural light, I almost was blind, squinting to see more than shapes. "Yes, the shield is mine," I said.

The two detectives moved up behind us. The other police had long since lowered their weapons and feigned an air of relaxation while the zombie continued to bang on the magical enclosure. With each passing moment, the zombie grew angrier and would have been foaming at the mouth if it had any saliva left in it's decaying body. My shield never so much as flickered.

"Nice shield," William said simply.

"Thanks."

"Mr. Dervish, what are your thoughts?" Detective Daniels asked.

"I'm not versed in necromancy, Detective. Those who deal with such black magic are... well, they keep to themselves. I wasn't aware there were even any necromancers around here," he added, a hint of anger coming through his words. He was more than a little irritated that someone had slipped into his territory without his knowing.

"Necromancers can work from great distances," I said, not knowing why I was wanting to appease William Dervish.

"I thought they needed to touch the body to create a zombie."

Shaking my head, I said, "No, they just need to have something of the person, such as a strand of hair."

"Or blood?" Detective Daniels asked, his words sending a chill down my spine.

"Yes, blood would work very well," I replied. The detective was nodding, as though he already had all the pieces in place. "What do you suggest we do to take care of this problem, Mr. Dervish?"

William was staring at zombie still, but his eyes flicked to mine before he responded. "I believe Ms. Marchesi's magic will hold it forever, if that is what you wish. Or until her death, anyway. If that isn't an option, I suggest burning it. I don't think there's any other way to stop a zombie."

"Can you burn it? Magically?"

"Not unless Ms. Marchesi releases it, and I'm not sure I could be fast enough."

"Fast enough?"

"Fast enough to burn it before it attacks. That creature is growing in strength. Whoever is controlling it is pushing magic into it. Can't you feel that?"

William was speaking to the detective, but I knew exactly what he meant. The air had thickened over the past several minutes and a foul odor permeated the air, like a mix of ozone and blood. I looked over my shoulder, taking note of the way Detective Daniels wrinkled his nose. He sensed the magic, for sure, and William knew it. Whatever the detective was, he wasn't human. Not fully.

"Burning the magic out of a zombie until it is truly destroyed can take some time. Ten minutes, perhaps," I said, shrugging. I could do it, though, and probably in less than a minute, but not with witnesses.

"Perhaps if we work together," William whispered as he stepped up beside me. "Remove the shield and together we can burn it out. I've done similar things with certain members of my coven."

Work with him? He was an arrogant warlock of decent power, but he had no idea what I truly was. "I'm not sure that's wise," I said. "Perhaps you'd prefer to work with one of your own. Ian, for example."

"Ian is nowhere near your strength. If we combine our power, we can destroy it in quick order. Plus, as you mentioned, Ian is here. He can keep us safe while we take care of the zombie."

"Gia, can you do that? Can you two destroy that thing?" Detective McNeill asked.

On the other side, Detective Daniels leaned forward. "If you two can take care of this without incident, the police department would truly be in your debt."

They weren't equipped for this. None of them were. If I hadn't been so surprised by the zombie, I might have reacted differently. Who was I kidding? I hated fire magic. My precious store was extremely flammable, and not just because of the books. Some of my spell ingredients were flammable. And who cared if the police were in my debt? It was an empty line. The police would do whatever they wished, as always.

I was stalling, even to myself. I could just destroy the zombie, but with so many eyes watching, particularly those attuned to magic, I was loathe to attempt such a thing. William was waiting for my response. He was right, though, he and Ian couldn't take care of this. Not before it killed half the police force. Shivering, I looked back at the zombie. More magic filtered into it, making it seem larger than before even though it hadn't changed size. The creature bounced off the walls of the shield repeatedly, desperate to break through. The moment I lowered my shield, that thing would come barreling at me. We'd have seconds, and everyone would know that thing was gunning for me, and me alone. Unless I took care of it fast.

There were too many people... too many witnesses. "We should move everyone back, for their safety," I added. "William and I will be the creature's focus, but anyone in the way could get hurt."

"Ian can try to draw it away from us," William began, but I shook my head.

"No, we need him safe and out of the way. Like you said, he can protect us. The danger should rest in just us."

"Gia, you don't have to do this," Steven said, coming up beside me and placing a hand at the small of my back. It was an intimate gesture he hadn't earned, but that I liked just a little too much. It had been far too long since I'd been with a man, and he was hitting all the right buttons. "This is dangerous."

"I can take care of myself," I murmured, smiling up at him. "Besides, Mr. Dervish wouldn't let anything happen to me."

I felt William shift beside me and I couldn't help but smile. If I had to do this, I was going to do it right. Protecting myself and my secret came first. I wasn't opposed to killing everyone in sight, but is that what I really wanted? Then I'd have to move away, again. And I wouldn't be able to explore this attraction to the young detective. My eyes turned toward my shop, my true love. No, I wasn't ready to start over just yet.

"We'd really appreciate this, though. We don't have anyone on the police force who can do this sort of thing, and it would take time to call in the State troopers. Even then..."

I nodded, knowing it was true. It was one of the reasons I'd chosen to live in a small town, even if it was a tourist trap. The bigger cities had witches on their payroll, as did the State police, but small towns were slow to catch up. Besides, magic was expensive. Nodding, I sealed my fate. "Mr. Dervish, shall we?"

William took my hand and together we walked forward. The detectives shouted out orders, pulling their men back and out of the way. They weren't far enough for my liking, but it would have to do. The two detectives stood nearby, refusing to leave. Ian stood back with them, pulling magic into him. I rolled my shoulders, trying to loosen the feeling of anxiety as magic was spun behind me. He couldn't kill me directly with magic, but that didn't mean he couldn't hurt me.

We stopped walking, but William kept his hand around mine as he began drawing magic inside of him, as though he were taking large gulps of water. My magic was similar, but different. I was part of the energy flowing from the earth, through the air, and in every living thing. Magic rose up into me with each breath, filling my body with its natural energy. William turned his head and looked at me, awe clearly painted on his face as I pulled in twice the magic he held in a matter of seconds. He continued drawing magic up, filling himself to his max. I stopped, making it appear as though I was full. Even at that point, I held more than double what William held. If he only knew how much more I could draw and hold. For me, it was as easy as breathing.

"You're strong," he whispered as he began to weave fire before him.

I watched him, analyzing the intricate way he gathered the magic before imitating him. While I wasn't a fan of fire magic, I still knew hundreds of different ways to use it. William's way was strong, forming webs of fire that would interlace and lock down on the creature like a giant net. It would slow the creature down, but it wasn't enough to destroy it. He was testing me. I pooled in more magic, compressing it down into a bright blue flame. William nodded in appreciation and cast his spell out, careful to keep it above the sphere holding the zombie.

"Ready when you are," he said.

"Now," I said as I released the sphere. The zombie moved with amazing speed, but William's fire net dropped over him, slowing him. Blue flames shot from my hands, searing the zombie with its immense heat. William's hands moved furiously, crafting another web as the first one began to disintegrate, slowing the frantic creature. My blue flames stuck to the zombie, and I pushed more energy into them. Again, William's web unraveled and we repeated the process. I concentrated on what I was doing, making sure I moved slow enough to keep up appearances.

Something hit me, and I fell on my back, staring up at the sky. The smell of death and decay overpowered everything else, churning my stomach. William yelled, and Ian ran forward, casting spells in quick succession. Rolling to my side, I sat up and looked toward the zombie. He continued to move forward, despite the flames enveloping him. William was on the ground, holding his hand to his chest as Ian stood over him, casting small balls of flame back at the creature.

"Gia!" Steven yelled.

I held up my hand, not wanting him to get in the way. The smell of death came quick, but I was ready this time. Putting up a barrier, the necromancer's spell hit it instead of me. Crawling, I moved toward William, reaching out a hand to grasp the collar of his suit. I yanked him back to me and held out my hand. He took my hand, letting his magic flow into me. I channeled it, sending fire across the trail of magic. Flames ripped down the road, past buildings, scorching everything in its wake, running up the distant mountains, until it finally found the source. I pushed the magic back at the necromancer until I felt him release his magic.

The zombie dropped to the ground, his body smoking. The necromancer had pulled his magic back, but if he had the man's blood, he could make him walk again any time he wanted. Better to destroy the body completely. I threw another bolt of blue flame at the body, incinerating it. The stench of death, decay, and blood retreated with the necromancer's magic, leaving only the smell of burning flesh from the corpse and the crisp smell of ozone.

"Master?" Ian asked, kneeling over William.

William pulled his hand from mine and let Ian help him to his feet. His left hand was covered in black lines where the necromancer's magic had hit him. He turned to me, holding his good hand out to me. I took it, letting him help me up. "He got you too," he said, pointing at me.

"What?" I asked.

"You got hit," William replied, using his good hand to touch me lightly where black lines converged in a circle on my chest, just below my collarbone.

I reached a hand up, feeling the cold from the lingering magic still on my skin. "That's new," I said softly, running a finger across one of the raised lines. Each of the lines burned like ice.

"I've never felt anything like that," William murmured.

"Haven't met many necromancers, have you?" I mused, not expecting an answer.

"Only one," he replied, his voice soft as the police began to move in closer. "And I never want to meet another." I couldn't agree more.

CLUB WYVERN

BY THE TIME THE police had cleaned up and left, it was well after ten o'clock. One patrol car remained in the area, silently driving down the bay front and surrounding areas. I leaned up against Steven's sleek red convertible while he finished chatting with his partner. The two detectives were as different as could be, but they appeared to work well together. One tall and broad with a permanent scowl, the other slender and jovial. Ian had driven William home as soon as the zombie had disintegrated into nothing but a pile of ash. We hadn't spoken more of necromancers and magic, both deciding to keep to ourselves. That was fine with me.

Steven had asked me to stick around, if I was still up for a date. He'd offered to take me home first, but I didn't invite people I'd just met into my home. Besides, I wanted to stay and see what the police were up to. My store was once again warded with magic, but the police thankfully didn't seem interested in it. I suspected this was due to Steven keeping the full details of the creature's attack to himself. If he'd told them the creature had been in my store, the police would be all over me. That, if nothing else, kept me where I was.

Steven and Hunter shook hands and parted ways. As Steven walked back toward me, I admired his swagger. He was young for a detective, somewhere in his mid-twenties, and downright sexy. I shivered and looked up, feeling the eyes of his partner, Hunter, on me. The man stared at me, his expression unreadable. Turning my attention back to Steven, I smiled as the smell of his cologne reached my nose.

"You smell nice," I said softly.

He laughed and moved up beside me, taking my elbow gently. "Had to cover up the smell of barbecue." He shivered, his eyes glancing toward the cleanup crew removing the charred remnants of the zombie. "Are you still up for dinner?"

"I believe I mentioned earlier that I was starving," I replied as he led me around and opened the car door for me. I slid in, setting my cane on the floor in front of me as Steven gently shut the door. The seats were leather and the car smelled of lemon cleaner.

"I'm not sure what's still open," he said as he started the car. "The bars, for sure, but they're not what I had planned."

"At this point, I don't care where we go. Although, I'm guessing I'm a little overdressed."

"Well..." he began, twiddling his thumbs on the steering wheel. "There's a club about a thirty minute drive from here. I've heard they have amazing food, and they're open all night."

"You mean Club Wyvern?"

"Yeah, you know it?"

I laughed, surprised he was up for such a place. "Yes, I know the place. You've been there?"

"Uh, well, no, but some of the guys told me about it."

"The guys? You mean on the force?"

He nodded his head and pulled the car out onto the road. "Have you been there?"

"Yes," I replied simply.

"So, what do you think?"

"If you're up for that sort of place, I'm game."

"That sort of place?"

"Well, your friends told you all about it, right?" I pushed.

He shrugged and cast a glance at me. "They just told me I needed to check the place out. Said it's one of the hottest clubs around. Plus, I was told they have amazing food. And dancing, right?"

I sat back and relaxed. "Yes, they have it all. Club Wyvern is definitely one of the hottest clubs you could find. I wouldn't flash my badge around that place, though, if I were you."

He laughed and shook his head. "Oh, no, I wasn't born yesterday."

"And don't act like a cop."

"Gia, I'm hurt," he said, placing a hand on his chest.

I smiled and casually rested a hand on his thigh. A muscle in his leg twitched, but he said nothing as I let my hand curve naturally over his leg. He kept a tight grip on the steering wheel as he drove, casting glances in my direction. For my part, I stayed relaxed, with my hand slowly inching back and forth.

We reached the club in under thirty minutes and parked across the street. I waited while Steven jumped out and hurried around the car, holding the door open for me. I gripped his elbow and left my cane behind. The club would be packed enough without me trying to walk around with a cane in my hand. Steven seemed fine with the idea as he moved in closer, putting his hand at the small of my back once again.

"Shall we eat first?" I asked as we walked across the gravel parking lot. The club was in between two towns and three stories high, with a huge gravel parking lot at the south side and a paved lot on the north side. Construction seemed to be a constant affair at Club Wyvern. Currently the oceanside ground floor was undergoing renovations.

"Yeah, food would probably be a good idea."

"Then we need to go in through the north entrance," I said. "That's the restaurant side."

He steered me toward the main entrance, my heels clicking as we crossed onto the long sidewalk running around the building. At this hour, the club was just getting going and the restaurant side was still busy, but winding down. I stopped at the corner and reached a hand into my purse, pulling out the protection potion. Steven raised his eyebrows, but moved in front of me as I murmured the spell. It wasn't as good as the last time, but would still last about 3 or 4 hours. As I finished he simply smiled and took my arm again, not even questioning my use of the spell.

We continued around the corner to the main restaurant doors. The front doors were steel, as was the framework of most of the building. A man in a suit stood at the door, opening it as we walked up. He raised his eyebrows at Steven, but ushered us inside without a word. Steven immediately took the lead, speaking to the hostess to get us a table. I had my power muted, appearing almost as ordinarily human as Steven.

"I'm sorry, oceanside ground floor is under construction," she said. "It's about an hour wait for any other tables on the first floor."

"Anything else in the restaurant?"

"The second floor has a few tables, but..." she stopped talking, eyeing him up and down. "Is this your first time here?"

He didn't answer her question, instead pulling out a five dollar bill and sliding it over to her. "We'll take the second floor. Is there a good view?"

"Not as good as the top floor," she said softly, a smile on her lips as she pocketed the bill. "I could get you seated up there."

I stepped up beside Steven and pushed a small fraction of power at the hostess. "Second floor will do," I stated sharply. "Oceanside."

The girl sneered at me and I pushed a second burst of power at her. I felt one of the bouncers step closer. "Is there a problem?" asked the deep rumble behind me.

"No problem."

"No magic on the staff," he said.

"Then tell your staff not to offer my date up for food," I replied tartly. The bouncer looked over at the hostess, who had the audacity to blush. "We'll take our table now. Second floor, oceanside."

The hostess waved her hand and a young werewolf moved forward. We followed him into the elevator and up to the second floor, where he moved us to a table. The second floor was busy, but there were a few empty tables spaced out. He sat us at a table with a view of the ocean. There wasn't much to see at night unless it was a full moon, and thankfully it wasn't. Coming to Club Wyvern on a full moon wasn't advised, even if most of the working shifters were older and supposedly stable. Still, the oceanside was the best side, even if there wasn't much to see. The tables were spaced further apart and given more privacy on this side. The only better spot was the third floor, and that wasn't advised with a human in tow.

"You've definitely been here before," Steven stated as he looked at the menu. His voice was steady, even, giving nothing away.

"A few times," I admitted.

He nodded and set the menu down, leaning back. "So, what do I need to know? The guys told me to go to the club, and that the higher the floor, the more exciting it was. Is that true?"

I chuckled and leaned toward him. "And what floors did these men claim to go to?"

"Second floor, but one said he went to the third. They all laughed like it was a big joke."

"Are these men human?"

He sat up at that and looked around. "No," he said softly. "Does that make a difference?"

"Yes," I replied, taking a drink of water. The waiter came back and we both ordered steak and drinks. As soon as we were alone, I spoke again. "The restaurant side is safer than the club, for starters. As a human, it's best if you stay on the first floor. Basic rules are no blood and no biting on the ground floor. Second floor means no non-consensual biting, but a little bit of blood is allowed. Blood sharing is common, and expected, and fights can and do break out. Third floor is anything goes, except killing. Everyone who walked in alive better walk out alive. That's it. All staff at Club Wyvern are Other."

"Other?"

I shrugged and said, "Other than human. Mostly shifters, but some vampires work the top floor and there are a good number of witches. Some Fae, too."

"Fae? What are Fae?" he asked, leaning forward now.

"Keep your voice down," I said, glancing around. I immediately stopped, realizing what I was doing, but thankfully he hadn't noticed. He was too busy looking around at the staff himself to notice me looking. Damn, I was getting reckless. Securing my glasses, I leaned forward and reached a hand across the table until I found his fingers. He looked over at me, but I kept my head down.

"Sorry," he said, his voice softer. "So, this is a supernatural hot spot?"

I smiled as Steven laced his fingers through mine. "Yes, you could say that. Most humans are safe though, as long as they stick to the first floor. There are strict rules in place."

"We're on the second floor though," he said, stopping as our waiter returned with our drinks. I reached for mine, pulling it to me and taking a long drink.

"You're with me, though," I replied. "And we're in the restaurant, which is pretty safe on all floors."

"You..." he paused, his fingers playing with mine. "You're just a witch, though. Right?"

I began to pull my hand away, but Steven gripped my fingers tighter. "I'm no witch," I replied.

"But I thought... I mean, you can do witchy stuff."

"Witchy stuff?" I shook my head. "It doesn't mean I'm a witch, or wiccan, or anything else."

"Are you a Fae then?"

I shook my head. "No," I said simply. There was no further conversation as the waiter came back with a bread basket. The tables around us began to fill in, and Steven took my cue to keep silent. The restaurant side was mild this evening, and I had to wonder if he would push to go to the club. His eyes were wide, taking everything in. Yes, I decided, he would most definitely want to go to the club.

As soon as we finished our steaks and paid the bill, Steven stood and took my hand. "Club?" he asked simply.

"Are you sure you're up for that?"

"If I go back to work and tell the guys that I was here, but never made it into the club, I will never live it down."

"First floor," I said simply.

"There's a door right over there that says it leads to the club," he said, taking my hand.

"That will be the second floor."

"Didn't you say I was safe with you?" he murmured in my ear as he pulled me close to his body.

I nodded my head and let him lead me toward the club. Heads turned as we made our way to the door. The waiter moved toward us, stopping before we reached the club door. "This way goes to the club. The exit is over there," he added, pointing in the opposite direction.

"Oh, good. We want to go to the club," Steven said, pulling himself up to his full height which was still several inches below the werewolf.

"Elevator," the werewolf replied. "First floor."

"Can't we just go in there?" he asked, pointing back to the door.

"There are rules, human, for your safety," he stated.

Steven put an arm around my shoulder and nodded his head. "I'm with her, and she knows the rules."

The werewolf looked at the two of us, shrugged, and moved back. "It's your funeral," he said.

Steven grinned and steered me toward the club door. We made our way down a narrow hallway, following the sounds of thumping club music. A bouncer stood at the end of the hallway, eyeing us up and down before letting us pass. I let a trickle of magic float from me, letting anyone nearby know that I could handle myself. The last time I'd been at the club, I'd been with a werewolf. We'd spent most of our time on the second floor as well. I'd yet to go up to the third floor, but I'd been in clubs like this before. The top floor was mostly vampires and their blood donors, or shifters in various states of undress. It was one of the few places vampires, werewolves, witches, and Fae all mingled together.

The club was like most clubs. Loud music played from a massive stereo system, with speakers throughout. Two long bars sat at either end of the club, ensuring everyone had enough liquor in them at all times. The ocean side was similar to the restaurant portion, with tables spaced out and small, private booths here and there. The smell of sex and blood filled the air. The other side of the club was reserved for dancing.

"This place is huge," Steven commented, taking my hand and leading me to the closest bar. We ordered drinks and Steven leaned his body in close, pressing his mouth next to my ear. "Do you want to dance?"

I took my drink and nodded, letting him lead me to the dance floor. The dance floor was packed with shifters and humans alike. Two Fae danced nearby, their electric blue eyes giving them away as some sort of fairy. I moved in time to the music, letting Steven lead as I held my drink up with one hand. The dress was a little too fancy for a regular club, but here, anything worked. Steven leaned in close to me, his breath hot on my neck. The tingle of necromancy magic still radiated across my chest along the black lines. They had faded enough that they appeared to be a strange tattoo, but the cold chill from the magic was much more noticeable in the hot club.

Steven moved against me as the music changed, and I downed my drink, setting it on a nearby table and letting him wrap both his arms around me. Several shifters danced behind us, shedding articles of clothing with each song. Steven scanned the dance floor, his eyes wide as he watched the shifters dance. On the second floor, most shifters preferred minimal clothing. Two female shifters beside us wore nothing but thongs as they danced around a human male. The human had already lost most of his clothing, leaving him in a tie, one shoe, and a pair of boxers.

"It's a good thing you can't see much," Steven whispered as he pulled me close to his body. "A bunch of naked people dancing?" I mused.

"Is that normal?" he asked, pulling me to the edge of the dance floor.

"It is for shifters," I replied. "This is a slow night."

He nodded, but I wasn't sure he heard me. His attention shifted to someone behind me and he steered me further away from the center of the dancing. I could feel the heat of a shifter behind me, following us. Hands encircled my waist, not from Steven. "Hands off," Steven said as he pulled me against him.

"If it's hands off, you better mark your territory better," the shifter replied.

"I don't have your scent on me," I said to ease Steven's confusion. "Shifters rely on smell. You and I both smell single."

"We smell single?"

I shrugged and ran my hands across Steven's chest, undoing the buttons one by one. His dancing slowed, but his heartbeat sped up as I pulled his shirt open and pressed myself against him. "This should help a little," I replied as I rested my head on his shoulder.

It didn't last long before another pair of shifters moved up behind us, pressing their sweaty bodies against ours. Steven pushed them away, which only excited them more. Two more shifters moved in, their half naked bodies drenched in sweat. I wasn't afraid, but I could sense the anxiety in Steven. This could get out of hand fast. Wanting to end this, I reached out and took his hand, pulling it down to caress my thigh. I wrapped my leg around his, pulling myself closer to him and allowing the fabric of my dress to slide upward considerably. His hand stayed in place, as though glued to my thigh.

"Steven," I whispered, taking his hand and sliding it up my backside. His eyes widened as he touched my bare skin. I pressed myself closer, leaning in until he closed the distance with a kiss. His lips were soft on mine and tender. I leaned back, giving him access to my neck as he continued his kisses. The shifters moved away as our scents began to mingle, but they were no longer on my mind. Steven's hand explored underneath my dress, searching for underwear that wasn't there. He groaned in desire and I felt him press his hardness against me. We moved further away from the dance floor until we had backed up against a wall. Desire filled us, as it was known to do in Club Wyvern. Steven held himself in check though, pressing his fully clothed body against mine and keeping his hands tight to my thighs.

While Steven was trying to be a gentleman, I was riding a wave of growing desire. Reaching down, I unzipped his pants and reached my hand inside, drawing a small cry from him as I pulled him free. He had a moment of clarity as he darted looks around the room. "Gia, we're in public," he managed to croak out.

"I don't care," I responded, caressing him and cutting off his argument briefly.

"What about protection?" he continued as I moved my leg higher and pressed myself against him.

"I can't get pregnant, or anything else for that matter." Desire had grown to such a peak I didn't care where I was or who I was with.

One of Steven's hand stayed on my upper thigh, holding me in place, while the other hand moved to capture mine. "Why don't we get out of here?" he said, pulling my hand from him. "Back to my place."

"I don't want to wait," I murmured, struggling to reach him.

"Gia." He pushed me so my back was against the wall, then stepped back, fixing himself and zipping up his pants. "This isn't the place for this. I think we should leave."

"Sure it is. Everyone else is..." I trailed off as my words came back to me. Moans filled the room and the shifters who had been dancing now seemed to be in some very unique states of sex. Clothes were strewn about the room, some little more than pieces of torn fabric. "Shit."

"What is it?" he asked, suddenly on high alert, his arm snaking around my waist.

I shook my head as desire raced through me once more. The urge to pull my clothes from my body became overwhelming. "Vampire," I whispered, clasping hold of Steven's hand on my waist.

"Where?" he asked, his hand moving to the gun at his back.

"No, don't," I said. "Club rules, remember?"

"Gia," he said my name again, in a condescending tone that immediately pissed me off.

"This isn't your normal vampire. Look around the club. Do you see anyone who works here?"

Steven did as I asked as I pulled him toward the exit, my free hand clenching my skirt tightly. "The bouncer that blocked the hallway," Steven whispered in my ear. "He's...uh... busy."

The bouncer was lying on the floor by the hallway with two woman atop him. "Get me out of here."

He took a firm grip around my waist and guided me to the staircase, leading me carefully downward. Desire rippled through my body and I almost fell. Steven caught me and picked me up, carrying me through the club. The music on the first floor had stopped, leaving only the sounds of a hundred people writhing across the floor. I wriggled against Steven, fighting against the vampire magic spilling through the air.

The cold night air helped, but Steven didn't set me down until we were back across the street at his car. "Are you okay?" he asked as I slumped against the hood of his car.

"Oh, no," I said, shaking my head. He moved over me, his body pressed tantalizingly close. "We're still under the vampire's influence out here. Or, rather, I am."

"What do you mean?"

"Have you heard of succubi and incubi?" I asked as I laid down on the hood of his car, letting the cold metal cool my fevered skin even as I lifted the hem of my skirt.

"In stories," he said as he moved in closer and grasped my hands, keeping me from lifting my dress further.

"They're a type of vampire. Instead of feeding on blood, they feed on sex. Only a very powerful one could take down the entire club," I said, waving my hand back in the general direction of the building. "Or maybe a coven of them."

"Fuck!" he said, shaking his head. "He's feeding on all those people inside?"

"Yes."

"And you?" he asked. His body pressed against mine so one of my legs was between his legs, my other leg wrapped around his waist, and I had begun unzipping his pants again.

"He's trying to, yes," I replied as I concentrated on stilling my hands.

"What about me?"

I took my hands from his zipper and ran them up and down his thighs, trying to stave off the desire still circling through me. "I can't think," I said. "Maybe if you just..." I stopped talking and pulled him down for a kiss.

He kissed me back briefly before using both his hands to press me back down onto the hood of is car. "As much as I want to, I don't think that's a good idea," he said. "If we have sex, aren't we just feeding the vampires?"

"Yes, I would be. Pretty sure I already am, but this would just be... more. I think if I give in, I won't be able to stop. Just like those people in there. They'll have sex until they die. You...you... oh you're sexy. Kiss me... no... the protection spell."

"The spell? It's keeping me safe?" I nodded my head and closed my eyes, struggling to fight against the overwhelming feelings. I couldn't give in. Already, they could be aware of me, or rather, my power. I needed to think. "Get me away from here."

Steven pulled me to my feet and settled me into the passenger seat of his car, buckling me in before running around and jumping in. He drove off in a hurry, speeding away from the club. After just a few minutes, the magic snapped and I gasped as the sensation left me. My thoughts, which had been a jumble just moments before, rebounded with clarity. I knew just what to do. "Take me to my shop."

Succubus

STEVEN PULLED UP NEXT to my store and helped me out, opening the door as I took down the spells. Inside, I hurried to the store room, searching through the potions I'd already made. I only had one bottle of vampire repellent left, which I transferred into a squirt bottle. It might be enough to wake people up. I didn't like the fact that I'd been overcome by the magic as well. It shouldn't have happened at all. What was wrong with me?

I touched the mark still on my chest, feeling the cold lines. They had sunk in and lightened in color, but I could still feel the icy magic beneath the surface. Could the necromancy be messing with my magic? I didn't have time to deal with that. In the back of the cabinet, I pulled out an amulet. I hadn't worn the thing in centuries, examining the dark purple gem set on the silver chain. It was meant to protect against low level demons, like vampires and succubi, but being what I was, it had interesting side effects. For humans, the amulet did as it was supposed to and offered protection from vampire magic. For me, being a Gorgon, a cursed reincarnation of Medusa, it not only accentuated my powers but accentuated my anger and violence. The last time I'd worn this around a vampire, I had slaughtered half a town.

I was a different person now, and these weren't normal vampires. Taking the amulet, I slipped it around my neck, hoping it would help. I closed the cabinet and returned to the main store, stopping dead in my tracks as I heard Steven on the phone. He was sending police up to the club.

"What are you doing?" I hissed.

He covered the phone with his hand and turned toward me. "We barely escaped. I can't just let innocent people be fed to a succubus, or whatever it is."

"So instead you're going to send a bunch of untrained humans in?"

"We're the police, Gia," he said, as though that explained everything. "I was hoping you'd do your protection spell on them first. You'll be reimbursed."

I fingered the amulet around my neck. They were the police, after all. I could put a protection spell on them and let them do their job. The first police car pulled in, followed by a second unmarked car. His partner got out of the unmarked car and made his way straight to my door.

"Steven?" he said, his unspoken question speaking volumes. The two men looked at each other, nodded, then turned toward me.

"I'm coming with you," I said, the words leaving my mouth in a rush. What was I thinking? Immediately, I regretted it, fingering the amulet. This thing made me a bit reckless too.

"Gia, it's not safe. Just, please, give us your protection spell and we'll take care of things," Steven said as he moved forward, wrapping his arms around my waist. He moved his mouth next to my ear, kissing my cheek before speaking softly. "I can't risk you."

"That's sweet, but I'm coming," I said, pushing him back. His eyes widened in surprise, but I held up the amulet. "This is my protection. Don't worry about me."

The other detective spoke, his voice a stern, deep rumble. "Ms. Marchesi, we can't let a civilian..."

I cut him off, holding up a hand. "You let this civilian take care of a zombie for you, in case you already forgot. Besides, you don't know what you're doing."

"Steven briefed me already. I've dealt with vamps before. This is just a different kind."

I tossed the bottle of repellent into the air. Detective Daniels caught it with supernatural speed. "What's this?" he asked.

"Spray anyone afflicted and they should come out of it. It won't last long, so you'll need to spray them and get them away fast." He nodded as I continued. "My guess, considering the power involved, is that there is a coven in that building. Take out the leader, and the rest will usually fall into line."

"Take out?" Steven asked, his hands still around my waist. "Like any vampire?"

I nodded. "They're a type of demon, just like vampires. Cursed, in a way. Holy items or silver are best. Help yourself to a cross," I added, pointing to the display case.

"You mean kill them?" Detective Daniels asked, his deep voice quiet.

I shrugged and moved past them, holding my arms in front of me so I didn't bump into anything. The glasses were really helpful for my ruse. More police cars pulled in and men in flak jackets stepped out. Most of the men were the ones who'd been here earlier, watching me take out a zombie. Most were human, but a few were werewolves. Reaching into my purse, I pulled out the small vial. There wouldn't be any left after tonight. I wasn't sure where I was going to get more ingredients, either.

The police officers lined up under Steven's orders. One by one, I placed the protection spell on them. The majority would last three hours, which made me feel better about our police force. These were good men. A few, however, just couldn't get the magic to stick. I'd never had that happen before. They were both human, too. I advised the detectives to leave them behind, but I noticed Detective Daniels taking note of them. Lastly was Detective Daniels himself. Steven was still protected and getting everyone up to speed on the plan.

"I don't like magic," the detective said as he stood before me.

"Those who don't understand it never do," I replied, tracing his forehead with the solution. I murmured the incantation and watched as the magic took hold, swirling and coalescing across his body. "You'll be good for..." I stopped, gasping as the magic took hold and seemed to multiply before my very eyes.

"What? How long?" he asked.

"What are you?" I whispered, not sure about what I was seeing.

"How long?" he growled.

"A day, a week, maybe more," I replied, shrugging my shoulders. "I've never seen anything like it."

He grunted and turned away, jumping in his car and hollering out the window to the rest of the men. I hurried toward Steven, my heels clicking loudly in my haste. "Don't you dare," I murmured, watching Steven start his car.

"Sorry, Gia, but this is police business. I'll call you after," he added.

I stood back, watching as the police cars sped off. I had faith in my magic, but it would still only last a few hours. All the succubi and incubi had to do was wait. "Not my problem, not my problem, not my problem," I murmured to myself, fingering the purple gem of the amulet. "Damn it."

Stomping back into the store, I picked up the phone. I had a car, despite my blindness ruse, but it was still best not to be seen in it. Club Wyvern would be crawling with cops soon, and they'd be dead if I didn't do something. The people in the club might already be dead, for all I knew, or new recruits. While succubi and incubi fed off sex, they also drained the person's energy. Just like blood, energy could be replenished, but if too much was taken too fast, a person could die.

Club Wyvern's reputation was on the line, but so was mine. If word got out that I'd been there and I was the reason for the police, I'd have to pack up and move towns. Again. Damn it, I'd barely gotten settled here. I had at least a dozen years here before I needed to move again, unless things went downhill like the last town. I looked at the phone in my hand and dialed one of the only people I knew in the area.

"Maggie, I need your help," I said as soon as the line opened. It wasn't Maggie, though, it was Mike.

"It's a little late for a work issue, isn't it? Can't this wait until morning?"

Damn, just what I needed. "I need a ride," I said slowly. "Is Maggie there?"

"Maggie's in bed, sleeping. What's so important you need a ride in the middle of the night?"

"There's a succubus at Club Wyvern stirring up trouble."

I had his attention now. "What? At the club? What's going on? You'd better start talking."

"Can you give me a ride?"

"Damn it... I have friends working at the club."

"Give me a ride and I'll explain everything. I need to get there before things get bad."

"I'll be there in five."

He hung up and I immediately regretted my phone call. I had just enough solution for two or three more people, but I wasn't sure the werewolf would accept my magic. If only Maggie had answered. She could have just dropped me off and I would have taken care of the situation. Now, I was dragging more people into it. What the hell was I thinking?

It had barely been three minutes when a loud truck barreled down the street. I stepped out of the store, placed my wards, and hurried to the truck. Three werewolves were in the back seat, with guns out. I climbed in and Mike drove off, swerving onto the road.

"Start talking," he growled.

"I was at the club earlier when some succubi or incubi started taking over the club. I barely got away, but now the police are on their way there."

"Police? You called the police?" one of the werewolves in the back asked.

"I was on a date with one at the time," I replied.

"You just gave that vamp more food," he mumbled.

"I put a temporary protection spell on them. I have just enough to protect maybe three of you, then I'm out," I said, pulling the bottle out and showing them.

"Magic? You can count me out," the same werewolf said.

"Fine, I'll show you where the magic takes hold. You can stop the car there. Anyone without protection will be useless past that point."

"What do you plan on doing?" Mike asked, turning to look at me.

I sat back, his words sinking in. What was I planning? I shrugged, not sure if I should voice it out loud. These were werewolves, but I still wasn't sure what they'd think of my plan. Taking a deep breath, I said, "Just get me there and take care of your friends."

Mike grunted and we were quiet for several minutes as he drove. I pointed to a spot five miles from the club, where I had felt the edge of the spell. He pulled over and parked the truck, turning to look at me. "You can protect us from the vamp?" he asked.

"It'll protect you from harm and vampire magic for a short time, yes."

"Do it."

I placed the protection on three of the four werewolves. The last man chose to stay behind, not wanting me to touch him with magic. We left him there grumbling to himself as we drove toward the club. I placed the last remnants of solution back in my purse. Enough for maybe one more person. I felt the magic hit my amulet and soak in a few minutes later. It was hard to tell, but I thought the power had grown in strength. Not good. Mike drove around the back side of the club, avoiding the police cars parked along the sides of the road. There were no officers to be seen though and all the cars were empty. Everyone was inside.

The werewolves knew their way around, leading us to a side door hidden by the construction plastic. The magic hit me, melting into my amulet. The werewolves sniffed the air and I was glad I didn't have their heightened sense of smell. From the sounds of moaning, groaning, and thumping coming from the club, the succubi were still working their magic. The werewolves split up, but Mike followed me as I hurried to the stairs. I didn't like the werewolf with me, but I didn't have much of a choice.

I kept climbing right past the second floor, making my way straight to the top. The sounds of gunfire stopped me in my tracks. Mike didn't hesitate as he raced past me, heading straight for the gunfire and yelling. I hurried after him, lifting my glasses slightly so I could see the stairs beneath my feet. At the top landing, a police officer hunkered down, sighting around the corner. He started when I came up beside him.

"I thought Steve left you behind?" he said.

I shrugged. "He did. I got a ride," I said simply. "What's the situation?"

"Detective Daniels figured the vamps would be up here on the top floor. A couple of us came up and something grabbed Steve. He's over there somewhere. I'm not sure where Hunter went. He's like a fu...friggin' ghost."

I patted the man's forehead. "They can't hurt you. See if you can find Steven," I said, pushing him toward the left.

I stood and walked around the corner, not waiting to see what the officer would do. The amulet tingled against my skin, sucking in the vampire magic.

"Who do we have here?" a man's voice asked. I stepped further into the room, listening for the speaker. The darkness was thicker here, and even worse with my glasses, making me virtually blind.

"Those sunglasses are so out of style," a woman said.

"Those are glasses blind people wear," the man drawled.

"A blind woman?" the woman's voice laughed. I kept walking, hands held out in front of me.

"Is she deaf too?" the man asked.

This time I stopped. I knew they were close by, even if I couldn't see them. "I seem to be late to the party," I mused, resting my arm against what I assumed was the bar thanks to the overpowering smell of liquor. My arm touched something wet and sticky, and I only hoped it was alcohol.

"She's wearing an amulet. Naughty girl," the woman's voice said.

"Oh, I think you have plenty to feast on without me," I replied.

"You're a witch!" the woman screeched, startling me with her proximity. The air moved around me and I felt something touch my arm. "You gave those police some sort of protection. You're spoiling our fun."

"Well, you ruined my date," I replied. The woman moved around me and a man stood several feet away, lounging against the bar. I kept my head down, surveying the situation.

"Date? I can be your date," the woman said as she traced a hand across my neck. The man suddenly moved, standing before me. He was tall, well over 6', and smelled of cigarettes, liquor, and sex.

"Mmm, no, this one is mine," the man said. He trailed a hand across my cheek, lifting my chin. "Your little amulet won't help you," he whispered. His lips touched mine at the same time the amulet snapped from around my neck. The woman cackled behind me, but they had no idea what they were getting into.

Desire raced through me as the man, the incubus, pushed his need into me. His hands moved across my body, tearing fabric while he touched and teased my breasts, drawing gasps of pleasure from my mouth between the kisses he pressed to my mouth. The woman closed in, her body against my back, pushing me closer to the incubus while lifting the bottom of my dress. Her breath was hot on my neck as her teeth grazed my skin, drawing out a small amount of blood.

"Oh, you taste good," she murmured.

The incubus leaned forward, his tongue tickling the wound at my neck. "Mmm, what are you?" he murmured. "You don't taste like a witch."

"Let's take her home," the woman urged, her mouth going back to my neck.

"She's certainly pretty enough to join our menagerie," he mused. "Would you like that? Do you want to come home with us?"

His magic dissipated slightly, and I let out a breath of relief, quickly reaching up to my glasses, tearing them from my face. "Where's home?" I croaked.

"Anywhere we are," the succubus replied, her power pushing back into me as she sucked on my neck again. "Oh, that's funny. The wound closed already."

I smiled, feeling a sense of carelessness run through me. The incubus took my head in his hands turning my face toward his. "What are you?" he asked.

They always asked that, I thought, chuckling as I lifted my eyes up to his and stared back at him. His hands stilled on my body and try as he might, he couldn't pull his gaze from mine. The spell broke, and I felt his power spill into me in frightening waves. All the power and energy he had consumed over the course of the evening was now mine. I dragged that energy into me, sucking it down in great gulps. The energy flowed like a river straight into me and I reveled in it even as his body turned gray and crumbled at my feet. The woman stilled behind me, one hand around my waist as she shoved all her remaining power into me, trying to get me under control. Desire flashed through me, but she was too late. Turning fast, I grabbed her, holding her until she faced me in all my snake-ringed glory. Again, I pulled energy into me with just a look. Her power was less than the man's, but still full of juicy goodness. Within minutes, she was nothing more than a statue with a shocked expression. With a flick of magic, both turned to dust at my feet.

I knelt on the ground, feeling around through the ash in the darkness until my hands found the amulet. The chain was broken, but the amulet still worked. I slipped it into my purse and brushed my hands on the bottom of my skirt before slipping my glasses back on. I could feel the magic of the incubi dissipate throughout the club as the rest of the coven released their hold. There had been more here than just the two, but they were fleeing now, taking the remnants of their power with them.

"Gia?" Steven hurried across the room, stopping before me where I still knelt in a pile of ash. "What are you doing here?"

I ignored his question and stood up. "They're fleeing," I said simply.

"I know. Some of the men are giving chase," he replied with a shrug. "It was crazy. They were flinging us around like we were rag dolls, but I swear not one of us has a scratch." His eyes took me in, and I could only imagine what I looked like. "You're hurt."

"I'm fine," I replied.

"But your dress.." My dress was beyond repair, littered with tears and holes and showing a good deal more skin than I would ever show in public. I moved the dress around, trying to at least cover my breasts. "It's fine. I'm fine."

"You're sure? Is that blood?"

"Steve."

"Okay, I just don't like you putting yourself in danger like this."

"Well, don't get used to it. I don't plan on making it a habit, plus I'm out of protectant."

"Gia, are you hurt?" Mike asked, coming up behind Steven. Steve straightened, turning and eyeing the werewolf skeptically. One hand still held a gun and it looked like he was doing his best not to raise it.

"Thanks, Mike, I'm fine. This is Detective McNeill. Steven, this is Maggie's husband."

"Maggie... oh, right, the girl who works for you. What are you doing here?" Mike flicked a glance at me, which was enough for

Steven. "Gia?

"I asked Mike for a ride," I said simply. "That protection spell only lasts so long, and I would have regretted not coming to make sure you were okay." The lie rolled off my tongue easily.

He smiled and put an arm around my waist, pulling me toward him. "You were worried about me?"

I nodded and rested my head against his shoulder. "I was worried about all of you, actually," I replied, surprised to hear a hint of truth in my words. I didn't make a habit of protecting humans, especially police, but they had trusted me. It was a strange feeling.

"There was a woman in here. She seemed like the leader," Steven said. "She was over here somewhere right before I went flying through the air."

"She's gone," I said softly, kicking at the dust caking my shoes.

"Gone or dead?" he asked, but luckily the other detective walked up just then.

"We rounded up a couple of them. They said their coven leader died, which is why they fled. They blame him for the error of their ways," Detective Daniels stated as he walked up behind Steven. Mike discretely stepped away and back down the stairs, leaving me alone with the police. The detective looked at me briefly, a frown marring his forehead, before continuing. "The owner of the club is here now, and he's not happy. He's going to have some lawsuits on his hands."

"I should leave you," I said, pulling myself from Steven's embrace. "Sounds like you're going to have a busy night."

I stepped past them, hurrying toward the stairs. Steven moved up beside me, placing a hand at my elbow and guiding me to the elevator. We had just stepped into the elevator when the other detective joined us. He hit the number for the first floor and leaned back against the wall, watching me. Steven wrapped his arms around me in what I supposed was meant to be comforting. I stood stiffly, my mind racing as the other man stared me down.

As soon as the elevator stopped, I pulled away and stepped out. Mike was near the door speaking to one of the police officers. He looked anxious to leave and actually pointed in my direction. "I should find my ride," I said as Steven put his arm on my waist once more.

"He's by the door. I'll help you," he said. His partner followed us like a silent shadow as Steven led me to the door. "Make sure she gets home," he said to Mike, who nodded his head in response.

"Of course," he replied, taking my elbow.

"Can I call on you tomorrow?" Steven asked as I walked toward the door.

"Sure... tomorrow," I replied, smiling. Steven nodded and smiled back. I turned and let Mike help me out, with Detective Daniels' eyes on my back the whole time.

STEVEN

POWER THRUMMED THROUGH ME, making it hard to sleep. Normally, I would have been exhausted by the numerous protection spells I'd enacted, but the incubus and succubus packed a serious punch. I hadn't tangled with a supernatural in some time, and I'd forgotten how much energy I could pull from one, let alone two. After tossing and turning most of the night, I finally got up and decided to start the day early. My house had two visible stories and a third underground, which held not only the wine cellar, but most of my more important artifacts. The upstairs held three bedrooms and two bathrooms. The largest was my bedroom, the secondary was a guest room which I doubted I'd ever use, and the third had been converted into a home gym.

After getting strange looks at the gym in the last town I'd resided, I had decided the only way to get a good workout was at home. I ran ten miles on the treadmill before moving on to weights. Being immortal didn't mean letting yourself go. My metabolism seemed linked to my magic...curse.... The more energy I consumed from others, the more powerful I became. I was faster, stronger, and more alluring. Full of power, I could eat an entire pizza and not gain an ounce, then turn around and bench press a small car. When I was fasting, I tended to react more like an average human. It was a trade off that I'd played with many times over the centuries. Currently, I was trying to be better... meaning I killed less. Usually. That also meant staying in shape the old fashioned way and keeping energized with regular food. Habits are built with time, and this was a habit I'd found I actually enjoyed.

By the time I finished my workout and showered, the sun was just beginning to rise. The buzz at the gate so early surprised me. I walked to the gate camera, raising my eyebrows to see Steven sitting in his car.

"Who is it?" I asked into the intercom.

"Good morning, beautiful. I brought coffee," Steven said into the speaker. "And breakfast."

I pushed the buzzer, letting him in while I grabbed a pair of sunglasses and picked up my phone.

Maggie's phone rang three times before she sleepily answered. "Hullo," she mumbled.

"Maggie, it's Gia. Sorry if I woke you."

"Oh, no, it's okay. I heard about last night. Crazy," she said, sounding more alert by the minute.

"It was," I said, watching as Steven parked his car and bound up the front steps. "Do you think you'll be okay opening the store without me this morning? I'll be in later, but I have a few things I need to take care of."

"Really? You trust me to open up by myself?" she asked, sounding way too excited. Mornings were the easiest and slowest part of the day. "I'd love to."

"Yeah, of course. I'll take the security wards down from here."

"You can do that?"

I laughed and walked toward the front door as Steven pushed the doorbell. "Yes, I'll do it right now. Make sure Mike takes you to work. I'll see you this afternoon. Call if you need anything."

"Sure thing. Bye!"

"Bye," I said, hanging up and reaching out with my magic. Spells were easiest to take down on site, but this full of energy I barely had to blink and the protection magic surrounding my store was down. I lowered the wards around my house while I was at it before hurrying toward the door. While the wards were down to allow entry, I still had other spells in place at both my business and my home. The years had made me cautious, or paranoid, depending how you looked at it.

I opened the front door and smiled out at Steven. He was dressed casually in jeans and a short-sleeved shirt, with dark sunglasses on to rival my own. He held a bag in one hand and a drink carrier in the other. "Morning," he said. "I hope you like coffee, because I have a variety here."

"Come in," I said, stepping back to let him in. The smell of coffee came first, followed by the tangy scent of his cologne. I closed the door behind him and headed straight to the breakfast nook off the kitchen. It was one of my favorite spots, with a great view of the ocean.

"Wow, that's quite the view," he said, immediately heading toward the large window. He cleared his throat a moment later and turned around, setting the coffee and bag on the breakfast bar. "How do you like your coffee? I have three different levels here: black, creamy and slightly sweet, and diabetes in a cup. What's your poison?"

"Tea, actually," I replied. "While I love the smell of coffee, I can't stand the taste."

"Tea? Um..."

"Don't worry about it," I said, turning toward the kitchen.

"Well, I do have one chai tea," he said.

I stopped in my tracks and turned around. "You do?"

"Yeah, it's one of those coffee place versions full of creamy goodness. This one is the spicy kind."

I grinned at his description and moved toward him. He pulled a cup free and I wrapped my hands around the warm cup. Pulling it toward me, I breathed in the sweet and savory scents before taking a tentative sip. "Mmm, that's good," I said, licking my lips. I'd had true chai before and this was surprisingly close. "It *is* spicy. I don't think I've had one this good in a long time. Then again, I don't go to coffee stands."

"This one is from the coffee shop right down the street. Ask for the spicy house chai."

"I'll have to do that," I replied, moving to the breakfast bar and sitting down.

Steven pulled out one of the coffees and took a drink before opening the bag. He pulled out a bagel, scone, muffin, and donut. "So... I wasn't sure what you ate for breakfast either. The selection wasn't great."

I shook my head and leaned back, watching while Steven settled himself across from me. "I already ate," I lied.

"Oh, so no bagel?"

"No, I'm not a big breakfast eater. Usually it's just a bowl of fruit or some yogurt after my morning workout."

"Yogurt and fruit, and you work out in the morning. Got it."

I chuckled. "What are you doing? Making a list? Is this a cop thing?"

"No, just wanted to know what to make you for breakfast. Just in case."

"Just in case. I see," I murmured, taking a sip to hide my smile.

He packed the food back in the bag, with the exception of the donut, which he proceeded to eat. "I wasn't sure if you'd be up this early," he said as he licked icing from his fingers.

"Couldn't sleep," I said, shrugging.

Nodding, he leaned back in the chair and stared at me. "I get that. It was a busy night."

"Did you sleep?"

"Not yet," he replied. "I'll be running on coffee until noon. Then I'll probably crash."

"Are you on duty?"

"Yes."

The one word answer was all I needed to know. He was there on official police business, while trying to disguise it as post-date breakfast. "Ask your questions, Detective."

He sighed loudly and leaned forward, placing both of his arms on the table. "Gia, it's not like that."

"Oh, really? You come here with breakfast acting so casual, but you're really here on police business. How else should I be taking this, Detective?"

"If I didn't come down here first thing, Hunter would be here instead, dragging you down to the station."

My heartbeat sped up at his words, but I managed to keep my expression calm. "Why is that?" I asked, my voice relaying my irritation.

"What happened at the club? You were in the middle of that room, all alone, and the vampires that had been there were gone. I know they were there. One of them flung me across the room, and one of the other officers swears he shot at a male. The others vamps we managed to catch said they felt their leaders...die," he finished, but I heard the unspoken words. There was more he wasn't saying.

"What do you think happened?"

"Damn it, Gia, this isn't a game," he said, his voice rising with each word. "I've got half the police force singing your praises asking for you to be brought on as a consultant, and the other half condemning you and wanting to burn you at the stake. You saved us with that protection spell, and that should have been it. Then you, a blind woman who does magic but isn't a witch, shows up out of nowhere! It doesn't make any fucking sense! Why were you there? Talk to me."

As he'd spoken, he had moved to his feet until he was standing with his hands pressed firmly against the table top. He stared down at me with his piercing blue eyes, his breathing fast. He took a deep breath, which didn't diminish the flush to his cheeks. What the hell had I been thinking getting mixed up with cops? Toying with my glasses, I debated my next move. If he disappeared, his partner would be after me next. Followed by the next cop, then the next.

Then I'd have to leave town, just like last time, looking over my shoulder for the next thirty years.

Pushing my glasses back firmly on my face, I shrugged and sat back. "You want to know what happened? Are you sure?"

"Gia... you killed them, didn't you?"

"That protection spell I put on you and your men was just that—protection. You were still flung around. You were still pinned down. Eventually, the protection would have worn off and you all would have succumbed to the succubus magic. You would have been just as vulnerable as everyone else in that room. You do remember what that was like, don't you?"

"Lots of sex."

He laughed at his words, but I shook my head. "That's how the succubi feed. They gather the sexual energy, fueling themselves. One succubus, you might have been able to handle. She wasn't much. The incubus, though, was the real threat. He was the one controlling all the vamps in that club. He was the reason I fell victim. That wouldn't have happened with just one little succubus. Those two together could have brought down a town, if they'd wanted to." I laughed, but the smile was long gone from Steven's face. "You call them vampires, and you're right, in a way. They are a breed of vampire, but far superior. They are intelligent, strong, powerful, and able to control any vamps in their coven. Lucky for you, they are also very rare. Now, there are two less terrorizing your neighborhood."

He stared at me for several minutes, digesting all I'd told him. I was prepared to kill him, and I think he finally sensed the danger growing in the room. He moved back casually, but his right hand fidgeted, as though he were itching to pull out his gun. "You killed both of them?" His voice cracked, just slightly. I took a sip of the delicious drink and nodded my head once. "What are you?"

I shook my head. "That question's not on the table, Detective."

"You're not a witch."

"No, I'm not. As I stated before."

"And you're not human." I smiled at him, which was answer enough. "How did they die?"

"Does it matter? An incubus and a succubus walked into a bar. Everyone had sex. Then it was over."

"Sounds like a bad joke. What's the punch line?"

"They were never seen again."

"Gia, I can't go back to my superiors with that story."

"Why not? They're supernatural creatures that you know very little about. In a fight against a succubus, you will always lose. You're just a human. With two of them, and the amount of energy they were powering, I almost lost. I don't think you understand what that means."

"I saw your dress," he mumbled.

"You didn't see enough."

He threw his arms in the air and turned in a circle. "I'm a cop, Gia. Fuck!"

I sat back, watching him curse and slam his hand onto the table. When his breathing slowed and the curses had tapered off, I spoke into the silence. "You would be dead if I hadn't intervened."

"Maybe," he murmured.

"Definitely. It was only a matter of time."

"Damn it, one of the officers saw you. Fuck!"

"Saw me? Someone saw me? What do you mean?" My voice rose in pitch.

"One of the officers saw you go into that room with the two... creatures. He tried moving toward you, but by the time he got to you, he said..." he swallowed, shaking his head.

"He said what?"

"He saw that woman turn to dust at your feet."

"Is that all he saw?" In my full powers, I looked much like the creature of mythology, glowing eyes and scales coating my skin. It had been extremely dark in the room, but he'd seen enough if he saw the woman turn to dust. How close had he been that I hadn't noticed him?

"Yes, but that's enough. I mean, it was self defense. Wasn't it?"

"She still has the fangs of a normal vampire. She bit me."

"She bit you?" his eyes trailed over my neck.

"I heal fast, but yes, she bit me."

He nodded his head. "Was it magic? Did you have some kind of holy item?"

"What?"

"Just tell me how you dusted them? They die like vamps, right? Stab them in the heart or something? Throw some holy water at them."

"Yes," I replied, leaning back and feeling a strange sense of calm wash over me. They didn't know. No one had seen me. If they had, there would have been a lot more police in my home and they wouldn't have come with coffee. "Yes, they can be killed like vampires. I hit her with a silver dagger dipped in holy water, stabbed through the heart."

Steven stopped moving and stared at me. A deep breath filled him and as he released it, he moved toward me, his arms outstretched. "I can't believe you did something so crazy," he choked out as he wrapped his arms around me. I stiffened, then forced myself to relax into his arms. "Promise me you won't do anything like that again."

"Oh, I promise," I replied immediately. I meant every word of it. Helping the police had almost cost me everything. Next time, I'd just let them take care of themselves. If they died, it wasn't my problem. They signed up for this job.

Steven stepped back, his bright eyes searching my face. "I wish I could see your eyes," he said.

"Sorry, but that's not a good idea."

He nodded and ran a hand down my arm, sending shivers across my skin. "So, about that second date..."

I laughed, like he knew I would. "Date? Did that qualify as a first date?"

"We had dinner, we danced, and we even made out. I'd say it qualified."

"Hmm, I'll give you dinner, but the rest of the night was under the influence of an incubus. I don't think that counts."

"Oh, no, we were dancing before anything weird happened."

"Maybe, but the kissing didn't count. As far as I'm concerned, we had dinner, danced a little, then things went to shit."

"We had dinner, danced, and you had to call it an early night. So, I came over the next morning with breakfast and tea."

I laughed and shook my head, surprised he was still flirting with me. Part of me hoped it was real, and not some sort of police strategy. He moved in closer and ran a hand across my cheek. "So, technically, this is just a continuation of the first date?" I asked, turning my head into his hand.

He stepped in closer until he had me trapped in my chair. The bar stools were tall, putting him at the same height standing as I was sitting. His hand moved up and through my hair before caressing my cheek once more. I closed my eyes, bracing for the kiss that was coming. He leaned in until his lips just brushed mine. "Then he kissed her goodnight," he whispered.

"Don't you mean good morning?"

He kissed me again, letting his tongue play across my lips until I opened my mouth. The kiss grew, but I could feel him holding back. "Can't do a good morning kiss quite yet," he said between kisses.

"Mmm, why's that?" I asked, leaning forward and pursuing his kiss. He obliged, kissing me deeper. One hand rested gently at the back of my neck, while his other had a firm grip on the table. He stepped in closer until his legs brushed mine and his hand moved from my neck to trail down my back.

"Good morning kisses are for after bed," he said, finally pulling back. "What are you doing tonight?"

"Just because you saw me act a certain way under the influence of succubus magic, doesn't mean I'm always like that," I said as he moved away.

He chuckled at that and picked up the coffee carrier, making it clear he was leaving. I slid off the stool and walked him to the door. "Tonight?" he asked again, stopping with one hand on the front door handle.

"Fine, but how about a night in?"

"Your place or mine?" he asked, a grin splitting his face.

"Here." I'd already broken most of my rules, and I felt better in my home. "Does eight o'clock work?"

"I'll see you then, beautiful." He turned and walked back to his car, pausing with his hand on the handle. "You may still have to give a statement, officially, but I don't think anyone is going to bother you over this."

I hoped he was right. I put a smile on my face and waved in his direction. "You'd better get some sleep," I admonished.

"Are you planning on keeping me up all night again?"

I laughed but he didn't wait for an answer before climbing in his car and driving away. I stood in the doorway watching him for several minutes as the weight of everything came crashing back on me. No matter how interested he appeared to be in me, Steven was still a cop. I wasn't sure if he trusted me or not. He could be playing me, but I was playing him just as much. I touched my lips, feeling the lingering traces of his kiss. I'd liked his kisses far too much. Things could get dangerous if I wasn't careful. Dangerous for him.

Painting

THE LAST FEW DAYS had been strange, but the most worrisome aspect were not succubi and necromancers. No, for me it was the pieces of artwork. These, were personal. After Steven left, I made my way to the door in the corner of the living room. The door led down the cool stairs to a vast wine cellar, full of bottles and casks of various wines, and a few choice pieces of liquor. To the right, behind what appeared to be another wine rack, was a hidden room. I pulled on the rack, sliding it outward to reveal the hidden room. The room was long and narrow and wouldn't look like much more than an antique hoarder's secret stash to the casual observer. Five statues of men lined the wall to the left. To the right were racks filled with jars, glasses, vases, and a variety of other antiques.

I stepped into the room and passed the first four statues, running a hand across each. Michael had been tall and strong, and a masterful lover. Turning him had been an accident, and I was only thankful that I'd been able to turn my cursed stare into a slow process. He lounged eternally, his mouth open in excitement and surprise. I smiled as I knelt down and touched the full beard of his jaw, down his heavily muscled chest and further down before moving on. The next man was Josiah. He stood still with ropes wrapped around his arms. I flicked a finger at his nose, sneering at the man who had tried to force himself on me after one date. He was my newest addition, but I thought heavily about just draining him completely. The third man was the oldest of my collection, dating back well over a hundred years. He was dressed in a long, hooded robe. I didn't know his name, but he'd attacked me with magic and I had retaliated. I'd never figured out exactly what he was, with his strange gray eyes and magic so different from my own. The fourth man was seated in a chair. He was from the last town I'd lived in. We'd dated for a few months before he got irritated I wouldn't take off my glasses, even in bed. I finally obliged. I smiled as I looked at him, completely naked with his legs spread wide. He'd been waiting for me.

The last statue wasn't one of my own. I ran my hands over his face, feeling memory stir. Was this him? Was it truly the man I had loved all those years ago? To all appearances, it was him, but I couldn't fathom how he was still encased in stone. I flicked a glance to the hooded man. At over one hundred years, he was one of the oldest I'd ever heard of. I never knew why some statues disappeared after a few hours or days and others remained for years. To me, it was all the same. I could either drain them instantly, or I could choose a slow drain. Mostly I chose the slow drain, even if it did mean carting around statues everywhere I went. Better to keep a few around than having to drain and kill on a weekly basis. It was the lesser evil, to my mind.

I walked around the statue, running my hands over the stone and imagining it was flesh once more. The height felt right to me, but after 600 years, I could be wrong. Stepping away from the statue, I turned to the painting, now hanging on the wall opposite the statues. Over the centuries, I had sat for several portraits, but I didn't recall this one. My eyes lingered on the cross in my hands. I did, however, remember exactly when and where the details of this painting had originated.

Theda moved ahead of me, dancing up the stone steps, her powdered hair elegantly coiffed in the latest fashion. Her dress was simple with little adornment, like mine, helping us blend into the crowd. The protestors had already surged forward, finding a breach in the palace's defenses. Already, the head of a guard had been mounted atop a pike. Blood flowed down the stairs, coming from guards and peasants alike. I smiled as a peasant woman ran past me, shouting loudly in French.

"Now isn't this much more fun, Giavanna?"

I raced up the steps, passing Theda and grabbing a guard, pulling the sword from his hands. The young man he had cornered was already dying in a mess of blood. Raising my eyes to him, I captured his gaze, pulling the life force from his body. Within seconds he was nothing more than a statue. Theda knelt beside the dying young man, speaking softly to him. Anyone walking by would think she was comforting the dying young man, but Theda's actions were for her and her alone. I grabbed the statue and shoved it down the stairs, watching as bits and pieces of it broke on the way down. More men and women raced up the stairs past me. Lowering my eyes, I let them go.

"What are you planning to do with the sword?" Theda asked as she walked up beside me. Blood coated her hands and dress, but she didn't seem to mind. In fact, I think she had purposely put more there. Lines of blood trailed down her small breasts, showing where she'd wiped her hands. Behind her, the young man was nothing more than a pile of dust.

I shrugged and flicked my wrist, listening to the sound of the sword cutting through the air. "I'm not afraid of getting my hands dirty, either," I replied.

She laughed and wrapped her arms around me, kissing my cheek. "That's my girl! Let's help these peasants with their rebellions."

"Maybe if we move fast enough, we can even catch ourselves a king."

Theda laughed louder at that and together we surged after the crowd. Blood led the way. More peasants had died at the hands of the guards, but still more had pushed through. We stopped periodically, filling ourselves on the life force of those already dying. It was easy work. Power coursed through me, speeding me, strengthening me, and giving me a rush like nothing else could.

As the mob moved one way, Theda and I branched off. The mob had consisted of peasants with little to no skills other than brawling, and they were quickly being defeated. More still stood outside the walls of the palace, shouting, but those who had made their way inside were being eliminated in short order. Theda and I moved away as the guards became more organized.

"It was a fun time whilst it lasted," I said as we made our way back outside. I was more than a little disappointed the guard had reassembled so quickly. Outside the palace, it even seemed there was some sort of talk happening.

"That looks too peaceful," Theda remarked, nodding with her chin toward the remaining peasants. "How many did you take?"

"Five guards," I said, shrugging but still watching the mob. "Some six or seven dying peasants."

"Only five guards? Giavanna, there were dozens more you could have fed on. You're getting slow."

I nodded, but I wasn't really listening. My eyes had spotted a priest running from the palace. Blood trailed behind him. I followed him easily, tracking the bloody smears he left behind. Behind the palace, the man finally stopped and looked back. I lowered my gaze, but I could feel his eyes on me.

"What do you want?" he asked, his voice a strained whisper.

I held up the sword, thinking about using it. "Shouldn't you be with the dead and the dying, priest?" I asked, using the sword to point back toward the palace. Theda moved up beside me, chuckling quietly but otherwise letting me have my fun.

"I...I'm not ... I'm not a priest," he whispered.

I flicked my eyes up, just enough to see him. While he wore the clothes of a priest and held a large cross in his hands, my initial observation had been wrong. Beneath the robes, his boots were worn and covered with mud. His pants had holes in the knees and appeared worn thin.

"What are you doing, then, in the robes of a priest?"

"Just trying to get away," he mumbled.

"Where did you get the cross?" Theda asked.

I took a closer look at the golden cross in his hands. The sharp bottom point of the cross was covered in thick, dark blood. As I looked him over further, I realized none of the blood I saw came from him. "Where did you get the clothes?"

The man looked left and right, shaking his head. "Don't know why you care," he murmured, turning away.

I moved forward, sword held out in front of me. He heard my footsteps and glanced over his shoulder briefly before lifting up the robes and running away from me. I was too fast for him. My sword took him first, in the back, plunging in deep. He stopped in his tracks, a strange gurgle coming from his mouth. Letting go of the handle, I moved around to the front of him, my eyes on the tip of the sword peeking through his chest.

"You killed a priest and took his clothes, just so you could get away," I said, snatching the cross from his dying hands. "And they say I'm evil."

The man stumbled forward, collapsing against me as blood bubbled from his mouth. I stepped back, letting his body fall forward. The thought of draining him held no appeal. I looked down at the cross in my hands, feeling it's heavy weight. Theda leaned back, watching me silently. After several minutes, I finally turned away from the body, pulling the chain around my neck and tucking the cross in close to my chest.

Leaning forward, I looked closely at the cross in the painting. It was mostly plain gold, with a single ruby encrusted in the center and blood dripping from the pointed bottom. I turned back toward the racks, pulling open drawers filled with a variety of tokens I'd picked up over the years. In the second drawer I found it. Ancient dried blood still clung to the cross in spots, but most of it had flaked off over the years. Picking it up, I walked back to the painting, comparing the crosses. They were the same.

Only Theda had been with me at that time, I'd thought. Perhaps someone had seen us. After the mob had quieted down and the king had returned to Paris, I left France. Theda had insisted on seeing how things played out with Napoleon and we'd parted ways. Theda thrived on power and money, while I was content to lay down roots and really get to know the citizens of every area we moved to. After Napoleon's defeat, Theda had sought me out again. We spent another five years together before parting ways again. It was like that with us. We traveled together, killing and destroying, before finally growing tired of each other and choosing to part ways. Over the centuries, we spent less and less time together, and our time apart grew longer. When was the last time we'd been together? It had been during the Great Depression, but even that had been short-lived.

The painting only confirmed my suspicions that Theda was sending me messages. I wasn't sure what the message was, though. Did she want to reunite? Times were different now. We couldn't just run around arbitrarily killing, not that I ever had. I was more of an opportunist. I thought of my shop. This was the first time I felt like I could really be myself. Here, I could relax. I wasn't hunted. I wasn't running from anything or anyone. Of course there was the usual discord in the world, which made it possible for monsters like me to hide. Monster. I wasn't sure I liked that word anymore.

I was at peace, or the closest I could get to peace. Perhaps I was just comfortable, but even that was an elusive idea. No matter, Theda would destroy what I had. She was chaos and rage, and had never shown the slightest inkling that she wanted to settle in any one place.

I shoved the cross back in the drawer and left the room, casting one last glance back at the painting. My eyes, inevitably, traveled to the newest statue. It couldn't be him. And if it was, what did it matter? I couldn't change his fate any more than I could change my own. Closing the door, I made my way back upstairs and grabbed my phone. Theda had to be in town, and there were only three hotels she would stay at. She had expensive taste.

"Good morning, do you have a Theda Castellanos registered?" I asked of the first hotel on my list.

"Why yes, we do, room 313," the woman on the other line responded cheerfully. "In fact, I just recommended Dottie's to her for breakfast. It's right on the bay front. Do you know the place? Are you local?"

"Yes, I know the place. Thanks," I replied, hanging up.

Grabbing my jacket, I pulled it on and left my house. Dottie's was a short walk from my house in the opposite direction of my shop. It was a small restaurant situated on a hill overlooking the bay. It had become one of my favorite spots since moving to this town, which I'm sure Theda had figured out. She always seemed to find me, which was something easily done with magic. How she found out the little details of my life so easily was something that always bothered me. Then there was the statue and the painting. I walked faster, climbing the steep incline up to the restaurant.

"Good morning," the hostess said as I stepped inside. "Just one?"

"I think someone was meeting me here," I said slowly, trying to surreptitiously look around.

"Oh, of course, right this way," she said, turning and leading me to the back of the restaurant. Seated in a corner overlooking the bay, sat Theda and another woman I didn't know. Theda looked like she'd stepped off Hollywood Boulevard, an expensive diamond necklace gleaming between her small breasts that had been overly accentuated by her dress, and a touch of glamour magic. The other woman wore dark glasses as well and had her brown hair pulled back in a long braid. Both women smiled widely at me as I sat down with my back to the restaurant. I didn't like it, but there wasn't much I could do about it. The only other seat was in the corner, and I wasn't about to trap myself like that.

"Theda," I said by way of greeting. "What brings you here?"

"Well, you haven't met Amathela yet, our newest sister," she replied, indicating the other woman with a brightly polished red fingernail that matched her dress.

I frowned at the brown haired woman, taking in her sunglasses, slacks, and name brand jacket. She'd obviously been spending time shopping with Theda. "Amathela?" I asked.

"Well, it's much better than Amy Stevens. Now I am called Amathela Stefano," she replied, holding out a hand to me. Her nails were just as long, pointed, and bright red as Theda's.

I shook her hand and stretched out my senses, feeling for her magic. It was there, far beneath the surface, but faint. "Did you manage to dye your hair?" I asked. The only way to change our hair color was an exceptional glamour charm.

She blushed and pulled her hand from mine, shaking her head. "Uh, no," she said softly.

I looked back at Theda. Her lips were pursed together and a faint blush tinted her pale skin. Her hair was curled and wound intricately about her head, but the color was similar to mine- vibrant green mixed with black. Dainty glasses covered her eyes. "I felt the death of Nefeli some seven years ago now," I said slowly.

"Yes, that sounds right," Theda replied softly.

"Yet her hair..." I said slowly. "Is that why you're here?"

"Well, it is time you met your new sister. But, I thought perhaps you had some insight. You were close to Nefeli, especially toward the end," Theda replied.

I was quiet as the waitress came over and took our orders. I had become a Gorgon, cursed like Medusa, several hundred years ago. Until seven years ago, I had been the youngest of the three. It had been Nefeli, Theda, and me for so long. Nefeli had been the oldest of the three of us, and the most knowledgeable, yet she had been secretive. During her final years, she had secluded herself in Greece, praying to ancient Gods.

"It shouldn't take this long for her to come into her powers," Theda said softly, her words barely above a whisper, yet startling me from my thoughts. "It took you less than a year."

"And you?" I asked.

She shook her head. "That is so long ago I hardly remember, but I think less than one full turning of the seasons."

I sighed and sat back, trying to remember those days so long ago. "Yes, less than a year for me. I turned during the spring, and by the end of the summer heat, my hair had turned. My skin changed next and by the end of winter, I was wholly as I am, though not as learned."

Theda chuckled and shook her head. "You were a wild thing." She grew serious again almost immediately. "Amy cannot draw energy into her. She can turn others to stone, but the energy stays still inside the statue. Except for her eyes, she is human."

"Your gaze turns men to stone, though?" I asked, eyeing her once again.

"Yes, sometimes. It is strange. Sometimes they burst, but other times they just turn and stay there, like they're frozen."

"She doesn't show any sign when she is turning them to stone, either," Theda whispered. "Her hair, eyes, and skin are normal. Human."

"You do not feed?"

She shook her head and pointed at the plate of food the waitress set before her. "Normal food," she said, shrugging.

"I've never seen anyone eat so much," Theda grumbled.

"Why not just come here and speak to me?" I asked as I picked at the bowl of fruit before me. "Instead, you have to send strange paintings and statues."

"Paintings?"

"Let's not play games, Theda."

Theda huffed and crossed her arms, looking sullen. "Amy has been one of us for five years," she said softly.

"Five? But Nefeli died seven years ago?"

"She did, and Amy is the second since that time. Meagan was before her."

"I didn't feel anything," I said, frowning.

"She wasn't a Gorgon long, but I was with her when it happened."

"How?"

Theda took a drink of water and stared at Amy as though she held answers. "Meagan was with me for less than two years, but she was never fully one of us. Her hair began turning after about a year, but, like Amy, she was never fully instilled with powers. She turned men to stone and seemed to suck in their energy, but it left almost immediately. Every time. We met a werewolf pack in Texas and they were just a little too knowledgeable. They stalked us for days until they had us cornered. I wasn't concerned, not really, but then they attacked. One of the wolves bit Meagan. Her screams will haunt me forever."

"A werewolf bite?" I asked, my heart beating fast at her tale. "It killed her? How is that possible?"

She shook her head. "I don't know. I killed most of the pack, and the rest ran off, but it was too late. She... she turned to stone. Right there before my eyes. Then, she was gone. Nothing. She crumbled to dust and I felt her life force leave. Moments later, I felt Amy awaken. I figured you wouldn't pay attention to the awakening of another of our kind, so I sought Amy out on my own and never told you."

"Five years ago?" I murmured, thinking back. There had been a moment five years ago where I had felt a strange shiver, but it was nothing like I'd felt with Nefeli. It had been enough to cause me pause, but I hadn't pursued it.

"You did feel something."

I shrugged, "I think so, but it was not as it was with Nefeli. Not even close."

"No, it was not, and I was there with Meagan. Perhaps if I had not, I wouldn't have noticed either. Something is happening to us, I fear. That is why I'm here. We need your help, Gia," Theda said softly. The plea in her voice touched me, and I looked up at her in surprise. Only once in my 600 years had I heard Theda plead, and then, like now, it didn't bode well.

THEDA

THE RESTAURANT WASN'T A good place to talk freely, so I brought Amy and Theda back to my home. It was a sign of my concern that I allowed them into my home, but they couldn't access any areas I didn't allow. I had always been better with earth magic than Theda, especially with spells of warding, and I had no fear of Amy. Theda was all about flash and show, and illusion. She hated walking around appearing as a blind woman, and had spent centuries perfecting her illusions so she could appear any way she wished. To me, though, she would appear as she was, though I could see her illusion if I wished. Today her illusion showed a young woman in her mid-twenties with long auburn hair and bright green eyes.

"Nice place," Theda said as I led her past the breakfast nook I'd sat at with Steven just hours before. I looked up at her, watching her reaction, but she gave nothing away.

"I like the view," I said, pointing out the window. Overlooking the bay and the ocean beyond was something I couldn't get enough of.

"Oh, yes, you always did love the ocean." Her condescension was easy to hear in her words and tone, but I chose to ignore it. She hated the ocean and always made it clear she was above me and my fishing village origins.

"I have some texts in the library," I said, leading them past the formal dining room and into the living room I had converted into a massive library. The room took up a corner of the house, with views of the bay and ocean. Two full walls were dedicated to books, from floor to ceiling. I walked up to the first bookcase and pulled it open, revealing ancient texts I didn't like leaving lying about for just anyone to pick up. Not that I entertained much. "I've never heard of anything like this, but perhaps we can find something obscure."

"What do you think you could find? I have been alive longer than most of your books and I've never heard such a thing," Theda snapped.

I took a book out, looked at it, then set it on the coffee table in the middle of the room. Amy made herself comfortable on the couch as I handed her a book. I didn't know her well enough to trust her with my ancient texts, but she had more reason than any of us to look for a solution. Still, I would be picky about the books I let her touch. I pulled out several more, stacking them up on the table before closing my book case and sitting on the couch. Theda grumbled, but eventually sat down beside me and grabbed a book.

"I don't suggest looking for information on Gorgons," I said as I carefully opened a book. "Instead, I suggest anything about changes to supernatural creatures. Anything not normal."

"We're not normal," Amy murmured softly and I turned to look at her. "None of this is normal. Why me? Why us?"

"I have asked myself that many times," I replied and Theda loudly huffed beside me. I ignored her and continued. "We didn't do anything. Nefeli called us sisters, and she's closer to truth than I think she realized. We are sisters, in a way. I have traced my lineage back as far as I can, and I believe we are all related."

"Oh, this again," Theda mumbled. "You spent too much time with Nefeli. She, too, had so many theories."

"I have done much research on this, and why would you dismiss Nefeli's theories? She was alive far before you, and you're already older than dirt."

Theda placed a hand to her chest and gasped. "How dare you call me old!" Theda had become a Gorgon at the ripe old age of 32, and she hated the fact that she had stopped aging at such an age, when the rest of us were all in our 20s when we'd become Gorgons.

I rolled my eyes and turned back to Amy. "Nefeli's theory was that we were all descended from Medusa, and when another of the Gorgon sisters dies, a new one must take her place."

"Wait... *the* Medusa?"

"The one and only. There are many different stories about Medusa, but Nefeli insisted that the true story was that Medusa, and her two sisters, were cursed by Athena."

"Oh, I heard about that. She got busy in Athena's temple," Amy replied.

I turned around to glare at Theda, who cringed slightly. "Got busy? Really? Have you taught her nothing?" I said, feeling my anger grow. I took several deep breaths to calm myself before turning back to Amy. "Medusa was raped, by the god Poseidon, in Athena's temple. Athena only saw, like you said, Medusa getting busy with Poseidon in her temple. Poseidon was outside her realm, but Athena could easily punish the beautiful and very human Medusa, and she did."

"Snakes for hair," Amy replied.

"I believe her punishment was like ours, but after so much time, the tale has become warped. Or, perhaps Medusa didn't feed often enough. Maybe she even liked being a feared creature, and purposely walked around in her cursed form. Who's to say? As far as our memories go, there have always been three of us though. Forever. Before me, there were many others, going back hundreds of years. Before Theda there was Narissa and Scilla. But before Scilla was Stheno. I have kept many texts on this, keeping great accounts during my talks with Nefeli. She spoke of her early days as a Gorgon with Stheno and Delfine, before Stheno killed herself."

"Nefeli told many stories," Theda said, cutting me off. "You don't actually believe she knew Stheno, one of the original Gorgons."

"Nefeli knew a great deal of information that is not in any texts but hers."

"You have her books?"

"Of course I have her books!" I said, standing up.

"Where are they?"

"What?"

"Where are they?" Theda asked, standing and moving before me. Amy's arms wrapped around mine from behind, holding me in place. I raised an eyebrow in surprise. "Where are Nefeli's belongings? I knew you spent many years with her, whispering in her ear. Where are her things?"

"Theda, you should know better than to threaten me, especially in my own home."

"Amathela, follow the statue," Theda said, and I felt a small trickle of energy coming from the woman behind me.

"It's not really him, is it?" I asked, pulling in energy, readying myself.

Theda leaned in close. "Wouldn't you like to know?" I cursed myself for a fool just before something hit me on the head, knocking me out.

Theda would never really hurt me, especially now, but she did know how to hurt me emotionally. When I woke several hours later, my house had been ransacked. All the books I had pulled out were gone, along with the rest that had been hidden behind my bookcase. The rest of my regular books had been tossed about the room. A few loose pages had been scattered around the room and the spines of several books deliberately bent backward.

I quickly made my way down to the cellar, stepping carefully. The wine casks that had been guarding my secret room had been destroyed, and wine filled the bottom of my cellar two inches thick. Cursing Theda, I hurried to the room and peered inside. The majority of the room was fine, with the exception of the wine coating the floor. My spells had worked, guarding my most sacred treasures while leaving just enough valuables to make the room appear full. The items they could see, they took. There were a few belongings I was irritated they had stolen, but the fact that they had taken my books angered me more than anything. I should have kept them warded, but I'd foolishly removed the spell when I'd opened the bookcase. Theda really should have known better than to touch my books, and I should have known better than to let my guard down.

The secret door no longer closed properly and thanks to the wine, I had a huge mess. I made my way back upstairs, left my shoes on the top step so I wouldn't bring the mess onto the carpet, and picked up my phone. First things first, I needed an emergency clean up. Over three hours had passed, and I had twenty missed calls. All were from Maggie. The cleanup would have to wait. I dialed Maggie and waited. "Gia, oh thank goodness," she said, her voice breathless.

"Maggie, what's wrong?"

There was a commotion and Mike's voice came on the phone. "Maggie has been trying to call you for the last hour. I was just about to drive over to your house."

"What's the problem?" I asked, cutting him off before he continued his rant.

"You were robbed," he said bluntly.

"What?"

"Two women came in here and held Maggie up at gunpoint!"

"Damn, is she okay?" I asked, cursing Theda once more. She had a lot of nerve. My protection spells in the shop would have kept Maggie safe from most things, but I had no way of testing that theory against other Gorgons. "Put Maggie back on."

He muttered angrily, but Maggie's voice came on the phone almost immediately. "The police are on their way to your house, I think. I'm okay. It's weird. They went straight to the store room and I could hear them in there bashing things around. I ran down the street to the pub and called the police."

The buzzer to the front gate rang and I hurried to the monitor. Detective Daniels peeked out at me and I cursed loudly. Just what I needed. I buzzed him in and made my way back to the front door, grabbing a pair of sunglasses on my way. My house was a disaster. They hadn't just ransacked my library, but my entire home. Broken dishes littered the floor of my kitchen. They'd been irritated they couldn't find Nefeli's belongings, and took their anger out on my house. I didn't have time to explore further.

"Maggie, Detective Daniels is here now."

"Okay, the police are still at the shop. Do you want me to stay here until they're done."

I sighed and ran a hand through my hair. Sticky blood met my hand. Damn, they'd hit me hard. I couldn't die unless someone chose to chop off my head, but I could still be injured, and knocked unconscious. "Only if you want to. I'll be down as soon as I can."

"I'll stay another hour," she said. "They have to take my statement anyway."

"Thanks, Maggie. Bye."

"Bye."

I hung up and opened the front door at the first knock. Detective Daniels looked up at me, mouth open, apparently about to say something. From the dark look in his eyes, it was going to be something angry. He clamped his mouth shut and stepped into the doorway, pulling his gun out and pushing me against the wall. "What happened?" he whispered, his mouth close to my ear.

I shrugged and said, "I was robbed."

"Stay here," he said, pressing me physically against the wall. He was tall and muscular, covering my body easily with his own. I nodded my head and he peeled away from me to drift through my house on silent feet. I could have told him no one was in the house, but I was pretty sure he would have insisted on searching anyway. He returned several minutes later. "It's clear," he said, holstering his gun.

"I figured, since they left here to go rob my shop."

He nodded and took my elbow, leading me through the wreckage and into the library, where he settled me onto the couch. He turned and walked back into my kitchen, returning a moment later with a damp rag he pressed gently to my head. I took the towel and he stepped back, looking around the room. "Lot of books," he mused, picking up a handful and rifling through them before sitting down on the couch beside me. He stacked the books on the coffee table and turned toward me. "So, you know the robbers?"

I sighed and sat back. "I know one of them and met the other today. They wanted my help with some research. We were looking over some of my older books when one of them hit me over the head. When I woke up, the place looked like this." It was mostly the truth.

"What's missing?" he asked, pulling out a notepad.

I shrugged. "Not sure. Several antique books, for starters."

"What was in the cellar? They made quite the mess down there."

"You didn't track wine back through my house, did you?" I asked, alarmed. I glanced down at his feet, noting the black socks.

"Took my shoes off on the steps next to yours," he said softly. "We can arrange a cleaner, after the investigation. I'll have to call the crew to come here as soon as they're done with your shop."

Damn it, the last thing I needed was a bunch of cops combing through my house. Not that they could see anything I didn't want them to see. My magic was strong. "Okay," I said resignedly.

"So, what did they take from the cellar?"

I shook my head. "I'm not sure yet."

"Couldn't have been much. Looked like you still had statues, paintings, and some pretty expensive looking artifacts in there."

"What?" I asked, my heartbeat speeding up at his words. My magic was strong. My magic was strong. Strong enough to deter Theda and Amy. Strong enough to deter anyone I'd ever met before.

"I can't see them trying to cart those big statues out of there, but that cupboard right inside the door looked untouched. Looked like some pretty pricey stuff."

I stared at him, trying to slow my heartbeat. He saw through my enchantments. It was the only explanation. "Did you touch anything?"

"No, everything needs to be checked and dusted for prints. I'm no rookie," he said, crossing his arms angrily.

"That's not what I meant," I whispered, turning to stare at my bookcase. There was still one hidden storage area that appeared to be untouched. Inside it were Nefeli's books. I was sure that's what they'd been after, although I couldn't understand why. Theda had read them before.

I pointed across the room at the hidden case, making up my mind to trust the detective. I could always kill him later. "See the dark blue book over there?"

He nodded and walked across the room in three quick strides, hovering his hand over the spine. "This one with the weird silver lines on the spine?"

"Yes that's the one. Pull it out. What do you see?"

He crouched down and peered behind the book, shuffling the other books out of his way. "Looks like a lever."

"You can see that?" He frowned and looked at me, but I shook my head. "Pull the lever."

He reached out, hesitating just a moment before pulling the lever. The bookcase slid to the right, revealing a hidden set of shelves. I tested my magic, feeling it still in place. He shouldn't have been able to see the lever, let alone pull it. Additional spells covered the books.

"On the top shelf, there's a small silver cup. Bring it here," I said softly.

He stood up and grabbed the cup, walking back toward me with it. "What's this?" he asked.

"A cursed cup," I said.

The detective swore and set it on the table, his voice lowering an octave. "Cursed? What kind of curse?"

I smiled and picked up the cup. "Calm down. It only works on vampires."

"Why did you want me to pick it up?"

"To see if you could."

"What? What do you mean? I'm not a vampire."

I stood and carried the cup back to the shelf, putting it back in its place. "This cup, this shelf, this bookcase, and that lever all had spells on them. And you just walked over plain as day and pushed through all of them like it was nothing. What are you?"

He backed up, rubbing his hands on his pants. He darted a look at the bookcase before planting his pale blue eyes back on me. "I'll call the crew over here to investigate."

"Don't bother," I said. "I'll take care of it myself."

"This is a crime scene," he said, pointing at me. "More than just the robbery. They hurt you, too."

"I'm fine, and there's nothing the police can do but get themselves killed. Stay out of this."

"What *are* you that you think you can take care of this yourself?" he asked, hands on his hips.

I chuckled and closed up my hidden bookcase with a wave of my hand. He watched me with narrowed eyes, and I had to wonder if he could see the threads of magic as well. "Don't you worry yourself about me. Now, if you'll excuse me, I need to check on my shop. And Maggie."

"You're not going anywhere," he said, grabbing my arm.

I looked down at his hand on my arm and really debated pulling the sunglasses off. "A gentleman never manhandles a lady, Detective."

He immediately let go and pulled himself up. "My apologies," he said softly. "Please, I'll take you to the shop as soon as I get a crew set up over here."

Please? "You tell no one about the bookcase, or anything else you've seen here for that matter," I said, crossing my arms. I shouldn't have shown it to him in the first place, but curiosity had gotten the best of me. Now I'd have to move anything valuable out of there. I had other hidden places, not that they'd work against him. Damn Theda for taking my books. And damn the detective. He was just another mystery I didn't need right now.

"Your secret is safe with me." He paused, with his mouth slightly open as though he was debating his next words.

"Your secrets are safe with me as well, detective. I won't tell anyone, if you won't."

He snapped his mouth closed, nodded his head, and mumbled his thanks before picking up his phone. Within minutes, my house was full of cops. I gave them descriptions of Theda and Amy, along with their names. Amy, I figured, could probably be found. Not with fingerprints. There wouldn't be any, unless that part of the transformation wasn't working on Amy either. Yet another thing I needed to research. Great.

BeTRAYAL

LEAVING MY HOUSE UNATTENDED sounded like a bad idea, but the only person I knew that could break through my magic was driving me to my shop. Detective Daniels drove me in his black unmarked police car the short distance to my store. He hadn't suggested I sit in the back seat behind the bullet proof glass, so he must have been warming up to me. I had changed clothes, deciding to go with a white skirt that just hit at the knees and a pale blue blouse with the first three buttons undone. I'd washed my hair quickly to get the blood out, thankful the wound had healed, and let it air dry. Before leaving, I'd slipped into a pair of blue heels that matched my shirt perfectly. The detective had eyed me up and down before leading me to his car, but hadn't said a word. I wasn't sure what to make of the look, but I guessed he didn't approve of my outfit. Like I cared. His idea of style was yet another rumpled suit with that just slept in feel.

Only one police car remained at my shop when we arrived, probably since the rest had moved their operation to my house. Maggie stood in the doorway chatting with one of the officers when we parked. She looked relieved when I stepped out, but her eyes darted frantically behind me. Turning, I saw what had caught her eye. Mike and another man- no, werewolf- were stalking down the street toward us on long legs. The other man had a smattering of gray at the temples, but that didn't lower his danger level at all. If anything, it upped it a notch. Still, I couldn't let a couple werewolves get under my skin.

I turned my back on the two werewolves and waited beside my car door as the detective moved around and took my elbow. I hadn't grabbed a cane, and one must keep up appearances for the general public. Detective Daniels eyed the two men as he walked me toward the door, and I couldn't help but feel like I was caught in the middle of a pissing match. Did he really just puff out his chest? I rolled my eyes behind my glasses, glad no one could see it, and put a smile on my face.

"Gia, I think they're mostly done here. There were cops everywhere, but they almost all left a few minutes ago," Maggie said as she hurried toward me and took my elbow from the detective.

"They all went to my place," I said as we walked inside. The place had been ransacked, just like my house. If it had been after hours, I doubt the two could have gotten through my defenses. Being broad daylight, and my store open for business, I couldn't restrict access like I normally would. My store room, where my more expensive spelling equipment was, had additional wards. I let Maggie chatter on as she led me to the storage. They had indeed made it through some of my lower level wards, but none of the truly dangerous, or expensive, items had been touched. There wasn't anything here they needed or wanted anyway.

I moved around the room, mentally tallying the things they had taken. They had stolen all of my basic spelling equipment, which I'd need to replace immediately. I had a few ready-made potions and my more expensive spelling ingredients remaining, but all my standard supplies were gone. Even the most basic equipment was costly, and took time to order. If they hadn't stolen it, I had a small backup kit at the house. One more thing I needed to check.

Maggie had been clutching my elbow as we walked back to the front of the store. "They didn't take any money," she murmured.

"No, they weren't after money," I replied.

"What were they after, Miss Marchesi?"

I took a deep breath before turning back to face Detective Daniels, who wasn't alone. Steven stood beside him, along with an older man with graying hair. Steven looked nervous, Detective Daniels looked nervous, and Maggie was shaking like a leaf. "Books," I replied simply.

"Magic books?"

"No," I said, shaking my head. "Just very old, very rare, and very expensive books."

"So, you're the owner?" the older man said. "You've made yourself quite well-known recently, haven't you?"

"You know me, but we have yet to be introduced."

"Joe," he said as he took my hand and shook it. He held my hand too long and too hard for a proper handshake and his jaw was set tight, working back and forth as though he were grinding his teeth. Just as suddenly he dropped my hand and put a bland smile on his face as he spoke. "Now we've met."

"Who exactly are you, Joe?"

"Uh, Gia, this is my boss," Steven said, taking my elbow and pulling me back from Joe a few steps. "Captain Hall insisted on coming down when he heard what happened here."

Joe shook his head and glared at Steven. "Don't sugar-coat things, McNeill. I came here to make sure Miss Marchesi isn't causing problems in my town." He turned back to look at me, the scowl on his face only diminishing slightly. "Are you the cause of all these problems in my town?"

"I think I've proven that I'm more of a solution to problems."

"Maybe. Or you're just good at covering your tracks."

"The only reason I bought this place was because it was a good deal. And why was it such a good deal?" I waited a heartbeat before answering my own question. "Oh, yes, because of the arsonist who tried to destroy this part of town. Did you ever catch him?"

He stared back at me, took a slow breath, then cleared his throat. "No, we didn't."

"And how long ago was that? A year now? Two? I've been here two months."

"You've made your point."

"I certainly hope so, and I hope this means your men will be on this case searching for my missing artifacts."

"Get a list of missing items to us."

"Sure thing."

He nodded one last time and stomped away. Steven blew out a breath and moved his hand across my back, tugging me closer to him. "Damn, he's scary. You handled yourself well."

"Not much scares me," I replied.

"What about these two women? You said you knew one of them?"

I let out a sigh. "Yes, she came by asking me for help. I took out books for her research and as soon as I did they knocked me out, took the books, and made a disaster of my home."

"Books? Like Braille?"

I held my breath and put a small smile on my face. "No, regular books. Well, not so regular. Old, very old, and unique."

"But..." he trailed off, glancing at me and then back to the floor.

"She's not blind, Steve," Hunter said, frowning at the two of us.

"What?" Steve's hand dropped from my back as he looked back and forth at the two of us.

"She's not blind. She has some eye thing that hurts her eyes."

"You're not blind?"

I turned toward him and shook my head. "Not totally, no. Detective Daniels is correct."

"What color eyes do you have?" he asked, leaning toward me and putting a hand out.

I cringed backward and clutched the glasses to my face. "Don't!" He jerked back as though he'd been burned. "Sorry, I don't take these off. Ever. The repercussions just aren't worth it."

"Oh," he said, nodding as though he understood. "Sure, sure."

"Green," I said. "My eyes are green."

He smiled and patted my arm, but the warmth had left his face. "I have to go finish this up. Catch you later."

After he walked away I turned towards Detective Daniels. "How did you know?"

"I'm a damn good detective, that's how," he said, smirking at me. "Not that Steve's not, but he tends to overlook things when there's a pretty face involved."

"And you don't?"

"I always do my research. No matter how attractive the subject."

"Are you saying I'm attractive, Detective?"

He laughed, a nice, deep full laugh. "I'll get Steve to come write down what's missing."

I frowned as he walked away and jumped when Maggie touched my arm. "I'm sorry, but I was listening to your conversation," she said softly. "How much can you see?"

"In a brightly lit room, I can see shapes. Outlines, really. My doctor says I'm about seventy percent blind," I lied, hoping this wouldn't come back to bite me on the ass later. "The more light my eyes get exposed to, the more damage is done, so I just don't ever take these glasses off."

"Not even at home?"

I shook my head. "I can't risk it. Being able to see shapes and movement is all I have left."

"What do the doctors say? Is there a cure? Surgery?"

"No," I replied simply, relieved as Steve came back into the shop and walked up to us.

"I'll need to take down an official list of anything missing, Miss Marchesi. Maggie, you're free to go home. Your husband is waiting for you."

Maggie patted my arm before leaving, letting the shop door close gently behind her. I moved my back to the counter and leaned against it, trying to get a read on the detective. "What do you need to know, Detective McNeill?"

"What exactly is missing from the shop, for starters?"

"My basic spell kit and some common ingredients. I can make a list."

"That would be helpful. Are any of these ingredients rare, or used in any specific spells?"

I shrugged. "Not that I can think of right now. I'll get you a list."

"Of course," he replied, tapping the stylus to the tablet. "These other women are witches?"

"No."

"Yet they do magic?"

"Yes."

He looked up, his lips pursed. "Are they like you?"

"What do you mean by that?"

"Maggie stated both the women had glasses like yours, indicating they were blind, but they both moved around the shop as though they could very easily see." I felt my heart speed up at his line of questioning. Already my lies were coming back to bite me in the ass. That didn't take long. "Is this eye condition of yours genetic? Are you related to these women?" Or maybe not.

I felt a wave or relief wash over me. "Yes, I believe so. Theda and I go way back, and I've long suspected we were related due to our similarities. I just met Amy, so I couldn't confirm anything."

"The other night..." he trailed off, lowering the tablet and finally looking back up at me. "Are you Fae?"

"No, but I'm Other," I replied.

"But not Fae?"

"You don't even know what Fae are."

"I looked it up after our... date."

Perhaps he paid more attention than his partner gave him credit for. "I'm not Fae, Detective McNeill. I'm also not human. I'm just... something else. Other."

"What is that?"

"It's not important."

"Okay, what do you mean by Other?"

"Other than human."

"So werewolves are Other?"

"Yes."

"And vampires."

"Yes."

"And Fae."

"Fae are Fae."

"What does that mean?"

"It means don't meddle in things you don't understand."

He crossed his arms and exhaled loudly. "Miss Marchesi, I am a detective assigned to the supernatural. This is my job. The more I know, the better prepared I can be."

"Believe it or not, I'm trying to help you, *Detective*."

"Gia."

"Oh, are we back on a first name basis?"

"Gia," he said again, stepping toward me. "I'm trying."

"Well, try harder," I snapped.

"Is there anything else missing from the shop?"

"Not that I've noticed yet. I'll have to take an official inventory to see, and close my shop to do so. I also have to take care of my house." I took a deep breath, trying to calm my rising anger.

"I'm sorry about your shop, and your house."

"Thanks."

He stood quietly before taking another step closer to me. "Why didn't you tell me about your eyesight?"

"It's just a part of who I am, and honestly I get tired of explaining myself to everyone I meet. It's just easier if everyone thinks I'm blind. It's close enough to the truth."

"Hunter knew," he murmured.

"Your partner obviously has a lot of time on his hands for snooping."

"You mean you didn't tell him?"

I frowned and turned my face toward his. "Why would I have told him?"

He shrugged and looked at his tablet again, the frown on his face deepening. "How long do you need to get a list of inventory to me?"

"A few days, I suppose."

"Do you need help?"

"Maggie will help me with the shop tomorrow. I need to get back to my house and get a cleanup crew set to take care of the wine disaster."

"I can take you home."

"Sure, thanks," I muttered, pushing away from the counter and heading toward the door. I could still see Maggie outside, waiting for me, with Mike just a step behind her.

"Gia?" I stopped at the door and turned around. "I have to take care of some paperwork, but I'd still like to see you tonight. I can come by and help you clean up. We can order take out."

He smiled at me and his voice had taken on a lighter, friendlier note, as though it would take the sting out of the way he'd been treating me for the past thirty minutes. I wasn't sure what to make of it. "Well that depends. Are you Detective McNeill or Steven?"

"Just Steve, the confused one."

"Sure," I said, pushing the door open. "I need to talk to Maggie real quick, then you can drop me off and take care of your police stuff."

"And then?"

"Then leave Detective McNeill at the station. I'd prefer to see Steve tonight."

"I think that can be arranged."

I smiled, hoping that was true before stepping outside and walking toward Maggie. Before I reached her, Mike moved forward, his chest puffed out more than usual. "I don't think my wife should be working here alone any more," he said before I had a chance to speak.

"Darn it, Mike," Maggie said, pushing him aside. "Would you stop?"

"I didn't say you couldn't work here. I said not alone." He turned back toward me. "Jerry will accompany my wife whenever I'm not available. He will be like a ghost. You won't even know he's there."

"I know he's here now," I replied tersely.

"Mike, I do not need a bodyguard," Maggie said, tugging on her husband's arm.

"If you want to keep working here, you obviously do."

"It was a one time thing."

"You're human!"

"I'll make a compromise with you," I said, interrupting the two before their argument escalated further. Mike turned toward me with his eyebrows raised, while Maggie looked more defeated than ever. "For the time being, I will allow Jerry or you to accompany Maggie only if I am not here. Outside the shop, though. I can't have werewolves cramping my business."

Mike stared at me for a long moment before curtly nodding his head. "That's acceptable."

I turned toward Maggie. "Does that work for you, Maggie?"

She shrugged her shoulder and looked up at me with red-rimmed eyes. "It doesn't seem like I have much say in the matter. You all think I'm some frail thing that will just shatter into a million pieces. I guess that's what I get for marrying a werewolf."

"Maggs," Mike said, turning toward her with a look of utter devastation on his face.

"What time should I be here tomorrow?" she asked me.

"Let's meet here at nine."

She nodded once before storming off, tears rolling silently down her cheeks. Mike stared after her, his mouth hanging open. "Mike," I said, stopping him before he chased after her.

He turned and glared at me, his eyes glowing golden, but he stopped moving. "What?"

"It's not my place," I said, retreating back a step.

"Just spit it out."

"Maggie knows she's human, and weak compared to a werewolf, but she doesn't need that thrown in her face. She's a lot stronger than you give her credit for."

"I know how strong my wife is." He stormed after her before I could say another word. Not my place.

Clean Up

STEVE DROPPED ME OFF with promises of a drama-free evening. I was trying to be hopeful and looking forward to the evening, but I wasn't looking forward to the cleanup. The first thing I did was phone companies searching for someone to come clean up the mess. The police had left me a list of agencies they used, so I knew they'd been vetted already. The first company agreed to send someone right away, for a substantial fee. I agreed and hurried down to the cellar before they arrived. My secreted items were all still there, but Hunter had already seen them, and their location. I made trips stashing various items in new locations throughout my house. I'd need to try out some new protection spells, but for that I'd need more equipment. Amy and Theda had in fact stolen my extra spelling kit, so I'd have to either find them to get all my equipment back, or just order a couple more sets. A third choice popped into my head, but I didn't like it, even if it would be faster.

Sighing, I opened my phone and dialed Ian's phone number from his application. "Ian here," he said by way of greeting.

"Hi, Ian, it's Gia. I'd like to speak to William."

He didn't respond right away, but I could hear a muffled conversation. After a moment he came back on and rattled off a new phone number for me. I jotted it down and redialed. William picked up on the first ring.

"Gia, to what do I owe this pleasure?" his voice dripped with sincerity and a touch of humor.

"You may have heard that I was robbed earlier today."

"Hmm, yes, I did hear that." I wasn't surprised. William seemed the type to stay connected to anything in his town.

"Well, they stole some personal equipment that is rather difficult and time-consuming to replace. Would you happen to have a spell kit and some basic supplies I could buy from you, or borrow until I can replenish my supplies?"

"A woman like you doesn't have an extra kit lying around?"

"I did, actually, but that was stolen as well."

"Well, that is unfortunate. Thankfully for you, I always have at least one extra kit on hand. I'll send Ian over with a kit and any ingredients we can spare. It should be enough to get you by until you can order more." I heard the clinking of vials in the background and could imagine William standing over his supplies, sorting through the ingredients in between long drags of brandy. "It looks like I have enough ingredients to do a locater spell, if you'd like me to include those."

I smiled into the phone. "Thank you, I'd appreciate it."

"I'll be over in ten minutes."

"You? I thought you were sending Ian?"

"I changed my mind." He hung up without another word. I looked at the time. The cleaning crew would be arriving within the hour, William would be here in ten, and Steve said he'd be there in two hours with takeout.

Precisely ten minutes later, William's sleek black Mercedes pulled up at my house. I'd left the front gate open, but my gate alarm still alerted me to his car. To my surprise, he was alone and carrying a large black case. I opened the door and he stepped right inside, taking a quick survey of my entryway as I led him to the kitchen. I pointed to the far counter, and he set the case down before clicking it open. Inside was an entire basic spell kit, complete with a small cauldron, stirring spoons of various materials, and small containers of ingredients all labeled in a precise hand. He pulled a small leather bag from inside his jacket and set that down as well, showing me the extra ingredients inside that would make a basic level locater spell.

"Thanks for this," I said, pulling out the ingredients and sorting them. Theda had known what she was doing when she took my basic potion ingredients. It hindered me more than I liked to admit. "You make your locater spells with fir?" I asked.

He chuckled and leaned back against the counter. "How else would I make them? Is this some sort of quiz to see if I know how to do my own potions?"

"No, it's just I've found if I substitute a few ingredients and use oak instead, I get a more precise location." I tried to sound casual as I pulled out the ingredients I'd need to do my location spell. Theda hadn't taken all my ingredients, thankfully, since I had a small store warded in my kitchen. I unlocked the ward with a wave of my hand and pulled open the small cabinet. The supplies were expensive or rare, which is why I had them warded and not my basic kit. It was an error I wasn't about to repeat.

William watched me as I pulled the supplies together and carried them to my stove, turning the burner on with a flick. The gate buzzed, and I cursed, remembering the cleanup crew. "Can you start this?" I asked, pointing to the first three ingredients. "Just these three, bring to a boil. Stir constantly, but only with the oak stick. As soon as it boils, remove it from the heat."

"I know the basics of a location spell," he replied tersely, shuffling my ingredients around. I moved the supplies back into the correct order and looked at him pointedly. "Fine, I'll do it your way," he replied.

I hurried to the door and let the cleaning crew in, setting them to work in the cellar. The man and one woman were human, but the other woman was Fae. She stared at me with wide eyes, and I would have been uneasy if she'd been anything dangerous. I didn't have time to stand over them with William cooking up a potion in my kitchen, so I gave them explicit instructions and left them to the now empty cellar.

William was just taking the cauldron off the heat when I walked back into the kitchen. He'd removed his gray suit jacket, folding it across the back of the nearest chair, and had rolled up the sleeves of his crisp white shirt. Over the shirt he wore a matching gray vest that somehow looked even better with his sleeves rolled up. He set the cauldron down and stepped back. "Just in time," he said, reaching for the next ingredient in my lineup.

I nodded and moved up beside him, letting him continue with the potion. "Two drops, stir once, then two more drops." He obliged and I picked up the final bottle, opening it carefully. "Hold up the spoon." He held it up and I carefully dropped a single drop of the blue-green liquid onto the spoon. "Put the spoon back in, stir one turn in each direction, then remove the spoon." He nodded, doing as he was told precisely. As soon as he removed the spoon, the potion turned bright green, indicating it had been done correctly. I pulled out four vials, filling them carefully using a copper ladle before stoppering them.

William moved around the kitchen, helping me clean up in record time. We moved in time with each other, dancing around the kitchen, and I found myself appreciating the extra set of hands. I hadn't had this good of a spelling partner since Nefili, and the last time we'd done a potion together was when I'd visited her in Greece in the late 1800s. I sighed at the memory, missing my favorite mentor, as I packed up the kit nicely.

"Thanks again," I said to William, handing him one of the vials.

He raised an eyebrow before smiling and taking the vial. "Thank you," he said as he tucked the vial into a pocket on his jacket. "I'm anxious to see this potion in action, but I don't have anything or anyone I'm currently looking for."

I grinned and held the potion up, swirling the contents. "You want to help." It was a statement.

"Well, I did give you all these supplies. Free of charge," he added with a wink.

"Not so free, I think." I put the vials and my new equipment away, warding it from prying eyes. "Are you available tomorrow night?"

"A night hunt? I think I could clear my schedule."

"You're not tagging along," I chided. "I'll do the spell, you can watch, and then you go home."

"Why?"

"Why? First, this doesn't really concern you. Second, it could be dangerous."

"So nice that you're concerned for my safety."

I chuckled and said, "I'm not. I just want you out of my way. I usually work alone."

He grinned and moved toward my living room, taking stock of my book-strewn room. I followed him as he made himself comfortable on my couch. "What are you doing?"

"Convincing you to let me join you tomorrow," he replied, tapping the couch. I sat down beside him, watching as he flipped through a few of my books, closing the spines carefully. "Animals," he said, shaking his head at one book that had a broken spine.

"I completely agree," I replied. "Which is why you shouldn't involve yourself."

"I'm already involved, and I find myself becoming... invested in you." He paused, and I could tell he was thinking through his next words carefully. "You really shouldn't let Fae in your home, especially unguarded."

"I'm not worried about the girl."

He smiled widely, obviously pleased. "You knew, and you still let her in."

"Fairies are good at cleanup," I replied simply, shrugging my shoulders.

"But letting her in..."

"I'm not a fool, William."

"And choosing to work the potion with me instead of watching her. I didn't feel you cast any spells either."

"Because I haven't."

He turned sideways, leaning one arm on the back of the couch and looking very at home. "You are either very foolish, or very egotistical."

I flicked my wrist and the books in the room flew into the air, zooming around until they had all settled back in their places on my shelves. The magic it took was minimal, but William shivered and the Fae poked her head out of the cellar to look at me. Her big brown eyes widened as I snapped my fingers, cleaning up the rest of my living room in a flash. She made a movement with her fingers, tracing over her eyes before bowing her head and backing up into the cellar.

"What do you think of me now, William? Foolish or egotistical?"

"I'm leaning toward egotistical," he said slowly. "Do you even need a cleanup crew?"

"Wine cellar," I replied, pointing toward the doorway. "Have you ever tried to use magic to clean up wine? Organizing books on shelves is child's play. Cleaning up a room two inches deep in wine deserves a special touch."

"I imagine you could do it."

"I have done it before. No thanks." Wine, like blood, was messy clean up, and the wine had to go somewhere.

He laughed suddenly and relaxed back into the couch. "You are an interesting woman. Maybe you're not foolish or egotistical."

"Oh, really? What am I?

"Talented, definitely, and knowledgeable."

I laughed and snapped my fingers again, sending a book soaring across the room to land in my lap. I picked it up and handed it to William. He took it and opened it carefully, running a hand over the smooth leather cover. "It's in Gaelic," he mused.

"Do you read Gaelic?"

"I do, actually," he replied as he browsed the first page, running his finger down the text. "It's a book of potions?"

"It is. There's nothing inherently dangerous inside, and I've personally tested every potion. You may borrow this. I want it back, but I think even you might learn a thing or two."

He smiled and turned the page carefully. "Thank you. I'd like that." I waited for the sarcasm, but none came.

"Consider it an investment."

"Investment?" he asked, stopping to look up at me, one eyebrow raised. "An investment in what, exactly?"

"A mutual partnership, so to speak."

"I scratch your back, you scratch mine?"

"Sure."

He closed the book and stared at me, his hands casually running over the book. "How about a friendship?"

"Friendship? I don't have many friends."

He grinned. "Neither do I. That's what makes this perfect."

"One step at a time."

"You don't want me coming with you to track down the thieves," he stated simply.

"I don't. If you were my friend, I wouldn't want you coming with me. It will be dangerous."

"Fine, but I still want to see this spell in action."

"Sure thing." I stood up and stared at him, hoping he would get the hint that our conversation was over. He stayed where he was and opened the book back up. "This might take me a while to go through. My Gaelic is a bit rusty, and this requires precision."

"You can have it a month," I said, grabbing a Gaelic to old English translation book off the shelf and handing that to him as well.

He took the book, flipped through it, and grinned at me. "That should work. Two months?"

"Fine, two months. I have company coming."

"As friends, or future friends, I can't in good conscience leave you alone with a Fae. I'll stay until she leaves."

"She can't hurt me."

He shrugged but didn't look up from the book. "The Fae are crafty. I've had a few dealings with them, and they really can't be trusted. It's best if I just stick around."

"This was a police-recommended cleaning company. The police wouldn't use them if they couldn't trust them."

"Did you know that some faerie magic is impossible to feel, even for the most talented warlock, or witch."

"I did know that, actually, but only in the high Fae. I'm not worried about the pixie."

"How do you know she's a pixie?"

"You know she's Fae but didn't know what type?" I retorted.

He shrugged and cast a glance toward the cellar, running a hand across his goatee. "Fae feel distinctly different, but unless they are in their natural form I can't tell a pixie from a brownie."

"You just have to know how to look past their glamour."

"And you know how to do that?"

It was as easy as breathing to me, but then again, I wasn't human. "I wouldn't suggest trying to learn. It's enough that you can sense them. The Fae use glamour for a reason. It would be unwise to try and see beyond it."

"Yet you do."

I shrugged. "People have different talents. Think of this as one of mine."

He nodded in agreement. "I'll just take your word for it."

"That's a good idea."

"Still, it doesn't make sense. What is a Fae doing working with humans, especially doing something mundane like cleaning houses?"

"Perhaps she's on a quest."

"Or exile."

"There is that possibility. I wouldn't bring it up," I said, moving toward the cellar door as the Fae and two humans walked out, removing the protective booties from their shoes.

"Summer is going to finish up the detailing, but we got the wine all cleaned up. Do you want us to take care of the rest of the house? Looks like you cleaned up in here," the man said as he looked around the living room.

"No, thanks, I can take care of the rest. The wine was the big issue," I replied.

"Sure thing." The man handed me the bill as he and the human woman began loading up their cleaning supplies. As soon as they left, the pixie showed her face.

"Summer?" I asked.

She nodded, glancing briefly at William before stepping forward and speaking in a soft voice. "My lady, if you allow, I will use my gifts to clean your home."

"You may use your gifts to clean the cellar only. You may not leave anything behind, and you will not alter anything in my home," I replied, hoping I was choosing my words carefully enough.

She knelt on the floor and stretched out her arms, palms up. "My lady, I would not cross you. On my word."

"Very well," I said, hurrying to touch her outstretched palms briefly with the fingertip of each hand. "No more of this, though."

She hurriedly stood up and I felt her mind touch mine briefly. *I know what you are.*

I didn't respond as she turned and scurried back into the cellar. After a moment, I felt the gathering of her magic like the wind before a storm. William and I were both silent as her Faerie magic spun through the house, gathering to her in the cellar. I resisted the urge to open up all the doors and windows so I could feel the wind on my face. William moved to his feet and was halfway to the door before I stopped him. He shook his head, trying to free himself from the effects of Fae magic as he gathered his own magic inside him.

"You should probably go," I said as the pixie began weaving her magic.

"I said I'd stay, and I'll stay." His voice was strained as he fought against the Fae. "It's been a while since I've been around any Fae. I forgot how alluring their magic was. How do you resist?"

I shrugged and moved toward the gate alarm panel as it chirped, indicating someone had entered my driveway. "I have a sort of natural resistance," I replied. "Damn."

William moved up beside me and looked at the screen. "The police bring takeout now?"

"He's early."

"Your company?"

I nodded, watching Steve walk toward the door, a look of awe and wonder on his face. "He's already enthralled. Great." I opened the door before Steve had a chance to knock, but his eyes seemed to look past me as he stepped inside. I took the bags of food from his hands, but he hardly registered my presence as he walked purposely toward the cellar door. I set the food down and hurried after him, throwing up a quick shield to stop his movement.

William walked forward, his fingers twitching as he reached toward the shield I'd put around Steven. "I didn't even feel you put that up."

I ignored his comment as I walked toward Steve. He looked at me, a sliver of recognition lighting his face. "Gia," he said, a frown forming between his brows.

"Just stay there," I said, looking over at William. "You too."

I hurried to the cellar and went down the first few steps. A thick fog enveloped the room, evidence of the Faerie magic. I didn't want to interfere, but even though Steve was currently enthralled, there was the possibility he would remember this. "Summer, there's a human here."

Her voice came back in my mind. *Just a few minutes more and I'll be done.*

I nodded, even though I had no way of knowing if she saw me, turned and went back upstairs. Steve was pushing against the magical barrier, his eyes growing wilder by the minute. William had followed me toward the cellar, but I pushed him back. "She'll be done in a minute."

"I was just keeping an eye on you," he said.

"Sure," I replied. William held his magic tightly in check, but it was a losing battle. Summer's magic had grown, creating a wind that whistled through my house and sent my hair flying in all directions. William turned his face toward the cellar and took a step forward. He stopped, shook his head, backed up, then stepped forward again. "Would you like me to put a ward on you as well?"

That got his attention, and he turned his steel gray eyes on me. "I'm perfectly in control of myself."

I grinned as Summer's magic ratcheted up a notch and William stumbled to the ground. A second later, the wind died and her magic dissipated, leaving the scent of honeysuckle and lavender in its wake. She walked up the stairs, a smile on her face. "I am done, my lady."

"Please, enjoy my garden. It's on the side of the house."

Her eyes lit up, but she quickly bowed her head and shuffled out of the house. William stood up, brushing off his slacks. "Are you okay?" I asked him.

"Better than your cop," he retorted.

I turned around and quickly moved toward Steve, who had pulled his gun out and was testing the ward with his foot. "What's this?" he asked, hitting it with his foot.

"A shield. I was just protecting you," I replied.

"Can you take it down?"

"I will, if you put your gun away. The danger is gone, I assure you."

He didn't look like he believed me, but he holstered the gun anyway. I removed the shield and he quickly stepped forward, grabbing William around the collar of his shirt and slamming him into the wall behind him. "What are you playing at, wizard?"

"Warlock," William corrected.

"Steve, William hasn't done anything."

"Then why is he here? You can't trust him, Gia."

"I am hardly worried about William," I replied, which got a frown from William and an exasperated sigh from Steve. Steve slowly removed his hands from William and stepped back, keeping his hands ready as though he were a gunslinger in the old west. "William, you can leave now."

He straightened his jacket and turned toward me, letting his magic dwindle down. "I'm not afraid of you either," he stated.

"You should be."

He laughed and stepped forward, wrapping his arms around me in an awkward hug while I stood stiffly. "Dating a human is dangerous," he whispered in my ear. "You'd be better off with a warlock."

I felt my face flush at his words. Was he referring to himself? He kissed my cheek, sending a shiver down my spine before stepping back. "I'll see you tomorrow night."

I stood where I was as William casually moved to the kitchen to retrieve his jacket before gathering the books and strolling out the front door. As soon as the door clicked shut Steve sighed loudly. "What was he doing here?"

"He's loaning me some supplies, since mine were stolen," I replied.

"Supplies? Like magic stuff?"

"Yes, like magic stuff," I retorted as I walked toward the kitchen, grabbing the bag of takeout on my way.

Steve followed me, his steps loud and angry. "Why is he seeing you tomorrow?"

"Not really your concern," I snapped.

He frowned and opened his mouth several times before speaking. "What was the magic shit going on when I got here? Why can't I remember anything?"

"More magic stuff, Steve. Nothing to worry about."

"Nothing to worry about? I don't remember parking my car, or coming in the house, or anything." He looked at his watch and frowned. "I swear I lost like twenty minutes of time."

"More like ten, and don't worry, you weren't abducted by aliens."

His frown deepened. "So what was it?"

"Magic," I said, shrugging. "Aren't you hungry?" I moved around the kitchen opening drawers until I found a couple paper plates since all of my dishes had been broken.

Steve stood in the center of my kitchen, arms crossed, as he watched me dish food onto plates. After a moment he sighed loudly and moved in beside me, his arms brushing mine as he helped me pile food onto our plates. "I guess I have to get used to all this," he mumbled.

"If you're going to spend time with me, yes," I replied.

I took the plates to my small table and sat down. Steve followed and sat down opposite me. "Sorry," he mumbled.

"Mmm," I replied, smiling at my first bite. "Thanks for dinner, although you're a little early."

"I got sent home early."

"You were sent home early?"

"I have to go in early tomorrow morning for a training session, and I've already been on duty for I don't know how long. I may be a detective, but I'm still the new guy."

"What did you do before this assignment?"

"I used to work in Seattle, before my mom got sick and I moved back here. That's a fun city, but truth be told I'm glad I left when I did. They hired five werewolves and a witch not even a month after I moved. That was a bad move."

"Bad move?" I stabbed at a piece of sweet and sour chicken.

"Well, you heard about that, didn't you?"

I raised my eyebrow at him. "About what?"

"The witch. Look, I'm not saying all witches are bad. But bringing someone with that kind of power onto a police force is a recipe for disaster. They should use Seattle as an example to the rest of the world."

"The Pike Street Disaster," I said softly, closing my eyes. How could I forget? It was just two years earlier.

"Yeah," he murmured. "They were supposed to be going after a vampire den, not destroying the heart of the city. That witch was out of control."

"I remember hearing about that. They said the witch had a personal vendetta against the vampires."

"Oh, she sure did. She blew up vampires, police, civilians, and herself, all to get at one fucking vampire. She didn't even do that right. The vamp got away. Can you believe that shit?"

"Is that why you have such a problem with the supernatural?"

He started and looked at me, his eyes focusing on my face. "I lost a lot of good friends that day, but it could have just as easily been me."

"You said you moved back for your mom..." I began.

"She died three months after I moved back. My dad died in the line of duty when I was nineteen. It's just me now, and the job."

"I'm so sorry," I said, reaching across the table to take his hand. "Your dad was a police officer as well?"

"He was, and my mom was a dispatcher, until she got sick. It's a family thing, I guess."

"But after she died, you stayed here. Why? You obviously loved living in Seattle."

He shrugged and leaned back, pushing his empty plate away. "I did, and I miss it, but there was always one more thing to do around here. I had her house to sell, her cars, all my dad's stuff still. I guess it was just one excuse after another. Plus, here I was the big-shot city cop. I was practically running homicide before they moved me to the Special Cases Unit. It's supposed to be a promotion."

"You don't see it as one?"

He glanced up at me, shrugged again, then grinned widely. "If I had left, I wouldn't have met you."

"Because that's been a barrel of fun."

He stood and walked around the table, sliding a hand around my waist to gently turn me toward him. "You have been the first good thing I've come across since moving back. I know I was a jerk earlier today, and I'm really sorry. I'm determined to make it up to you."

"You are quite a man, Steven," I said, leaning my face up towards his. He took the cue and moved closer, gently pressing his mouth to mine. The kiss was soft and gentle, and over too fast.

"I promised I'd help you clean up your place first, and that's what I'll do. You take inventory of anything missing, and I'll help you clean things up. Deal?"

I grinned and pushed him back gently. "Sounds good. I only had the cleaning crew take care of the cellar. Wine is a bitch to clean up. The rest of the house is still a disaster."

"Shall we start in the bedroom?"

I laughed and pushed him again, turning back toward my almost untouched plate. "Let's save that for last, shall we?"

After we finished eating, Steven followed me upstairs with a bevy of cleaning supplies. So much of my home had been destroyed just for the sake of destruction. We started in the cleanest room and worked our way through the house. I used a speech recorder application to take notes on my phone of everything that had gone missing, not that I expected the police to actually do anything about it. I'd take care of them myself, but I had to keep up appearances, and any other person in my situation would do the same thing. In addition to my basic spell equipment, they had taken clothes, jewelry, and several pairs of shoes. Theda wasn't my size, so I could only guess Amy had taken them. It was a petty thing to do, but it only served to irritate me further. She did not know who she was messing with.

"Did they take any underwear?" Steve asked from across the room. I turned to see him pulling out the top drawer of my dresser. "Because if they did, that's fine. I'm pretty sure it's the new fashion anyway."

"New fashion?"

He turned and grinned at me. "Oh, yeah, all the ladies in New York are embracing this style. I think it started in Paris."

"Well I don't know if I'm sophisticated enough to keep up with Paris ladies."

"Oh, no, you definitely are. If you want, you can try on the new style now. That way I can be an impartial judge."

"What exactly does this style entail?"

He pushed my dresser closed and leaned back, his eyes going dark. "Well, no bra for starters. It's constricting. No underwear at all, actually. They like to move freely, usually in dresses or skirts, like you're wearing right now."

"That's a relief," I said, running my hands down my shirt, pulling it subtly lower so my cleavage showed better. "I guess I'm ahead of the curve. I adopted this new style months ago."

His eyebrows raised in surprise. "Did you?"

"It really is so freeing," I said, moving forward. He eyed me up and down, stopping at my breasts.

I'd barely made it three steps when he was moving forward, taking me in his arms and kissing me. His hand ran down my back and he pulled back from the kiss, chuckling. "That feels suspiciously like a bra."

I laughed and shrugged my shoulders. "Are you sure?"

"I know one way to find out." He moved his hands to the bottom of my shirt, pulling it up and over my head in one smooth motion. Next his hands slid to my waist as he carefully pulled my skirt down to pool on the floor at my feet. My matching bra and underwear were pale blue lace, and were more about showing than covering. "Hmm, I have to say I like this look too, but I bet you'd look even better naked."

Steve proceeded to kiss me as he fully unclothed me. He kept his clothes on for far too long, pushing my hands away any time I tried to undo a button. I was patient though, and little by little I managed to free him of his clothes as well. He was strong and muscular, compact for his frame that was only a few inches taller than my own. He didn't try to remove my glasses, for which I was grateful. Instead he focused on things much lower on my body, for which I was even more grateful. Our lovemaking was over too soon, and despite an excellent orgasm, I was far from satisfied. Steve was glowing, his chest lightly covered in sweat as he lay beside me, running his hands casually over my stomach.

"Do you ever take the glasses off?" he asked suddenly.

"No."

"Never?"

I turned my head toward his. "No, and don't ask again."

I was cold and cruel, but that was nothing new to me. He was just a thing. A fun plaything, but he'd never be more. They never were. They never could be. His lips suddenly pressed to my breast, startling me out of my melancholy thoughts. I glanced down, surprised to see he was already hard again. His hand moved down, pushing my legs apart. Round two was even better. We fell asleep in each others arms, content and exhausted.

SHIELDS

THE NEXT MORNING STEVE hurried off to his meeting, but not before a quick round of morning sex. I picked up the condom wrappers that littered my bedroom and finished cleaning. I couldn't get pregnant, or catch any diseases, but I still had appearances to keep up. I appreciated the fact that Steve was so concerned with safety. That would do him good in life. While Steve was working on my case with the list of missing items, I had a shop to take care of. After a quick shower, I walked to my business. The morning was cool and I'd be cleaning the mess of my shop, so I dressed accordingly in jeans and a black tank top, covered with a sweater for the morning chill.

Maggie was waiting for me outside the shop, with Mike at her side. She had her hair pulled into a neat ponytail and was wearing an outfit similar to my own, down to the black tank top. "Did you two plan your outfits again?" Mike asked, eyeing me up and down.

"I didn't know your husband was such a comedian," I said dryly.

He ignored my remark much like I ignored his. "Baby, call me as soon as you need me to pick you up."

"I'm fine," she snapped. "If you left me the truck, I could drive myself home."

I moved away from them and opened the shop. The last thing I needed was to hear more of their arguing. It didn't last long as Maggie followed me into the shop moments later. "Sorry about that," she said as she tossed her purse in the corner. "I'm just so sick of being treated like I'm this helpless little kitten. Did you hear him call me "baby"? Am I a little child? I am not his darn baby. I'm not. I'm a grown woman, dang it."

"He's just scared and overprotective."

"You got that right! Wait, scared? Mike's not scared of anything."

"He's scared of losing you."

Her head dropped and she fiddled with her short fingernails. "I know," she said softly. "I can't fix the fact that I'm human, or that he's a werewolf, or that this world is crazy. What can I do?"

"Learn to defend yourself however you can. As for Mike, he's just going to have to come to grips with things on his own."

"I read through that last book you gave me," she said, perking up. She hurried over to the purse and pulled out the book. "I even marked a few things I'd like to try, if you'll help me. Maybe after we've cleaned up this mess."

"Sounds like a good idea. As we clean, we'll do inventory so we can tell the police what's missing."

We cleaned and worked tidying up the shop. Theda and Amy had stolen almost ten thousand dollars worth of inventory. I'd have to be more careful with my stock in the future. From now on, everything not on the shelf was under wards. Maggie walked down the street to pick up our lunch while I put in orders for supplies. Most of them would be here within the week, but the rare ingredients would take much more time.

"Sorry it took so long," Maggie said as she walked in, bringing the aromas of fresh clam chowder with her. "Jerry followed me the entire way and wouldn't let me go into the restaurant until he had secured it first."

I stopped what I'd been doing and looked up at her. "Even though you're with me, he still sent Jerry?"

"He claims he was in the neighborhood and saw me leave the shop alone. I'm not sure if Jerry is taking this overboard, or if Mike told him to spy on me. Either way, I'm done."

"Done?" I asked as we moved to the table and set up lunch. There were two large containers of clam chowder, two orders of fish and chips, two drinks, as well as two pieces of cheesecake.

"I stress eat," she explained as we sat down and we both opened our clam chowder first. "I can't live like this, but I feel so stuck. I have an art degree I can't do anything with and this is the first job I've had in over five years. My last job was as a waitress. A waitress! I have no skills, no future, no... nothing."

I swallowed the hot bite of chowder and watched as Maggie cried around bites of clam chowder, apparently not even noticing the heat. Did her tears cool it down? I blew on the next bite and sat back, unsure what to say. I wasn't the best at relationships, or advice. Maggie devoured her chowder and moved onto the fish.

"Uh, Maggie, maybe you and Mike need to have a good long conversation."

"I've tried. I even suggested marriage counseling but he said the pack wouldn't allow that. We could meet with the Alpha and his wife though. Like that would help. She's a werewolf. She wouldn't understand."

"I'm not sure many people would."

"What do I do?"

I stared at my bowl, scraping up the last bite of clam chowder before setting it down. "I don't think I'm the best person to give advice."

She shook her head and wiped a tear with the back of her hand. "No, I'm sorry, I shouldn't have said that. I just don't really have any other friends. At all. Maybe that's the problem. I need someone to talk to."

"Well, listening I can do."

"Thanks, Gia." She paused, wiped her other cheek, and took a drink. "So, what's with you and that dreamy cop?"

I wasn't prepared for the change in subject, and normally wouldn't talk about my private life, but it was preferable to another round of tears. "You mean Steven?"

"Oh, is that his name? I heard you went to Club Wyvern with him."

"That didn't turn out as it should."

"I've never been there, but I've heard about it. Mike told me a little about what happened. Said a succubus was turning the place into a giant group orgy."

"Pretty much."

"He also said you killed the succubus."

My heart felt as though it stopped briefly at her words. I'd been so consumed with hiding from the police that I hadn't given enough thought to the werewolves who had been at the club. "He said that, did he?"

"Well, it wasn't any of the pack and it certainly wasn't the cops."

"He thinks I killed a succubus on my own and he still lets you work here?"

"Huh, he does," she murmured. "That's pretty big."

"I'd say so."

"He trusts you."

"What?" That was not where my thoughts had been going.

"He trusts you to protect me, but that means he also trusts that you wouldn't hurt me." "He still doesn't want you working here."

"But not really because of you."

"He doesn't know me. Neither do you."

"Did you do it? Did you kill the succubus?"

My fish had cooled down enough to eat and I took a slow, deliberate bite. This small town was supposed to have small town problems. "There were two, actually. Male and female. Incubus and succubus."

"Two? They're like vampires, right?"

"Similar, yes, and they can control other vampires. They are infinitely more dangerous though."

"And now we have two fewer of them to worry about."

I smiled. "That's one way of putting it."

"Will there be others? Will they retaliate?"

"Retaliation isn't really the vampire way. They're not that loyal. More could come to the area if no one is in charge, but most likely they'll be regular vampires. The succubi and incubi are rare. This area isn't exactly a hot spot."

"That's good." She finished her fish and pulled out the cheesecake, sliding one toward me even though I still had half my fish and all my fries. "So, back to Officer Hunky."

"What about him?"

"Are you two a thing?"

I shrugged and continued eating. "I suppose so."

"Have you gone on a lot of dates?"

"Standard dates haven't turned out very well. I like him, though," I admitted.

"Well that's exciting. It must be hard being in a new town and not really knowing anyone."

"I know a few people."

"Besides me, some cops and werewolves, who do you know?"

I cringed, but she was right. Mostly. "William Dervish. I know him and a few of his... associates."

She frowned and licked her fork. "The werewolves don't trust him."

"Well, he is a warlock."

"I don't trust him either."

"Do you know him?"

She shook her head and blinked at me. "No, he just gives me the creeps."

"Fair enough." I pushed my fish aside and took a bite of cheesecake. It was plain, simple, and delicious. I devoured it in a few bites. "I need to teach you something useful."

"Useful? Like how to not eat my feelings?"

"Shields, I think." We threw the garbage away and moved the table to its usual spot in the corner of the room. Maggie opened the book and read through the section on shields, murmuring softly to herself. "Are you ready?"

She nodded and turned to me. "I think so. It's sort of like that ball of energy from last time."

"In a way. You gather energy from inside yourself, as well as your surroundings. Pull it into yourself, hold it, then press it outward, surrounding yourself in a bubble of protection. If you can concentrate on the shield without distractions, it'll hold through almost anything. The thing is, if you're holding a shield then you probably have distractions. Some people can hold shields without thinking about it, but that takes time, and practice. For most people, the easiest thing is to shield yourself. It's much more difficult to shield someone else, and even harder if they move around. Possible, but it takes even more practice."

"Okay, I think I understand."

"Go slow. Pull in energy around you. Close your eyes. Feel the air, even if there's no breeze. Feel the earth beneath your feet. Feel the sun through the window. It all has energy. You'll always be tied to the earth, so that's where you should pull from to start. If you're not careful, you could pull energy from people around you, and that is a bad thing to do."

Maggie's eyes were closed and I could feel the energy slowly building in her. "Bad how?" she said softly.

"If you're not careful, you could kill someone by taking all their energy. It's not easy and would take a lot of effort, but it's possible. More likely you'd just drain a person to exhaustion. They'd be pretty angry with you though, and if any witches heard of you doing that, they'd be after you in a flash."

Her energy pulsed, and I felt her reach outward, like tiny bees searching for nectar. Her energy flared when she hit me and she visibly flinched as my energy lashed back at her. "Sorry."

"Don't be sorry, be careful. Earth. Feel the soil, the trees, the grass. Feel the energy pulsing upward."

She nodded and continued her energy pull, shifting her focus to the earth beneath us. When she had enough I spoke again. "Now that you're mostly full, you can create a shield. Imagine the energy as a wall around your body. It helps if you picture it as a color surrounding you. Blues and greens are safe colors. Let that color surround you, covering your skin. Good. Now push it gently away from you. This is usually the hard part. The energy doesn't want to be separate, it wants to merge with you. You're going to push it away and solidify it at the same time."

She was silent for several minutes, the pale blue of the sky seeming to swirl around her. "How do I get it to hold still and get solid?"

"Your energy is fluid, like water. If you put your hand in the water, it moves around you. Feel the current. If you jump into that water, it parts. If you jump from too high, it still parts, but it hurts. It stings. If you go higher still and jump in, it can feel like hitting a brick, and it can kill you. This is the same. The closer to you, the more fluid it is. The further away, the harsher it becomes. To make a shield, you need the energy to be separated from you. To solidify. Just an inch or two is enough."

Maggie opened her eyes as the swirling blue pushed slowly away from her body. Sweat beaded on her forehead with the exertion. The swirling stopped and solidified briefly before dissolving into nothingness. She looked at me, her dark eyes wide with fear and excitement. "Did I do it?"

"You did," I replied. "Briefly, but now you know how it feels. It'll get easier. Try again"

And we did. The shop had been cleaned, the new supplies ordered, and Maggie worked on her shield for hours until she could finally sustain a shield for five minutes straight. It wasn't great, and I could have shattered it in an instant, but it was a good start. It had been years since I'd tried to teach anyone magic, and it felt strangely good.

A knock on the door stopped us, and Maggie's shield shattered. "It's Mike," I said, smelling that earthy wolf scent as soon as he opened the door.

"Hey babe," he said, grinning at Maggie. He turned his golden eyes on me. "Gia."

"You're early," Maggie said, glancing at her watch.

"I got us reservations for dinner. I was hoping you wouldn't mind if I showed up thirty minutes early so you have time to go change first."

"Reservations? Where?"

He smiled and moved toward her, reaching an arm out to pull her close. "It's a surprise."

She held him back, the anger from earlier flashing in her eyes. "Why?" she asked bluntly.

Mike glanced at me and pulled her a few steps away. "Jerry called and told me about you leaving the shop for lunch. He also told me about how he followed you and that you seemed less than thrilled about it."

"You got that right."

"I worry about you, especially after the break-in here the other day, but..."

"But nothing, Mike, you can't spy on me all the time."

"But," he growled, his eyes flashing briefly. "I told Jerry it was absolutely *not* okay to follow you around."

"You did?"

"I did," Mike said, his voice softening. "I worry and I'm sorry I come across as an asshole. I wanted to take you out to dinner to apologize, and hopefully come up with a better solution. I can feel you pulling away from me." His voice cracked and he cleared his throat, his eyes cast downward.

Maggie stepped toward him and ran a hand across his stubbled chin. "I know you worry, but I can't stay cooped up all the time. I will lose my mind if I do."

Mike nodded and glanced at me, then back to his wife. "This town used to be safe, but lately…"

"It's like that everywhere," she interrupted.

"Unfortunately, I think you're right."

"I want to show you something," Maggie said, taking a step backward and looking over at me. I nodded and she took a deep breath, moving to the center of the room. Her energy grew as she pulled from the earth. She was getting quicker each time. Mike rubbed his arms, feeling the tingle of magic. The blue of her magic pulsed outward and solidified into a shimmering shield just inches from her body.

"What?"

"It's a shield, Mike," I said, stepping around the counter and holding out a penny. I tossed the penny toward Maggie and watched as the penny bounced off the shield and dropped to the ground.

He looked over at me, his eyes golden. "You're not doing this, are you?" I shook my head. "Maggie?" He turned back to look at Maggie, who was smiling timidly.

"I can't hold it for very long, but I'm still learning."

"You taught her this today?" he asked, still staring at his wife.

"Yes."

"This will protect her?"

"Eventually," I replied. "Right now it'll protect her from simple mundane threats. The penny, for example."

"A bullet?" he asked.

I shrugged my shoulders. "Most likely, but I don't think we should test that theory."

"Vampires?"

"Well, why don't you try?"

"Try what?"

"Try to get through her shield."

Maggie's eyes widened, but I could sense her bracing herself. The shield shifted as she thought about it and I smiled as it grew stronger still. She was a quick study. Mike moved with lightning speed, rushing at Maggie. He hit her and bounced backward, falling into a roll. He was used to fighting and easily regained his footing and went after her again. The second time he didn't fall as he hit the shield, but Maggie did stumble backwards a step. Her shield wavered, but she drew in more energy to solidify it further. Mike ran at her again and the shield flickered. Maggie's shoulders shook as she absorbed the impact. Energy flowed toward her, but not from the earth this time.

"Maggie, no!" I said, moving forward as she pulled energy from Mike. He staggered, but she didn't stop. Her eyes were wild and the energy swirled around her, cascading from blue to red. I raised my hand and sliced through her shield.

Both Maggie and Mike fell to the ground panting as Maggie's shield shattered. I moved over Mike, watching his eyes burn with a bright golden light. He growled up at me, but I could see his humanity fighting for control over the wolf. "Keep it together, wolf," I said as I grabbed Maggie and hauled her upright. "What the hell do you think you're doing?" My voice was low and surprisingly calm.

"I was just trying to keep my shield up."

"Keep your shield up? By draining your husband?"

"I didn't mean to."

"Did you see what happened? Did you see your shield? Think, Maggie," I said, shaking her.

"It turned red."

"Yes, it turned red. Blue is your color. Blue is safe. Red, not so much."

"I don't understand."

"If he wasn't a werewolf, he'd probably be dead right now."

"What?" she finally looked right at me, her eyes wide with fear. "From me?"

"Yes, from you. I told you before, never, ever pull energy from another person. Not from any living thing, do you understand me?"

"I didn't realize…"

"Yes you did. Don't play dumb with me. You felt the strength of the energy you were pulling. The earth has sustainable energy. It may not feel instantaneously strong, but it is. Pulling from living creatures will be like a flash of bright energy, but it dies just as quickly. And you will taint yourself."

"Taint myself?"

"Your aura, your soul, if you will. You are still pure and clean. Keep it that way. Use magic to protect. Use the earth to draw energy."

Mike stood up and walked toward us slowly, his breathing slow and steady. His eyes still glowed, but they had dimmed down. "She was taking my energy?" he asked softly.

"I didn't mean to," Maggie said, her wide eyes terrified. "Oh, Mike, I'm so sorry."

"That shield was pretty strong," he said slowly.

"You almost broke through. I was trying so hard to prove that I could protect myself."

"I hope you never need to use it."

She nodded, tears dripping steadily down her face. Mike looked at me, and I could see the questions clearly on his face, and a bit of fear. "She would have had a hard time killing you," I said.

"My wolf didn't like it. He was trying to come out and play."

I nodded. "Maggie and I will continue training. She needs time, and practice."

Mike took a deep breath and his shoulders relaxed as he exhaled. "I almost killed my brother," he said bluntly. "I'd been a werewolf for almost six months and my brother showed up unexpectedly. We didn't get along at the time and he knew all the right buttons to push. He didn't know I was a werewolf. I hadn't told any of my family. I lost control and shifted in front of him. If my Alpha hadn't been there..." he stopped and shook his head, grimacing. "I didn't trust myself to be alone with a human for a good ten years."

"Ten years?" Maggie sobbed. He pulled her toward him and brushed her forehead with a kiss. "I don't want you to have that fear, babe. Gia can help you." He looked up at me, the question still in his eyes.

"Yes, I can help her. She's a fast learner, and she definitely has the gift. You saw how strong her shield was."

"You cut through it like it was butter."

"Let's just say I'm the exception to the rule."

"Are you saying other witches wouldn't have been able to do that?"

I shrugged, feeling Mike's suspicion turn on me again. "Some would be able to, of course. With time, she should be able to keep out almost any magic."

"Almost any? But not yours, I bet."

I smiled briefly. "No, probably not."

"And why is that? How are you so strong?"

I shrugged and turned away, moving back toward the counter and grabbing my things. "I think it's time to close up and go home," I said.

Maggie grabbed her things and we all walked out of the shop. I spun the keys on my keyring and locked the doors, following that up with a quick spell of warding. Mike stood close behind me, his breath hot on my ear. "Are you Fae?" he whispered.

"No, I'm something else."

Magic

THAT NIGHT I WENT back home and tried to relax before I began preparing for my locater spell. William had called to confirm the time of our spell, and I had reluctantly agreed to meeting at midnight. In order to track another Gorgon, I needed to be careful. Theda was good with illusions and tracking spells, and if I wasn't careful she'd know I was coming. I also needed something of hers, to link me to her. Amy would have been a better target for my spell, if I'd had anything of hers, or something I knew she'd touched. That was the tricky part.

In order to properly track someone in particular, I needed something that was part of them, such as hair or blood, or something close to them. Theda was close to nothing and I had no hair or blood of hers, but I did have something that held her energy. I'd never tried it before, and I wasn't sure what would happen. I still had three vials of the locater solution to dabble with if I needed to.

Later, I decided, not wanting to pull the statue out of it's new hiding place. The locater spell could work with no hair or blood, just not as well and not as accurately. I grabbed one of the books that had been torn in half. It was a new book I hadn't even read yet, which meant it wouldn't cling to me and interfere with the locater. Either Theda or Amy, or even both, had touched it when they tore the book in two. For the spell work with William, this would have to do. A part of me was hopeful it wouldn't work at all. Then I could try it again, without the warlock hovering over me, and see what happened when I used the statue of my dead husband as a locater. If it was even him.

I pushed the thought away and looked at the clock. Time to go. I gathered the locater vials, the book, and a threw a few extra items into my purse before walking out the door and down the driveway. Right on time, William pulled up to my drive. I was still dressed as I had been earlier, just with a thicker black sweater over my tank top. William opened my car door with a wave of his hand and I suppressed the desire to roll my eyes as I climbed inside.

"What's the book for? Are you afraid you need something for entertainment? I hope I don't come across as boring," he added with a smirk before he turned the car around and drove down the road, headed toward the beach.

I held the book up, showing him the two broken pieces. "I don't have anything personal to do the locater spell with, but hopefully this will work."

"If you know these women, you shouldn't need an object at all."

"True, but an object works so much better. Besides, I'm not sure I know either of them very well. One of them I just met and the other, well, we've grown apart."

He grunted, but said nothing more as he drove to one of the smaller local parking lots just out of town with easy beach access. There was enough moonlight to easily guide our steps to the beach. Despite the late hour and the cool breeze, I took my shoes off so I could walk barefoot in the sand. William raised an eyebrow, but said nothing. He was dressed as he always was, impeccably in a suit. Today his suit was black with a deep burgundy tie. With each few steps, he had to stop and shake loose sand from his loafers.

"You knew we were coming to the beach and yet you still decided to wear a suit," I said, not turning to look at him as I carried my shoes in one hand. The tide was still high and just beginning to turn, leaving a long path of wet sand ahead of me. Wet sand made walking easier, but the it was cold on my feet.

I moved ahead of William down the beach toward a small cove out of sight of the town, and away from people. When I was satisfied with my location, I stopped and turned to wait for William. He had taken my words to heart and was several paces behind me carrying his shoes and socks in his hand, with the bottoms of his pants rolled up carefully. He shivered as he stepped up beside me.

"Such a great idea working the locater spell on the beach," he murmured as he set his shoes down and tucked the black socks inside. He reached up and loosened his tie before taking it off and carefully tucking it into the pocket of his suit jacket.

"It is," I replied, waving my arms around. "There is nothing to distract from the spell here."

"It would have been warmer in your house."

I shrugged and pulled the locater vial, a map, and the book out of my purse. I spread the map on the wet sand, holding it down with rocks and shells at the corners. I unstoppered the vial and gathered the magic into me, feeling the earth and water magic fill me. Air came next, a breeze pushing against me. I was glad I'd put my hair up so I could see what I was doing. Next was fire. Before I could reach for the lighter in my purse, William was there beside me, lit lighter in hand. I smiled in appreciation and pulled the energy into me. The locater spell didn't take a great deal of magic, but it did take a little of everything. I spun the magic around and through me, speaking the first words of the incantation as I dripped a single drop of the vial onto the book held in my left hand.

Magic raced through me, and I focused my thoughts on Theda and Amy, searching for them. They'd be together, I was sure. I dripped another drop on the book then held the book over the map, moving to the next part of the spell. I spoke the words and poured the remaining solution over the map. William was beside me, pressing the lighter into my hands without my needing to ask. I held the book to the flames, cringing just a bit as the book caught. The wind swirled around the flames before I lowered the book on the map. The map and book both burst into a swirl of flames, but there was no heat as the water and earth joined together, suffocating the fire. Within seconds, the spell was complete and all that remained was a small piece of the map, it's edges seared black.

William picked up the map and held it out to me, glancing at the location. "Not far," he mused.

"For one," I added, reaching down to pick up a second piece of the map. "Damn, they separated."

"You channeled both of them in the same spell?"

"I figured they'd be together," I said, looking at the two pieces.

One was in town at the same hotel they'd checked into earlier. I found it odd that either of them would stay some place so visible, but perhaps they guessed I wouldn't go looking for them there. The police would have though. I looked at the second piece. This one was further out of town, and by the line of fire behind it, she was on the move.

"Well, who do we go after."

"We? I said you could watch, not hunt."

"So the local blind woman is going to drive after her prey all alone?" he asked.

While I did have a car, it was hidden and not in my name. Not my current name, anyway. Plus, he had a point. The problem with small towns is that everyone knows who you are, and I couldn't very well use my eyesight excuse if I was seen driving around.

"What did you have in mind?" I asked, holding up the map in my hand. "She's on the move?"

"So the one on the move is the one you wish to target?"

I shrugged. "Seems logical," I replied.

He tapped the other map piece. "Or, this is so obvious it is the logical place to go."

"She wouldn't trap herself like that."

"But there are two of them, are there not? Who is the easier one to capture and get answers?"

"She's on the move," I murmured again. The piece of map fizzled as it moved with the car. It would continue on until she left the map, for as long as I held the spell in mind.

"She'll be off that map before we can catch up," he said, pointing for emphasis. "Sometimes we have to choose the opposite of what we wish."

I tucked both pieces of map into my pocket and picked up my shoes. William took my cue and followed suit. I loved the beach, the sand, the salty air, but the joy was gone for me this evening. I trudged back to the car, dusted the sand from my feet, and climbed in. William moved more slowly, getting every piece of sand off him before climbing in and starting the car.

We drove to the hotel and I led William to the elevator, hitting the button for the third floor. He said nothing as I walked directly to Theda's room, number 313, and knocked. No answer.

"Are you sure this is the right room?" he asked.

"This is the room she checked into but..." I trailed off, pulling the scrap of map from my pocket and letting my magic flow through it. The air shimmered around us and a faint glow turned my attention to the room across the hall. I stalked across the hall and pounded my fist against the door. No answer, but there was the distinct smell of ozone and the pull of magic in the air. I gathered a shield around me before pushing a burst of energy at the door, shattering it.

"You know, there's a handy spell that'll pick the lock," William murmured as he followed me into the room.

"Theda," I said, surprised as the woman glared at me. I pushed William backward, out the door. "Go check the other room," I added, slamming the door behind him and before Theda could kill him with her deadly stare. She chuckled and ran a hand through her hair.

"You brought a friend?"

"Not exactly," I said, holding a shield pressed tight against the door. "Where are my books Theda?" I asked, looking around the room.

"Nowhere you'll find them," she said, laughing.

"Does Amy have them? I know she's headed out of town."

"Locater spell? Really, you could have just called."

"Where are my books, Theda?" I looked around, noticing a few of my other belongings scattered around the room.

She shrugged. "They're with a friend. Not that they're very helpful without Nefeli's books, her journals."

"I agreed to help you."

"Oh, yes, Amy's problem." She shook her head and straightened her back, a sure sign she was about to leave. "It doesn't affect me, so why should I care?"

"What? Why are you here? And it does affect us, even if you can't see why yet."

"Hmm, maybe, but Amy can do the leg work on that particular problem. I have bigger things to deal with right now, and you are not being very helpful."

"If you want my help, maybe you should tell me exactly what's going on."

She shook her head and smiled, her blood-red lipstick making a striking contrast to her pale skin and black hair. "Sorry, dear, but you really shouldn't have come here." She moved quick as lightning, pushing her shield against my own. I fought against her as she held up a needle, pushing it through my shield. I blasted her with magic, sending her sailing across the room. The door behind me burst open and I stumbled forward. Theda took one last look at me before turning and jumping from the window.

William ran across the room, watching as Theda jumped from the third floor to land on the ground, in what I was sure was an impressive display. I stayed where I was, my eyes still on the needle she'd dropped before her dramatic exit. William turned and bent down, picking up the needle.

"It's empty," he said, holding it up.

"It wasn't for injecting," I replied.

"What do you mean?"

"She was trying to take my blood."

"Blood magic?"

I shrugged, feeling a sense of dread. Theda knew better than to mess with blood magic. Even the simplest thing, such as a locater spell, could go deadly wrong using blood. Plus, there was the taint, not that she worried about it. Not that I needed to either. Both of us were tainted from so many years of dark deeds, there was no coming back. But she wasn't making locater spells, of that I was sure. What could she do with a vial of my blood?

"She knocked me out the other day," I murmured.

"You think she took some of your blood already?" He asked, and I shrugged in response. "If she did, why does she need more?"

"If she didn't, why does she need it now?" I added.

William stalked toward me and grabbed my sweater, pulling it over my head in one quick move and grasping my arms, pulling them toward him. I stood numbly, trying to think through the repercussions of my blood floating around out there, waiting to be used in a spell. William's hands ran over my arms as he inspected my veins. "I don't see any needle marks," he said slowly.

"I heal quickly," I replied. "There might not be."

His arms suddenly wrapped around me and I straightened my back in surprise, but he did nothing but hug me. After a moment, I relaxed and put my arms around his waist, resting my head on his shoulder. His arms wrapped around me tighter and I found it strangely comforting. I'm not sure how long we stood like that, with the steady beat of his heart putting me me at ease, before he finally pulled back and looked down at me.

"You okay?" he asked.

I nodded and stepped back, shivering at the sudden cold. He handed my sweater back to me and I pulled it on before examining the room. A quick look told me Amy had been staying in this room. She had my shoes and some of my clothes, along with some jewelry. We walked across the hall and William showed me what he'd found in Theda's room, which was more of the same. I found a few books, but not all of them. I picked up my phone and called Steve.

"Hey, Steve, looks like I found some of my stuff. There's a lot still missing though."

"Where?"

"At their hotel."

"Their hotel?" he paused and there was a distinct change in his voice. "Did you go with Hunter?"

"With Hunter? No, why?" I turned at the sound of the elevator. Sure enough, Detective Hunter Daniels walked down the hall toward me, his perpetual scowl in place.

"He was headed to check out the hotel rooms."

"He's here," I said. "I'll call you later."

I hung up and turned toward the detective. "What a pleasant surprise," I said.

"What are you doing here?"

"Well, looking for my stolen belongings. Just like you, I presume."

"Did you find them?"

I nodded and pointed at the two rooms. "Most of them. Not all my books though," I added.

"We'll take it from here," he said, pointing at the two uniformed cops accompanying him. "Take inventory and bag it up."

"When will I get my things back?"

"After we're through with them."

"How long will that take?"

He smiled widely and shrugged. "As long as it takes. What about the two women?"

"Gone," I replied.

"Did one of them happen to jump out a window and walk away?"

I laughed and nodded my head. "In fact, she sure did."

"Figures. Do you need a ride home?"

"I will take her home," William said as he moved up beside me.

Hunter's eyes slid across William, then back to me. "As I said, do you need a ride home?"

"You don't need to worry about me," I replied.

He grunted, but said nothing else as William took my arm and led me back to the elevator. "Well, I don't think he likes me," William mused.

"Join the club."

"Oh, I think he likes you quite more than you think."

The ride back to my house was silent, both of us lost in our own thoughts. Steve called several more times, but I ignored them for the time being. The little scrap of map showing Amy's progress had reached the edge, and burned up in my pocket. No more tracking Amy. William pulled his car into my drive and walked around to the passenger door, this time manually opening the door for me. I smiled in appreciation, letting him hold my arm as he walked me to my front door.

"Well, Gia, this has been exciting. I would like to thank you for letting me come along, although I am a little miffed you didn't introduce me to your friend."

"You wouldn't have lived to speak about it if you had," I replied shortly.

He shrugged and leaned against the door frame. "Maybe. I like to think I can hold my own."

Not against a Gorgon, I thought, but didn't say anything. "Thanks, William."

"So, does this mean we're friends now?"

"I don't think it works like that."

He stepped forward, his body suddenly too close. I backed into the door and he moved with me, his body a warm presence not quite trapping me. He traced a hand across my cheek and I felt myself flush in response. Shit. "How does it work?"

"William, I'm dating Steve."

"Are you? Is that an official stance? Are you his and his alone?" His breath was warm on my face as he leaned in closer. His left hand encircled my waist, drawing me towards him, and I found myself melting against him. What was I doing? "I'm going to kiss you," he whispered.

I swallowed, knowing he was giving me a chance to get away. Instead, I closed my eyes and tilted my head toward his. His lips felt like warm honey brushing against mine, so soft and tender. My body ached in response, but I didn't move, didn't react, other than to kiss him back.

We stood there with nothing but our lips moving, while our hearts fluttered and our blood raced. The kiss was tender and soft, sending a slow burn across my body. No magic needed here. His lips were pure magic on their own. I opened my mouth, letting the kiss grow deeper as he pushed his tongue inside, exploring. I moaned in response, and he took the cue to press his body against mine, holding us tightly together. Certain parts of his body thrummed in tune with the blood pushing through his veins, throbbing and pulsing against my stomach.

He suddenly pulled away, releasing my swollen lips. His eyes grew distant, as though he were listening to something far away. I felt the echo of magic coming toward him. Magical phone call? "I have to go," he said, and regret filled his words. "Duty calls." I opened my mouth to respond, but he took the opportunity to press one last kiss on my lips before rushing off to his car and speeding away. When I had my breathing under control several minutes later, I let myself into the house. Later, as I unpacked my purse, I found his burgundy silk tie, neatly folded inside.

PΛTH

FIVE WEEKS AFTER THEDA and Amy had interrupted my life, I finally had my shop fully stocked once more. New wards were in place all over my shop and house, and business was thriving. Over my many years, I'd tried my hand at a variety of jobs, but owning a business where I didn't need to hide was almost magical. Of course, I still had to hide what I truly was, but it was better. Acceptance of the supernatural was at an all-time high.

October was my favorite month, and I delighted in decking out my shop for Halloween. The weather was still warm, and the local children excitedly talked about it being a great Halloween. With two weeks to go, my shop was busier than ever. Instead of the usual love potion requests, I had more and more requests for safety charms from anxious parents. These days, communities banded together more than ever to keep children safe so they could still enjoy the holiday. As a business owner, I joined in, adding my shop to the downtown daylight trick or treating event. Decorations were up, candy had been bought, and I had taken to wearing festive outfits as we counted down the days. Unfortunately, these days business closed up earlier and earlier. Before the sun had set, the crowds had dwindled and I found my mind wandering to the mystery statue of my dead husband.

"What do you think you're doing?"

I jumped and turned around, wiping at my face. "Nothing, Mistress Nefeli," I replied, lowering my face.

"Are you crying, child?"

I shook my head. "Of course not."

She stepped closer, until I could see her sandals peeking out beneath her long skirts and feel her breath on my bowed head. "It is alright to mourn. Do not let Theda tell you differently." A fingertip lifted my head up until I straightened. Nefeli's nose was long, as was her chin, but her cheekbones were her truly defining feature, making her look beautiful and striking at the same time. Her green eyes, so similar to my own, softened with a warmth Theda didn't possess.

"Do you miss Nitsa?" I asked.

"So Theda told you of her, did she? Of course she did. Nitsa was young and idealistic. She wanted to be good. She wanted to be different."

"Theda said a werewolf killed her."

"Indeed, a Pack, actually. We don't die easily, but..." she trailed off, a tear sliding down her cheek. "We are still allowed to mourn. She was our sister."

"She was a fool," Theda said as she opened the door to our small hut. She unwrapped the shawl from around her head and pushed the wooden door shut. "Nitsa was a Gorgon for only five years. Five! Is that the kind of life you want, Giavanna?"

"Five years or five hours, she was our sister," Nefeli snapped. "Now Giavanna is our sister."

"She is weak," Theda sneered.

I stepped backward, wanting nothing more than to disappear, until I felt stone behind me. I turned and caught my breath, staring at the face of the man I'd loved. My hair caught in the edge of the statue, and I worked to untangle chestnut locks. I glanced behind me as Theda and Nefeli continued their argument. The two women were so similar with their green and black hair. Soon, they said, my hair would look like theirs. My eyes, though, were the same color I'd been born with. Nefeli said it was a sign. We had all been born with our green eyes. She said we were related. My mother had the same color eyes.

"We should make her destroy it," Theda said suddenly, and I moved instinctually in front of the statue.

"You turned the boy, not her," Nefeli reminded her.

"It matters not. The last thing she needs is this reminder of her past."

"It has only been a few months."

"I turned my parents the moment I discovered what I was," Theda bragged, standing up to her full height. She was slender with small breasts and a slight frame, but taller than any woman I'd met before. Nefeli, despite being shorter, raised an eyebrow and seemed to look down on Theda. "And it has been more than a few months."

"Please, don't," I said softly, interrupting the two women. "I know I should let go, but I'm just not ready. I don't want him to die."

"He's already dead," Theda sneered.

"But you said..."

"He's not dead," Nefeli interrupted as she glided back toward me. "There is no way to return him, though. You need to accept that. He is gone from this realm, but he feels no pain. He knows nothing. Only his shell remains."

"How do you know. I can feel him," I said, touching a hand to the statue's breast.

"You feel my magic," Theda stated.

"You said in this state, you drain them slowly. What are you draining, if not their soul? And if their soul remains, they remain."

"Would you rather I had finished him at once and taken all his energy?"

I shook my head, stroking his cheek absentmindedly. "No, if you did I might not remember him, and I want to remember. I want to remember everything about him."

"Better if you forgot."

"No, I don't want to forget him. I love him."

"You were turned too late. Same problem we had with Nitsa."

"Too late? I have barely begun to live!"

"You haven't begun living at all!" Theda screamed at me. "Detach yourself from these humans. They are beneath us. We are like the gods themselves. We are power. We are life and we are death. The sooner you accept that, the better."

"I don't want to accept that."

"Then go find that werewolf pack and ask them to take you out of your misery."

Theda turned and stormed off, leaving her head covering behind. We watched her go, and I knew what would happen next. In the time I'd been with them, I'd seen her do this before. Immediately, I began packing our belongings. We wouldn't be staying in this place any longer.

"She's not entirely wrong," Nefeli said softly as she draped a blanket over the statues in the corner.

I stared at the blanket-covered shape of what was my husband. "I can't destroy him," I said softly. "I don't want to forget."

"You don't have to forget, but you need to move on. Even if he were alive, you would never be happy. He would grow old, you would not. He would want children and you could not provide them. We must feed constantly, and some day you would have made a mistake. It is better that Theda did it. It is better."

"And he will stay like this forever?"

"Until his energy runs out and he crumbles to dust."

Theda returned just as the sun was setting and we left the small hut behind. I had moved his statue to the garden beside a climbing rose bush and wrapped a few thorny branches around his arms. Before we left, I kissed his cheek and wished him well. My hair turned a week later.

"Hello, beautiful."

"Steve," I said, turning around and plastering a smile on my face. I stumbled into his arms, letting myself fall into his kisses.

He pulled away sooner than usual and ran a finger across my cheek. "Were you crying?"

I wiped at my face and smiled at him again. "Just getting a little melancholy I suppose."

"Melancholy?" he frowned and looked past me. "This place looks great. I bet all the kids are excited to come here for Halloween."

I shrugged and said, "I hope so. The holiday isn't the same anymore."

"Not with vampires running around at night."

"They've always been there. People just know about them now," I added morosely.

He turned around and grabbed me again, running his hands down my backside. "Are you ready for dinner?" he asked.

"Of course, where do you want to go?"

"Club Wyvern is back up and running," he replied.

"It is?" I asked, knowing it had been open for two weeks already.

"Shall we?" He smiled eagerly at me, a little too eagerly.

"I don't know if that's a good idea," I said, leading him out of the store room and throwing up a ward as I flicked off the lights.

"It's fine. I've been there a couple times. No problems."

"You've been there without me?" I shivered as a cold breeze ran through the shop from the open front door. "You could have shut the door behind you," I said as I moved toward it.

"I did."

We moved forward together and the wind picked up, flinging my hair into my face and wrapping around my neck. I pulled it back with one hand as I followed Steve outside. The wind died, but the cold air grew. Our breath fogged instantly and I found myself shivering as the temperature dropped suddenly. "What is this?" Steve whispered beside me.

"Magic," I replied, but what the source was I was unsure. Drawing from the earth, I pulled a shield up around Steve and me. Immediately, the temperature normalized and we stopped shivering. I wove magic around me, casting my spells beyond the shield, following the magic. A trail lit up before me, glowing orange and leading into the city.

"What's that?"

"A path," I replied.

"Let's follow it," Steve said, leading me toward his truck. I flung the door to my shop shut and cast my spells, sealing it off as I followed Steve. I should take more precautions, but there wasn't time. Steve would follow the path with or without me, and my best bet was to bring him along. I jumped into the truck and he sped off, following the beacon of my magic.

"Is it an attack?" he asked as he wound down various streets, trying to keep an eye on the magical path. "Do I need to call in backup?"

"I don't think so," I said slowly as I saw where the path was leading us. I'd been there a few weeks earlier returning spell equipment to Ian, and doing my best to avoid William. The drive was short as we stopped in front of a modest two-story home that looked like every other house on the block. "This is Ian's home."

"Ian? The warlock?"

"Yes," I replied, opening the truck door. Steve grabbed my arm before I had a chance to move. "What are you doing?"

"Me? I'm going in."

"This is a bad idea. Have you thought that this is a trap? Or some sort of magic attack?"

I took a breath and nodded. "You're right, it is a bad idea."

"Glad we agree," he replied, releasing my arm. "Let's have a plan in mind first. Should we call William? Isn't he in charge of the other warlocks and witches in the area?"

"He is, and that is an excellent idea. You call William." I jumped out of the truck before he could stop me, leaving the shield nice and tight around the truck. "I'm going inside."

Steve tried to reach after me, but the shield held him contained to his truck. "Damn it, Gia, don't do this. Let me out!"

"I don't think so," I replied, turning toward the house. "Call William," I called over my shoulder as I hurried toward the front door.

I let go of the magic spell of guiding, not needing it any longer. The feeling of cold air was stronger here, creeping through the shield I had wrapped around myself. Steve would be safe in his bubble, and I had little to fear in this world.

The front door was open, leading into a basic foyer with hardwood floors. Two pairs of large mens shoes sat right inside the front door, yet muddy bare footprints led into the home. Much smaller footprints. I followed the footprints as they wound into carpeted living room and up the stairs. The carpet crunched beneath my feet and icicles climbed the banister, thickening with each step. Despite the shield, my breath fogged before my eyes and I shivered in my pencil skirt and heels.

The house went dark. I stopped, hoping my eyes would adjust to the darkness. Cursing, I pulled off my glasses and put them in my hair before continuing my slow climb. No light filtered through the dark stairwell, so I trudged on in the darkness, feeling my way to each step. At the top of the stairs I stopped and looked around. An orange glow flickered underneath the door at the end of the hall, illuminating the snow covered hallway and reflecting eerily on the walls. I followed the faint light slowly and made it halfway down the hall when my heel stuck into the carpet and froze. I yanked on the shoe, but it wouldn't come free. After securing the shield tighter around my body, I pulled my foot free and stepped onto the carpet. My foot sunk through snow and ice, but my shield kept the wetness away. Pulling my other foot free, I continued until I reached the doorway. I didn't want to immediately kill anyone on the other side of the door, so I lowered my glasses before turning the knob.

The glow I had seen flickering came from two rings of candles. At the center of the room, surrounded by the innermost ring of white candles, sat Ian, hands on his thighs. His lips moved constantly, murmuring incantations, but his dark eyes darted around the room frantically. His sweat-drenched bare chest heaved with his labored breathing. The second ring of candles surrounded the white candles a foot away. Inside that ring a shadow moved. Outside both rings was the source of the footprints. The man had obviously been dead for quite a while; what little flesh remained dangled loosely from his bones. He paced the edge of the black candles in the snow, leaving a muddy path in his wake.

I moved into the room and shut the door softly, taking a look at the wards and runes plastered on the walls. "Ian?" I spoke softly, hoping the skeletal creature would ignore me.

"I don't know how long I can hold it off," Ian said, his voice strained. A black candle flickered and died, and the pacing creature shrieked in excitement. I counted candles. Eight white candles, all still lit, and sixteen black candles, four of which had already gone out.

"Did you summon this creature?"

"Not intentionally."

"What do you mean by that?"

"I was tracing the necromancer." He stopped talking to mutter another incantation and the candles grew in strength briefly. "It backfired. He sent this thing after me, and something else."

"Why were you tracing the necromancer?"

He shook his head and continued his spell. I took a step closer, flexing my toes to regain feeling. "Are you doing the snow?" He shook his head.

Channeling fire was easy enough, but I didn't necessarily want to burn his house down. I pulled in magic and spread it outward, creating heat instead of fire. The candles flickered and another black one went out, but the snow melted from the floor leaving wet carpet.

"Don't," he said. His arms shook and a trail of sweat trickled down the middle of his chest, soaking his shirt.

The creature shrieked and turned toward me, flinging its arms outward. I stepped back and muttered a single word, burning the creature with a mere thought. It screamed and grabbed my arm, shattering my shield. My scream joined it as its icy touch burned my skin. I pushed fire into it again until it let go and staggered into the wall, catching the curtain on fire. I stared at it until it crumbled to the floor.

The black candles flickered out and a foul wind filled the room. I held my breath as the odors of death and decay assaulted my senses. The unnatural wind careened through the room, pressing me against the door. I struggled against the force, pushing my magic back against it until I was able to step away from the door. The shadow that had been stalking between the candles moved, changed. Darkness filled the room and towered over me, engulfing me in the stench of death. My stomach churned and I vomited, unable to stop until there was nothing left in me. The wind grew louder, bringing the cold chill of death with it. Again the wind slashed through the room, pushing me to the ground. I fought to move, crawling slowly toward the center of the room. The light of the candles flared and Ian's voice rose with urgency. I crawled slowly toward those candles, seeking shelter, but the circle of candles kept me out as well. I pressed against the invisible wall, seeing Ian's sweat-drenched face behind the haze of magic. There would be no help from him.

I reached out and pulled on my magic, grabbing every last inch of energy I possessed, filling myself. I felt the shield around Steve snap, and I knew he'd be coming this way. It couldn't be helped. Energy gathered around me, red and purple and angry, and I solidified it, crafting a shield and a weapon together. The darkness attacked again, pressing me facedown into the wet carpet. I closed my eyes and formed the magic in my mind, then stopped. The darkness moved over me and I felt hands grasp my own and the weight of a body on top of mine. The darkness had form. If I could have smiled, I would have. In my mind, I imagined the fire net I had used before and lashed out with my magic toward that darkness, engulfing it in the net. I rolled over as my dress caught fire, dousing it in the drenched carpet. The net surrounded the shadow form, tightening until I could make out a manlike shape. The darkness screamed, a piercing wail that had me covering my ears, but I kept my concentration on the fire net, closing it down tighter and tighter around the form.

The smell of death and decay that I knew to be the necromancer engulfed the room once more and I screamed as the lines on my chest from my last encounter burned back to life in glowing lines. Pain I had never experienced before raked across my body, but I held tight to my magic and squeezed back on the darkness, pushing my magic back at the necromancer.

With a flash of light, my net burned up on itself and the darkness was gone. I fell back into the carpet and looked past the candles toward Ian. His eyes were open wide, the white candles burned out, and a series of red marks crisscrossed his chest. The door blast open, but I didn't have the energy to do more than turn my head. Men moved around the room and I had the vague recollection that someone was speaking my name. Arms lifted me up and I curled against the strength, breathing in the clean smell of cedar and mint. I closed my eyes and relaxed, feeling strangely safe.

Missing

"DO YOU KNOW WHAT happened to her?" a woman's voice asked.

"She was unconscious when we found her, but there was definitely some magic involved." I knew that voice. Detective Daniels. The other voice was unknown to me.

"Doctor, I think she's waking up," another woman's voice.

I felt hands on my face and I flinched back, covering my face with my hands in a panic. My glasses were gone! "Where are they? My glasses?"

Rough hands touched my arm and I shivered as he gently pulled my left hand away and placed the glasses in my palm. I took a deep breath and put the glasses on my face before slowly opening my eyes. The room was brightly lit and smelled of ammonia. A hospital, for sure. I looked down. My clothes were gone as well and I wore nothing but a standard hospital gown. I took stock of the room quickly. Detective Daniels stood beside my hospital bed. On the other side was a woman in a white coat and beside her was an older woman wearing scrubs covered in pink kittens. At the foot of my bed stood four police officers. One had his gun in his hands, arms crossed, glaring down at me. The other three appeared ready to draw their weapons if I so much as twitched.

"What's going on?" I asked as I slowly sat up. I wasn't cuffed to the bed like they did in the movies, so maybe that was a good sign. I glanced at the officers as I moved, watching them watch me. The youngest pulled his gun out and moved a few steps to the right.

"We need to check her out," the doctor said, glaring over at the young officer who had just pulled his gun out. "I can't do my job if I'm worried about being shot by a jumpy cop."

The young officer blushed red and opened his mouth, but Detective Daniels spoke instead. "All of you, get out. I've got this."

They didn't hesitate to leave the room, slamming the door behind them.

"Detective?" the doctor said.

"I'm not leaving."

She opened her mouth, but I waved my hand in the air. "It's fine, doctor. He can stay."

"If you say so." I sat up the rest of the way and obliged her as she listened to my heart and lungs and took my temperature. I was curious what the readings were, but neither woman gave any indication if they were normal or not.

"May I look in your eyes?" she asked, reaching a hand out.

"No," I said firmly, holding onto the glasses.

"Very well." Bandages covered my chest and she carefully pulled them back to examine them. I looked down, really taking stock of my own body. The black lines caused by the necromancer had faded into faint red marks like they had the first time. She pulled the bandage off and pressed gently on the lines. "They're cold," she said.

I nodded my head and lifted my arm. "What's this?"

"You were burnt rather badly," she said, carefully peeling back a corner of the bandage to show me. My skin looked normal and she continued peeling the bandage off until my arm was completely exposed, whole and normal. "You were burnt."

"It must have looked worse than it was," I said.

She swallowed visibly and opened the back of my gown. I could feel her removing the bandages, but there was no pain. Her hand ran across my back as though searching for injuries. "You're almost completely healed, except for the mark on your chest."

I nodded and leaned back in bed, glancing over at Detective Daniels, who stood quietly with his face turned toward the door. "Like I said, it must not have been that bad."

"Are you a werewolf?" she whispered, moving close to my ear. Detective Daniels turned his head and looked over at us.

Loudly I replied, "No, doctor, I'm not a werewolf."

She straightened and glanced at the detective, flushing slightly. "Your body temperature is lower than normal, but..." she trailed off and cleared her throat. "But, your heartbeat seems steady and regular. You have a heartbeat."

"I'm not a vampire either," I said.

"Fae?" she asked quickly.

"No." I sighed.

"Are you human?"

I shrugged and pulled the blankets up. "More or less."

"Have you been infected with vampire blood? I have heard it has healing powers, temporary of course, but nonetheless."

I wrinkled my nose in disgust. "Absolutely not."

"What are you? I mean, how do I treat you if I don't know what I'm treating? May I take blood samples?

"No, definitely not," I replied, looking suspiciously at the IV in my arm. "Take this out."

She nodded and the nurse scurried around the bed to remove the IV. I didn't think they'd get any info out of my blood, but I didn't like the idea of anyone trying to figure me out. "How is it you're healed already, but that other man..." she stopped as Detective Daniels cleared his throat loudly.

"Other man?" I asked. "Ian?"

The nurse removed the IV and I pulled my arm away. The detective moved closer and said, "Doctor, I need to speak with the patient alone now, if you're done."

She nodded and they both left without another word. "Is he okay?" I asked as soon as the door closed behind them. "Ian, I mean?"

"He's dead," he said bluntly.

"What? Shit," I closed my eyes and leaned back, remembering crisscrossed red lines covering Ian's chest and his eyes open wide and staring.

"Did you kill him?"

"Did I... are you kidding me? Why the hell would I kill him? I was there to help him. He sent for me."

"He sent for you?"

"Ask your partner! Steve was there."

"I already spoke to Steve," he replied. "He told us about the cold and your spell. Why do you say Ian sent for you?"

"Well who else would have sent that magic to me?" I grabbed an end of my hair, twirling it nervously around my finger. Did Ian send me? Had he looked surprised when I showed up?

"You've thought of something."

I touched the ice cold lines on my chest and looked over at Detective Daniels. "Ian said he'd been tracing the necromancer and something went wrong. What if Ian didn't reach out to me for help? What if it was the necromancer luring me there?"

"Why would he do that?"

"I don't know, revenge maybe? Damn it, I don't know why Ian would come to me for help either. He would have gone to William."

"Exactly what I thought."

"Well, where's William? Maybe he knows what's going on."

The detective grimaced and pulled out a piece of gum, chewing it purposefully. I waited, staring at the detective and willing him to explain. I was about to ask again when he finally spoke. "We can't find William."

"Did you go to his house?"

"It's covered in snow and ice, just like Ian's place. No tracks. No sign of anyone coming or going. His cars are all there and accounted for. We've reached out to the other witches and warlocks we know, but no one has seen him in days."

"Is anyone else missing?"

"It's funny you should ask that. In fact, there are two other warlocks and five witches missing. All of their homes look the same, covered in ice."

"And you think I have something to do with all this?"

He grinned suddenly and shook his head. "No, actually, I think you're telling the truth. I pride myself on being a good judge of character, and I know when someone's lying. You're not lying about this. Other things, yes, but not this."

"Well, thanks, Detective."

"It's Hunter, and don't thank me yet. I'm going to ask for your help."

I laughed and twirled my hair. "The other cops looked like they were ready to shoot me and you want to ask for my help. That's hilarious."

"Well, its been left in my hands. Steve vouches for you, but the boss will only agree if I vouch for you too."

"The boss? You mean the police department is officially asking for my help?"

"Only if I give the go ahead."

"And do you, Detective... Hunter? Do you vouch for me?"

He leaned forward, bringing the scent of mint with him. "I think you're hiding something behind those glasses of yours." I felt the blood drain from my face at his words, but I tried to keep my face neutral. "But do I think you're behind this problem? No. Do I think you can help? I think you might be the only one able to help. So, yes, I will vouch for you in this and you'd better not make me regret it."

"That's impressive. You vouch for me and threaten me all in one breath."

"Do you really expect any less?"

I raised an eyebrow and smiled. "From you, no, I don't. I think you'd be a pretty poor cop otherwise."

"Yet Steve trusts you implicitly. What does that say about him?"

"He's young."

"And far too trusting."

"I think he's more suspicious than you give him credit for."

He grinned and leaned back. "That's good to hear. I'll get some clothes brought for you. We have work to do, and I don't think you want to rack up a hospital bill when there's absolutely nothing wrong with you."

"I couldn't agree more."

He moved toward the door and stopped, his hand on the handle. "Just so you're aware, I kept them from looking at your eyes but they did take your blood." He turned to look at me, watching my reaction closely. I didn't know what to think, so I couldn't give much away. "I already destroyed the samples." With that, he walked out the door.

I stared at the place he'd been, wondering what to make of his comment. I believed him, but I couldn't figure out why he would have done it. Did he suspect what I was? Doubtful, since there were only three of us. Maybe because he would have wanted someone to do it for him. I was still sitting there staring at the door when it opened several minutes later and Steve came in, carrying one of my spare dresses that I kept at the shop and a pair of heels.

"Hey sexy," he said as he held up my red dress. "I hear you're getting out of this joint and need some clothes."

I laughed and threw back the blanket. "Yes, get me out of this hospital gown."

He raised his eyebrows and crossed the room, tossing down the dress and reaching around the back of the gown. His hand trailed down my back, sending a shiver down my spine. "Your wish is my command."

I laughed as he yanked the hospital gown off and pushed me back onto the bed. "I thought we had to go," I said as he fiddled with the hospital bed controls, angling us into various positions.

"We have a few minutes," he said, glancing at the clock on the wall. "Make that five."

"Well then you'd better quit playing with the bed," I said as I reached down and pulled at his belt buckle.

He made sure I appreciated the theatrics of the bed buttons before we dressed and regrouped with the other officers. I had nothing but the red dress and a pair of heels on, but it would have to do for the time being. I threw my hair into a quick braid and followed Steve and Hunter out of the hospital, along with several other police officers. In the time I'd been in the hospital, three other witches had gone missing under similar circumstances, and another two had been found dead. We had a list of houses to check out and no way of knowing who was next, or what we'd find.

Due to Theda and Amy, I had only recently replenished my potion ingredients, and hadn't had time to brew another batch of the expensive protection spell. No one took the news well, but these were police officers and they were used to danger. I couldn't spend my energy shielding everyone either, and I didn't suggest it. Time seemed to be against us. I could feel it against my skin.

We rode in Steve's truck to an apartment complex a few blocks from the hospital. Hunter followed us, along with another patrol car. Seven witches and warlocks resided in the small apartment, all in the same building. The moment we pulled up to the apartment, I knew it wouldn't be good. A thick sheet of ice covered the walkway leading up to the building. I stared at the building, counting seven doors coated in a thick layer of frost as the police officers piled out of their vehicles.

"Wait," I said as I pushed open the door to the truck and jumped out. "Let me see if anyone is here."

They didn't ask how I was going to check, simply stepped back and waited. Steve smiled encouragingly at me. I zipped up the police jacket Steve had loaned me and wriggled my hands free. The cold sent a shiver down my spine, but I ignored it as I reached out for the magic that was always there, always around. Energy flowed into me, enveloping me in a different kind of warmth. The magic I was going to do was simple and didn't need the amount of energy I pulled into myself. No, that was for the chance that someone, or something, was ready to attack me. I was thankful for the reserve energy I still had from the incubus and succubus, although I had already used a great deal of it healing myself. Tendrils of magic spread forth and I wove them through the apartment, seeking the energy of anyone, alive or dead. Empty. Empty. Empty. Dead. I opened my eyes and looked toward apartment C4. Further I reached out. Empty. Empty. Empty. Even the dark apartment with no ice was empty. Nothing was here.

"The woman in C4 is dead, but otherwise there is no one here. We should move on."

"Dead?" Steve asked, his hand going to the gun at his side. "You're sure?"

"Yes, I'm sure. There's nothing here, and we won't find any answers standing around. Whatever, or whoever, is doing this has moved on. We need to move down the list." I turned and walked back to the truck, not waiting as I slid into the passenger seat.

A moment later Steve joined me and started the truck. He didn't say anything as he drove down the road, flipping on the heater to take off the chill. We stopped five minutes later outside another apartment complex. "Three live here," he said, pointing unnecessarily to the scene of winter coating one building only.

I nodded and stepped out of the truck. Magic was easier with a little distance from technology. Once again, I reached outward, only to be disappointed again. I climbed back in the truck and shook my head. "They're all dead. Five, not three," I said.

"We only have a record of three witches and warlocks living here."

"Well, maybe they had visitors. I don't know what to tell you, Steve. There are five dead inside that building. Two women, three men."

"Fine," he snapped, pulling a sheet of paper from his pocket. He looked at it briefly before backing up and speeding off down the road. The other vehicles followed us as we drove in silence. He stopped us in front of another apartment. It was smaller than the others and run down, but equally coated in ice.

Without a word, I stepped out and repeated the process. Steve joined me a minute later. "There's no one here, and I don't sense any danger," I said.

"Better than dead, I suppose."

I shrugged, "You don't know that. If they've been taken by someone, or something, it could be so much worse."

"That's the last place on our list," Steve said as Hunter walked up.

Hunter nodded and ran a hand over his eyes. "We don't have any more places to look. I just checked in. All the other places are the same."

"You've checked the home of every witch and warlock in town?" I asked.

"Every one we know about."

"What about outside city limits? Or the next town over?"

"Everyone in a hundred miles has been checked," Hunter snapped. "City and county are working on this. The only reason we even had this many names to check was because William had supplied it to us."

"William told you where everyone in his coven lived?" I asked, surprised. Warlocks were notoriously secretive, and William had seemed no different to me.

"He was worried about them."

"When did he give you this list? Has it been updated?"

"Two days ago. He gave us this list two days ago," Hunter replied and I felt the blood drain from my face.

"He knew," I said softly. "William knew something was coming."

"He said he was worried about his coven and asked us to keep the list just in case."

"Did he say anything else? Ian had mentioned he was trying to find the necromancer."

Hunter scowled and shook his head slowly in the negative. "He wouldn't say anything else. Ian brought up the necromancer?"

"When I arrived at his house, he said he'd been tracking the necromancer. He didn't really have a chance to say much more." I leaned back against the truck, my eyes straying to the icy apartments. I ran a hand across my chest, feeling the cold lines of necromancer magic that still lingered on my skin. "There's only one way to find them. Take me home."

HUNT

STEVE GRUMBLED THE ENTIRE drive to my house, mumbling unintelligibly under his breath. For my part, I ignored everything and focused on my next steps. I couldn't just cast a spell and chase after the necromancer. That would do nothing but alert him. William, though, I was sure I could find. Normally, I needed something personal to find someone, but I was confident William and I had bonded enough. I ran a finger across my lips, remembering the kiss. I could trace him.

Outside the gate to my home another truck idled, the headlights shining on the gate. I rolled my eyes, even though no one could ever see me doing so and opened the gate with a wave of my hand. Steve made another grumble under his breath, but he followed the truck past the gate and parked. Hunter followed behind us in his own truck, parking on the other side of our vehicle. I climbed out as soon as we stopped and walked up to the first truck.

"Mike," I said as the driver's door opened.

"Hi, Gia," he said slowly.

Maggie jumped out of the passenger side of the truck and scurried over to me. She wore jeans, a sweatshirt underneath a thick jacket, gloves, and a beanie pulled over her head. Outside her jacket hung a large silver cross. "I'm here to help," she said.

"Help? With what exactly?"

She shrugged as Mike threw his hands into the air. "She doesn't know!" he shouted, pointing at her. "She started bundling up and told me I needed to drive over here right away to help you. It's maybe 60 degrees outside and she's dressed for the snow."

I stared at Maggie for a heartbeat before turning toward the house. "Come inside, we have work to do. You too, Mike."

They followed me into the house without question. That was a first. Steve mumbled a few choice words under his breath, Maggie bounced beside me, Mike scowled, and Hunter brought up the rear like a silent shadow. The other police officers had gone back to the station, or wherever it was police went when they were out of witch hunting to do. They were all worried. I could feel the anticipation, fear, and worry leeching off each of them. Except Hunter. I opened the house and flicked on the lights with a touch of magic, dropping wards without a thought. Filled with energy, I could feel each of their emotions, except the silent man bringing up the rear. Hunter followed behind the group, giving away nothing more than his shadow. No fear, no anger, no emotion. Nothing.

I moved straight into the kitchen, pulling out anything I thought could be of use. If I had more time to prepare, I'd have a dozen bottles of protection magic. I ran a finger across the ingredients, running through the spells each could create in my mind. The protection spell might help the others, but even I was unsure if it would work against a necromancer. Unfortunately, time was against us. In my long years I'd only met three necromancers personally. For the most part, they kept to the shadows. I saw their handiwork though, even if I didn't see them.

"Are there any vampire nests around here?" I asked as I pulled a bottle of holy water off the shelf.

"Sure," Hunter replied, shrugging his broad shoulders. "The closest one is just east of town about ten miles. They keep to themselves for the most part, but they've been known to kidnap travelers. The next closest is near Club Wyvern. The club employs several, but we haven't had any issues with them yet. Next closest nest is somewhere along the coast to the south of here about thirty miles or so. They're trouble for sure, but we haven't been able to find their home, or their leader."

"We? Isn't that outside your jurisdiction?" I asked.

"The various police agencies. We work together on all vamp-related issues. Most police units don't have the manpower alone to deal with a nest of vampires." He paused and slid the bottle of holy water toward himself. "I thought this was about the necromancer?"

"It is," I replied. I filled my newest pewter cauldron with six ounces of water, eight drops of lemon oil, two drops of lime juice, and a basil leaf.

"Are you making tea?" Mike asked.

I grinned and shook my head, taking the holy water from Hunter and dripping three drops into the cauldron. "No, I'm making an undead repellant."

"A what?" Steve asked, leaning over the cauldron as I dropped in three more ingredients, sliding the bottles quickly back into the cupboard. "What was that?"

"Just potion ingredients," I replied, stirring the mixture once before turning the stove on.

"So what does this do?" Steve asked again.

The potion boiled quickly, and I removed it from heat, tossing in one last ingredient. The potion turned bright yellow, the steam swirling up like rays of sunlight. "Hand me twelve of those bottles," I said, pointing to the line of bottles in the top cupboard. Steve grabbed the bottles down and set them in front of me, pulling off the stoppers. Carefully, I poured the mixture evenly between the containers, sealing the lids quickly. I pushed the glowing bottles across the counter and cleaned up my cauldron immediately.

"Are you going to tell us what these do?" Steve asked again, his voice tinged with irritation.

"They're undead repellant, like I said earlier," I replied as I wiped out the cauldron and set it on the back of the counter. "They'll protect you from anything dead, or undead. It won't last long, though. When you're ready, open the bottle and drink it fully. Vampires will avoid you, zombies will ignore you, and if you die, it ensures you won't come back as a zombie, or worse. Be careful, though, it'll only last a few hours after it's consumed."

"Can't you make more?"

I picked up the nearest bottle and swirled it around. "When the color goes away, the potion is dead. As long as there's still a glow, it'll work. It doesn't matter how many I make. These will lose potency in about seven hours. They must be drunk before that, and then they'll work for only a few hours."

"We drink this and we repel vampires and zombies?" Steve asked.

"Basically. It's not perfect, but it helps against your basic undead scum. Older vampires are another story. Not much works on them."

"Great, so now what?"

"Now, I find William. I'm guessing he's at one of these vampire dens. Let's hope it's a small one."

"Vampire den? Why would he be there?"

I glanced over at Steve, then the rest of the group. They were all looking to me for answers. This wasn't much more than a lucky guess, but I couldn't tell them that. "Necromancers raise dead things, right? Well, vampires are dead. Or undead, I suppose. They've been known to band together from time to time, and it's never pretty."

"They have? I've never heard of any such thing?" Steve mused.

"Well, you haven't been in this game long."

"I have," Hunter stated, his deep voice little more than a murmur. "This is the first time I've seen the work of a necromancer, but I've heard of them. Makes sense they'd seek a commonality with vamps."

I shrugged, not wanting to give too much away. "It does, although it usually isn't beneficial to the vampires. A powerful necromancer should be able to control any vampires it chooses."

"It's all a power play," Hunter rumbled.

"It always is."

"When have you seen this before?"

Oh, he was good. I grinned and pushed one of the bottles toward him. "I don't entangle with necromancers."

"Yet you've still seen this before. When?"

"It's been a few years."

"How many?"

I shrugged. "I don't know exactly."

Hunter leaned forward, his body casting a shadow over me and blocking out everyone else. "Liar," he whispered.

"1933," I breathed out. He straightened away from me and took a deliberate step backward, allowing me to move past him. I walked purposefully into the living room and sat down in my favorite chair situated in the corner. During the day, I could sit in the plush chair, read a book, and watch the waves crashing over rocks. I sat down and closed my eyes, feeling the swirl of magic I had been gathering for the past hour.

"I'm going to search for William," I said to the room in general. "Don't interrupt me."

I didn't need the quiet, but I longed for it. Why did I let these people into my home? Why was I helping them? Why was I helping William? I didn't have the answers to my own questions.

Kansas City, 1933

"It's going to be a bloodbath," Theda cooed as she led me toward the train station. "The perfect opportunity to cash in on some mayhem. I just hope we're not late."

"These humans are sick. It's one thing to kill, but to set people up on top of it, even if they are criminals. Hard to tell who the good guys are," I mused.

She laughed and pushed the sun hat further onto her head. "This is nothing new," she replied.

The loud pops of gunfire were unmistakable. Theda grabbed my hand, tugging me after her in sudden excitement. We rounded the corner and I pulled Theda to a halt, still several blocks from the train station and the sounds of gunfire. "Brandi, come on," she urged, using the name I had chosen for this era.

"Stop!" I hissed, pulling her against the nearest building. She glared at me and opened her mouth to speak, when the wind shifted, bringing the smell of death and decay.

"It's just garbage," she whispered. "Let's go."

"Don't you feel it?" I asked, shivering. "That's a necromancer."

"It's not," she insisted, tugging on my arm. "You're so jumpy anymore."

"How did you hear about this again?"

"I told you it was an old friend."

"Theda..."

"Your old friend actually."

"Damn it, Theda, I told you Pierre is not to be trusted. And if he's consorting with a necromancer."

"Oh, don't be silly. Vampires don't consort with necromancers. And besides, it's daytime. No vampires here."

"Necromancers don't fear the sun." I pulled away, stalking back the way I had come. Theda hurried to my side. "I don't know what you're playing at, but I want no part of it."

"You really are no fun anymore."

"I don't like being lied to," I snapped.

"Fine," she growled and I stopped, arms crossed as I waited for her to continue.

"Pierre said he was working with someone, but he didn't say who."

"You knew it was a necromancer though, didn't you?"

"I'm not stupid." She tucked her hair further under her hat. "I knew what he was the moment I met him, but there's just

something about him. He's brilliant, truly. Oh, you just need to meet him. We had this all planned out. He's going to animate one of the dead police officers and lead us straight inside their headquarters. That's where we come in. Just think about feasting on all those strong, delicious cops."

"A little much just to kill some cops, don't you think?"

She shook her head. "We won't kill all of them, and we have to leave a few for the necromancer to reanimate. This changes the game. No running and hiding. Slow takeover."

"This was Pierre's idea?" I asked and she shook her head. "The necromancer?"

"I told you he's brilliant."

"Who is he?"

She shook her head and tugged on my hand. "Come meet him. He's gorgeous and young. His dad was a necromancer, and his father before that. So much power."

I pulled my hand away. "A family of necromancers who consort with vampires? That's even worse. Sorry, but you're on your own. I think it's time for me to move on."

"Brandi, stop."

"Brandi's gone. Time for a new name and a new place." I ran a hand through my hair, trying to avoid the hurt look on Theda's face. "Don't look for me."

Someone moved toward me, the footsteps steady and purposeful. The smell of vanilla and lavender wafted toward me.

"You're not alone," Maggie whispered, touching a hand to my shoulder briefly. Her words soothed me, surprisingly, and I felt the magic swirl into me in a rush.

I opened my eyes, feeling calm. "Grab a map for me and one of those vials," I said, pointing at the pile of maps stacked on my bookcase. She glanced at them briefly, before grabbing what I asked for.

"We're going to do a locater spell," I said. "In order to do this, we need to pull on energy from all the elements. Normally, I do this on the beach. It makes it easier to gather earth, wind, and water. But, time is of the essence."

"What do you need me to do?"

"I can pull on earth and wind from anywhere, but I need some water and fire so I don't pull from the wrong sources."

"Wrong sources?" she asked.

"People hold water, this house holds water. You get the point."

"Oh, how much water and fire do you need?"

"Not much. Just a glass of water and a lighter will do."

She scurried to the kitchen, gathering the items I asked for and returning in quick order. "Now what?"

"We pull on the elements. Watch me, but do not interfere."

I gathered the energy into me, explaining the process I'd done on the beach with William. There were other ways I could find people, but the locater spell took the least amount of energy, and I had a bad feeling I would need every last ounce I could muster. At least I wasn't showing any signs of weakness, like green skin.

"Normally, it helps to have something of the person, to channel the magic. It makes it easier. Hair is the best, but blood works too.""I thought blood magic was bad."

"It is, which is why it's not a good idea to use it. Oh, wait."

"What is it?"

"His tie," I murmured. "It's hanging in the hall closet."

Maggie moved toward the closet and pulled out the tie William had placed in my purse. I took it, wondering if he'd known I'd need it to find him someday.

"What's that?" Steve asked from across the room, his eyebrows drawn down into a frown.

"A tie belonging to William. I can use it to find him a bit easier."

"Why do you have his tie?"

I ignored his question, and worked through the spell, guiding Maggie, and feeling the rest of our audience watch as well. Before the spell ended, I touched the crisp cold lines of magic on my chest, feeling the intertwined connections. There were two. One was dark and smelled of death. The other was bright and fractured, smelling of the air before a storm. I followed the tangled paths of the bright light, feeling it intertwined with the darkness. The path ended, as I had suspected. "William is with the necromancer," I said, opening my eyes.

"When you say he's with him..." Steve began.

"I only mean to say they are in the same location. More than that, I cannot say." I wiped my hand on my dress, trying to ease the chill in my fingertips.

"Do we have a direction?" Hunter asked.

I looked at what remained of the map. "South."

He nodded. "I had a feeling you were going to say that. That's good."

"Good?" Steve asked, frowning at Hunter. "You just said there was a large, unknown, and dangerous vampire nest there. How is this good?"

"First, we'll finally know where this nest is. Second, we get to take out that nest, of course!"

"We'd better call this in."

"No," I said, standing up. "You call any humans in, they'll be dead in no time."

"We have your potion."

"It's a temporary potion, and it doesn't work against regular injuries. Damn it, Steve, my magic can't keep everyone safe. Especially humans. I don't have time to make my protection potion for everyone, nor do I have the energy."

"Humans. You forget, I'm human. Hunter's human. Maggie's human. Mike's a werewolf and you're... well... you're whatever it is you are."

"And most of your police force is human. If you want them all dead, then by all means, invite them along. Who am I to stop you?" Hadn't I told myself I wouldn't get involved again with the police? If they want to get themselves killed, let them.

"Well, I think I've heard enough. Maggie, time to go home," Mike said, grabbing Maggie's arm.

Maggie pulled away from him, shaking her head. "No, I needed to come here for a reason, Mike. I have to help Gia."

"You just helped her with that spell. Plus, if it makes you feel better, I'll call in the Pack and we'll help Gia do whatever the hell it is we're doing."

"I have to go, Mike. Don't ask me why. I just know..." she trailed off, turning toward me. "Please."

A feeling of unease crept over me and grew with each passing moment. I thought of a dozen different scenarios and dismissed them all. My best bet was going alone, but this necromancer had already proven to be strong. Too strong, perhaps. Alone, even I might not survive. "Fine," I said. "I don't care. You all do what you want to do. There are twelve potions. Take them. Give them away. Do whatever you need to do. Detective Daniels and I will lead the way."

"We will?" he asked, crossing his arms.

"Yes. Steve is going back to tell your boss what's going on and send the cavalry in after us. I'll leave a path for everyone to follow."

Steve scowled and crossed the room, pulling me out of the chair and into his arms. "What are you talking about? You're not leaving my side."

"Yes, Steve, I am. You're human and I don't want you to get hurt. Please, just trust me in this."

"Yet you're okay running into danger with Hunter," he said, his voice rising a notch.

Hunter wasn't human, but I had the feeling no one knew that but me. "Someone has to drive me," I said, shrugging. "Plus, he's your partner. I figured if you trusted anyone, it would be him. If you'd rather I travel with a werewolf..."

"No, no, you're right," he said quickly, glancing over to see if Mike had heard. He most definitely heard every word, but Mike was good at feigning ignorance. "Still, I should take you."

"I think I'm going to pull rank on this one," Hunter said, moving in close behind us. "While I don't like the idea of involving civilians, I've been given clearance to bring Miss Marchesi into all this. That being said, I'm also responsible for her safety. It's my ass on the line. You get back to the station and update everyone."

"I'll bring the cavalry," he said softly, the frown deepening on his forehead. "We'll be right behind you."

Hunter patted him on the back. "Good. Make sure everyone is prepared for vampires."

"Follow the trail," I said, touching his forehead. He blinked and stepped backward, looking down at the ground. A faint line of red led southward. "Maggie?"

"I see it," she said softly.

"You lead Mike and the Pack. You're the shield. Don't forget. The path is linked to me, but I'll make sure to anchor it at the south end of town. From there, you should be able to follow us directly." Everyone nodded in what I hoped was understanding. "Detective Daniels?"

He nodded and moved toward the door. "Let's go."

"Hey, you'd better take one of those potions," Steve said, running into the kitchen to grab a potion and handing it to Hunter. Hunter took the potion in his hands and walked out the door. Steve and Mike gathered the remaining potions while I ran upstairs to change clothes. By the time I was done, everyone had left and Hunter waited for me in his truck. I'd dressed warmly in jeans and a thick jacket, shoving a pair of gloves into my pocket along with a few extra potions. I climbed into his truck and buckled in, shoving a black beanie down on my braided hair.

"Can you see the path?" I asked.

"Yes," he said simply, turning the truck out of my driveway and down the road.

We followed the trail of my magic out of town, stopping briefly at the edge of town to anchor the spell. Anyone with magical talent would see the path, but since all the witches and warlocks in the area were either dead or missing, I wasn't overly concerned. Fae could see it, but they wouldn't trouble themselves with anything that didn't apply to them. I climbed back into the truck and we took off.

"It's dark out," Hunter said, breaking the silence.

I turned my head toward his. "I'm not taking off the glasses."

"Whatever."

"Just trust me on this."

"Can you tell how far this goes?" he waved his hand in the general direction we were headed.

I had anchored the map's location to my guiding spell, but it was still hard to get a sense of distance. "When we get close, I'll let you know."

His phone rang and he answered immediately. "Yeah. What? Just left town about five minutes ago. Are you kidding me? Are they alright? Yeah, we're fine. Okay. Let me know." He tossed the phone down on the seat between us. "That was Steve. They got to the edge of town where your spell started and a tree fell down across the highway. A friggin' tree. Mike and his people are there too trying to get it cleared out. They'll let us know when they're back on the road."

"A tree? That's interesting."

"Interesting? That's strange as hell, if you ask me."

"If there was magic involved, Maggie will be able to tell."

"Well..."

"Well, what?"

"The tree fell on Mike's truck. They're okay, but only because Maggie had a shield up around them."

"She did?" I felt a swelling of pride. My phone rang and I answered. "Maggie, I just heard. Are you alright?"

"Yes, we're fine. Mike's freaking out, of course, but I did it, Gia. I felt something like freezing wind and I just reacted."

"I'm glad you're okay."

"The truck's a mess, but we're okay. We'll ride with Evan as soon as we get the tree out of the road."

"Be careful. Keep your shield up."

"You too."

I took Maggie's advice and hardened a shield around Hunter's truck. Five minutes after hanging up with Maggie, Steve called Hunter to tell them they were back on the road. Hunter grumbled and pressed on the accelerator, "They want us to wait."

My phone rang again. "Yeah, Maggie, what's up?"

"Gia!"

"Maggie? What's going on?"

"It's so cold."

"Use your shield. Keep them safe."

"I'm trying. There's snow everywhere. Look out!" Maggie screamed into the phone and I held my breath as I heard the sound of grinding metal and squealing tires. Maggie's voice was muffled on the phone as she spoke. "Mike, are you okay? What do you mean we're stuck? What about Gia? Darn it, hang on." The phone clicked off, then rang a moment later. "Sorry, Gia, we crashed into a tree. It's like a snowstorm here. I don't know if any of the other trucks got through, but we're stuck. I'm so sorry."

"No, Maggie, it's fine. Make sure you take that potion and get back to town as fast as possible. And whatever you do, don't lower your shield for anything. Keep it around as many people as possible."

"Okay. Be safe."

"You too."

I clicked off the phone and turned toward Hunter, who had his own phone to his face and was speaking quickly and quietly. After a minute he tossed the phone down again. "Steve and Billie are still behind us along with one car of werewolves."

"They should turn around."

"That's what I said, but they said either we all turn around, or we all push on."

"We're being separated for a reason."

"Easier to handle us like this."

I nodded in agreement and touched Hunter's arm. "We're getting close."

"Then let's get this done."

Necromancer

VAMPIRE DENS COME IN all shapes and sizes. I had seen ones that rivaled small cities and others that were full of ravaging, mindless blood-drinkers. From the outside, this appeared to be nothing more than a nomadic encampment. A narrow dirt path led us off the main road. No more than one vehicle could make the drive at a time, and even in Hunter's pickup we were having a difficult time traversing the rocky path in the dark. Our headlights bounced off trees and more than once I thought I caught a pale face peeking through the trees. The path ended abruptly, blocked by a boulder no human was capable of moving.

Hunter and I shared a look before stepping out of the truck. He held the potion in his hand as he walked around the front of the truck to stand beside me. "Will this work?" he asked, his voice just above a whisper.

I shrugged. "It'll work for most people."

"Side effects?"

"You're worried about side effects at a time like this?" I whispered back, trying not to laugh. "None that I know of, Detective. As I said, it's very temporary."

"What about you?"

I shook my head. "It doesn't work for me. If they're stupid, they'll still try to attack me."

He didn't say another word as he opened the bottle and drank the contents down in one swallow. "I guess we walk from here. How far do you think?"

"How far for what? How far until the end of my spell, and William? Or, how far will we make it before the vampires come out to play? Or perhaps it's how far until we meet our necromancer?"

He shrugged. "Whichever."

"Less than a mile to William. I imagine we'll be attacked any moment now."

"Well, at least we have plenty of light since its almost a full moon."

"Full moon?" I glanced up at the moon through the trees. It wasn't completely full, but very close. A few days off, perhaps. "Hopefully those werewolves keep their cool."

"That's assuming they arrive in time, or at all," he added as he pulled out his gun and chambered a round.

"Not much faith in your partner?"

"Steve will do what he says, or die trying. Werewolves are another matter."

I grinned and nodded. "They have one thing going for them that will definitely work in our favor."

"What's that?"

"They hate vampires."

Hunter grunted in agreement, but he didn't have time for more than that before the first vampires attacked. They were weak; young and inexperienced, running at us with mindlessness. The detective shot them both in the head in quick succession, his movements smooth and experienced. They dropped, their bodies turning to ash within moments. While this police department might be small, they had obviously put money in their budget toward the vampire problem.

"Nice," I commented. "Special bullets? Are those regulation?"

"They manufacturer these down in Texas," he said, his eyes scanning through the trees as we walked. "Made of iron and silver, dipped in holy water, and blessed. Triple Threat, they call them."

"Hmm, I can see why. Those will take down a werewolf too, depending on the amount of silver."

"And Fae," he added.

"Yes," I replied. "Some."

He stopped, his head cocked as he listened for something. "Some?" he asked after he had begun walking again. "I thought all Fae were allergic to iron."

"Common misconception," I stated. "For some, it is pure poison, but others it is a mere inconvenience. Still, there are those Fae who are completely immune. You don't seem to have any issues with iron."

"Of course I don't."

"Why would that be? You're Fae yourself, aren't you?"

He stopped and glared down at me. "No," he said angrily before turning and stalking through the woods.

I shrugged and decided to let it go for now. If he wanted to be in denial, that was his problem. I had been thinking on it for some time. He wasn't a vampire or werewolf or any sort of warlock. He felt magic, but he wasn't just attuned to magic. He was part magic. I felt it around him, like a shroud. To me, he felt like Fae, but what kind I had no idea. He was nothing I had ever encountered before.

Another vampire darted out of the trees, this one jumping behind tree after tree. Smarter, faster, but not quick enough. One shot and he was down. "I'm not sure why you needed me at all," I mused as we walked over the dust pile.

"I have been wondering something similar. Why did you want me to take you out here, and not Steve?"

"I thought that was obvious."

"No, and Steve was less than thrilled about it. He thought... well, never mind what he thought. Why did you want me here?"

I chuckled. "Oh, you men are all the same. So arrogant." He looked away and I nodded to myself. "I had a few reasons, Detective. First being that Steve is a headstrong, rash human and despite what you may think, I actually care about him quite a bit. I would be unhappy if he were killed. He would not casually walk through vampire-infested woods with me at his side. He would get himself killed trying to protect me at every snap of a twig in the darkness. You won't."

"Well, despite what *you* may think, I am a police officer. We are sworn to serve and protect."

"I don't need protection."

"Maybe." He walked on, just a few steps ahead of me the whole way. Perhaps he was, in his way, protecting me too. "What's the other reason?" he asked.

"Why you?" He nodded. "You're not human, at least not completely. You have a greater chance of walking out of these woods alive."

He stopped suddenly and turned to glare at me again. "I'm human and I'm not going to have you..."

"Oh, do shut up, Detective. I may not know exactly what you are, but I know what you're not. I've never seen a human react to magic the way you do."

"What about you?"

"What about me?"

"You're about as far from human as it gets. What are you? Why won't you take those glasses off? We're in the dark, in the middle of nowhere, and still you're wearing those damn sunglasses. What are you hiding?" he reached a hand out toward me and instead of backing up, I moved forward, closing the distance between us. His hand stopped, hovering inches from my face.

"If you're that eager for death, Detective, then by all means, go right ahead."

"Is that a threat?"

"Take it how you will."

He stilled, his hand twitching to remove my glasses. I was beyond caring. Magic filled me, and I knew he could sense that, if nothing else. Ten seconds. Twenty. A full minute he ran the knife's edge before finally lowering his hand. Had he known how close to death he had been in those moments? I longed for the energy he possessed. He was strong, powerful, and as a statue he would probably sustain me for a century. A yearning filled me. How long had it been since I'd fed? Since the incubus and succubus over a month ago? As strong as they were, it was temporary. Adding the recent attack and subsequent healing that had drained me more, I definitely needed to feed.

We walked on, adrenaline and magic coursing through my body, fueling me. The occasional vampire popped up, only to be silenced quickly by Hunter. It was pathetic, really. The sound of moaning stopped me in my tracks. Hunter raised an eyebrow, and a gun, and turned toward the noise.

My path of magic led up to a cave and at the center of the opening, chained to a boulder the size of a bed, was William. As one we moved toward him. His shirt had been torn open, and his arms and legs were spread across the boulder. His chest and stomach were nicely defined, but marred with lines of blood. An intricate design had been etched into his chest. It wasn't deep, but it wasn't simple either. With each step closer, I could feel the magic in those lines, pulsing outward in icy waves. Hunter grabbed the chains and gave a quick tug, breaking them easily, as though they weren't an inch thick. Human, he claimed. I looked at him pointedly but didn't say a word as William slid down the boulder.

"Are you alright?" I asked, keeping my distance.

He shook his head. "He did something to me. Some magic. I don't feel quite myself." He looked up at me, a frown between his pale gray eyes. "Shield me."

It took me a moment to register his words. Magic was forming, bubbling all around me from an unknown source. I flung a shield around William, tightening it down around him. Thick, black puss poured from the new gouges on William's chest. He screamed and I stumbled backward, falling on my ass. Hunter moved toward me, but I shook my head, hoping he'd take the hint and stay back. I filled myself with energy and tried to put a second shield up around myself, but I wasn't fast enough.

I screamed. The lines of magic came to life on my chest. Fire and ice coursed through my veins, alternating and growing in intensity with each passing moment. This was something new. I tried to bring my shield up again, but the magic within me was dying, leeching out of me and back into the earth. I touched the ground, feeling the energy and trying to draw it into me. Nothing came. I tried again, feeling a sense of helplessness I hadn't felt in centuries. The shield around William held, and I concentrated on that. I needed to contain him; keep him safe, or us safe from him. The pain increased, and I rolled onto my side to stare at William. He was fighting against my shield, his eyes black as night. Pain. Fire and ice, ice and fire. I screamed, and heard the answering howls of wolves in the distance. I'd lost sight of Hunter. I couldn't see him and couldn't sense him.

The putrid, rotting smell of death rolled across the breeze, coming from the mouth of the cave. The necromancer was coming closer, bringing more pain and taking away my strength, my energy. I was losing. How had it gotten like this? And where the hell was Hunter? I curled into a ball and rolled, fighting with every last bit of energy I had to stand. I stumbled to my feet and leaned against a tree, gasping for breath against the onslaught of fire and ice pulsing from the marks on my chest. Shapes moved from tree to tree and I heard the sharp snap of gunfire. Hunter was still out there, but so were the vampires. On the walk in, I'd wondered where they all were, thinking they'd simply stayed away from Hunter thanks to my potion. Now I had my answer. They were waiting for weakness. Another wolf howled, closer, but still too far away.

"Giavanna."

The man strolled out of the cave, dressed in long white robes that trailed behind him like a wedding dress. The robes draped loosely on his thin frame, allowing his ghastly pale skin to show through. Everything about this man was cold and pale, almost translucent, except his eyes. His face was long and thin with a nose that dripped over his mouth, emphasizing his pointed chin even further. I glanced at William, comparing the black eyes upon this man who seemed to know exactly who I was. The pain eased slightly, but the touch of ice remained.

"You know me, but I don't know you." I was pleased at how strong my voice sounded.

He smiled and turned his head in my direction, but kept his eyes trained on my feet. "Oh, we've met before. Long ago."

"I think I would have remembered that. I don't know many necromancers."

"Necromancer? Yes, I suppose that's what I've become, but I wasn't like this last time we met." He chuckled to himself.

"When was that?"

He opened his mouth, flashing fangs at me. "Just before I painted that portrait."

"Portrait?"

"The one from France. I sent it to the art gallery."

"That was your painting?" I stared at him in confusion. Not only did I not remember sitting for that portrait, but I certainly didn't remember this man... this vampire. "I'm afraid I'm at a loss. Do you have a name? Perhaps we have friends in common?"

"Yes, you are at a loss, in more ways than one. You may call me Master, and I don't have friends any more than you do," he laughed again at his own joke and darted toward me, wrapping a hand suddenly around my upper arm. "Don't even think about taking the glasses off. Not yet, anyway."

"What do you want with me? Why send that dead man after me?"

"Well, I needed some way to get your attention."

"You could have just called."

"Funny," he murmured, grinning at me widely and reaching a hand out to touch the marks lining my chest. "Consider this my phone call."

His magic hit me again and I would have fallen had he not been holding me up. He drug me toward the cave and I stumbled to maintain my footing against his speed and the overwhelming pain that wracked my body. I felt my magic failing me, for the first time in years... centuries. Energy leeched out of me and the shield I was carefully holding over William began to slip. I tied it off, letting it sustain itself, and hoping it would be strong enough to hold up against the necromancer's magic. It was weaker this way, but I didn't have a choice.

The necromancer must have felt it, because he gave me an abrupt angry tug. I fell, tearing a hole in my jeans as he yanked me up again. He moved with that superhuman speed vampires had, and I could do nothing but roll with it and hope he didn't pop my arm out of its socket. The cave branched off here and there, but onward the vampire pulled me. I tried to pay attention, so I could eventually find my way back out, but between the bouncing, the icy pain, and the lack of steady light, I was at a loss. A few minutes, and a dozen vampire-speed turns later, he stopped.

He let go of my arm and I briefly entertained the idea of running for help. I may have been a Gorgon, a descendant of Medusa, capable of fantastic feats, but super speed wasn't one of them. Still, a vampire could turn to stone as easily as a human. I rolled to my knees and managed to stand up, my left arm hanging limply at my side. Somewhere along the way I'd felt the pop, but I tried not to think of that at the moment. There were bigger things to concern myself with than a dislocated shoulder. This section of the cave was large and mostly circular, with a smaller opening the size of small car in the center that showed the night sky. That smaller opening was perfectly circular and appeared to have been made with magic. Where the rest of the cave had been cold as ice, this room felt like a sauna.

I pulled off my gloves and jacket as I roamed around the edge of the cave. Around the circular area were the missing witches and warlocks, and most of them were alive too. Even better. Except the living ones had black eyes, like William, and seemed under some sort of trance. What he'd done to them and what he planned now, I had no idea. All I wanted to do was rip off my sunglasses and fry this asshole. He knew what I was though, and was very cautious about avoiding my gaze as he moved about the cave, lighting candles and muttering incantations.

I tried reaching for my magic again, but nothing came to me. Nothing. I felt empty. Even the earth around me felt empty, as though all the energy in this place had been sucked dry. That wasn't something I thought possible. I moved closer to the nearest witch, feeling for any magic. Anything. She was alive, I felt her spark and her energy, but it was dull and muted. Her face was pale and drawn as she stared through me. I did a quick survey around the room, seeing the same thing. I debated again running back out the way I'd come.

"What did you do to them?" I asked.

"Oh, it's just a little spell I whipped up." He laughed again, that same self-satisfied laugh. "They'll do whatever I want, whenever I want it. They'll die to do my bidding, and then they'll be undead, still doing my bidding." He pointed at one of the witches he'd already turned into a zombie for emphasis.

I looked back at the witch beside me. Sure enough there was a stain of dried blood on her neck, almost hidden in the collar of her black shirt. "You bit them all?"

"Of course."

"So, what's next?"

"Next?" he stopped what he was doing and turned around. "Next, you get to be my conduit."

"Conduit?"

"You really don't remember me, do you?"

"Not at all."

"Do you remember France, and the bodies you piled behind you?"

I'd spent a great deal of time in France, piling a lot of bodies. "I take it we came across each other during this time?"

"No, not exactly. I watched you kill a man pretending to be a priest. You took the cross, the one I painted."

"You were there?"

"I was. You walked right past me. I was crouched beside the building, but you turned and looked right at me. Well, not right at me, since I didn't turn to stone, but you looked in my direction."

I shrugged. "Sorry, I still don't remember you."

He closed his eyes and took a deep breath. "No matter." He opened his eyes and looked in my direction. "After that night, I was desperate for an escape from this world. Demons like you walked the earth, and I didn't want any part of it. I sought out death, and he found me. But I didn't die. No, because I became a vampire. For years, I just existed. I had no purpose. I roamed and fed and killed. Then I killed my first witch. Oh, what a rush of power that was. I drank down her blood and her energy all at once. It was intoxicating. I felt more alive than I had in years. With each witch or warlock, I felt my own power growing. I found I could channel this new energy, and control other vampires. Eventually, I came across a necromancer. He was strong, powerful, and surprising. Together, we taught each other, and I became much as I am today."

"And what about him?"

"The other necromancer? Oh, I killed him when he outgrew his usefulness. Except, he was still useful even at the moment of his death. Draining him gave me even greater power."

"Well, that's an interesting story. You've obviously come a long way. If that's all true, then why are you here? You can control other vampires, so you choose this tiny little coastal town and hang out in a cave. Not exactly lofty goals."

"Choose this place? No, I did not. It was chosen for me, as were you. My next experiment."

"Excuse me?"

He laughed again, and I found myself wincing at the sound. "Oh, I don't want to spoil the surprise. Reunions are the best, after all."

"Reunions?"

"I know all about you and your little Gorgon curse. If I could become like you, now that would be fun, but I don't think men are meant to be Gorgons. Pity."

"So, you don't plan on draining me in order to absorb my power?"

"Of course not! No, I'm going to channel your energy into another. Then I'll drain you."

"Amy," I muttered.

"Oh, you figured it out!" He clapped his hands and went back to lighting candles. I took a better look around the cavern, but Theda and Amy weren't there. My books, though, were. I stalked across the cave and grabbed my books, cursing as I noticed the cauldron he was using. My cauldron. Potions and jars littered the cave, tossed about haphazardly. I had a list of everything recovered from the hotel and this appeared to cover the majority of what was remaining, minus a few shoes and outfits. I counted the books twice, reading off each title to myself. Yes, these were all my remaining books.

"Where are they?"

"Theda and Amathela? Oh, they're not here. Nope, can't have any other Gorgons in the room. That would be a bad idea. The spell might backfire on them."

"They're close, though."

He shook his head and snapped his finger. A nearby warlock walked over to the cauldron and began stirring while the necromancer dropped in ingredients. I cursed and ran toward the mouth of the cave. I didn't even make it to the tunnel. One of the warlocks grabbed me and carried me back, dropping me at the necromancer's feet. What was I thinking? I was a Gorgon, damn it. I stood, touching my sunglasses.

"Oh, I wouldn't do that, unless you want everyone in this room to know exactly what you are."

"You just called me a Gorgon. I think they already know."

"Not while they're under my control. Right now, they know nothing. They will remember nothing. But with a snap of my fingers, they're back online." He snapped his finger and the warlock who had carried me blinked and looked around, the black of his eyes receding to a nice chocolate brown.

"What's going on? Where am I?" He looked at the necromancer and took a step back. I could feel his faint magic pulse as he sought out an energy source. There was nothing in this cave. No life. No energy. He turned to run, but I grabbed him, tossing my sunglasses aside. He fell to my gaze easily, and I drained every last miniscule drop of energy he had in him. I felt alive again. I wiped the dust off my hands and turned toward the necromancer, a shield forming around me at a single thought.

"No." He backed up, stepping inside the circle of candles and lighting them with a word of magic. They flared brightly before burning with a black light.

"You forget who you're dealing with." I wasn't full of magic, but I had enough. Enough to sustain a shield and enough to blot out the pain the necromancer was throwing back at me. The lines on my chest flared, first blue, then black. "You dare mark me."

"I had to." There was fear in him now, but power too. The smell of rot and decay filled the cave as he pulled on his power. Then the vampires came.

Through the tunnels vampires swarmed, running at me with that super speed. I had seconds to act. I jumped toward the necromancer, hitting the shield around the candles. He flinched, but the shield held. The witches and warlocks under his control began closing in along with the vampires. I couldn't kill them all fast enough, but I could stop his plan. I flung all my energy at the cauldron, using the fire burning below it to scorch everything in sight. The warlock stirring the cauldron screamed, even as he continued to do his master's bidding. The bottles of potion exploded with the intense heat. The vampires shied away from the flames and the popping bottles. My energy was draining quickly. I tried to pull what energy I could from the flames, but there was nothing to grab. I ran toward the cauldron, fingers catching on my arms and legs. I lashed out, freed one leg and kicked, spilling the cauldron contents across two warlocks and a vampire. The purple liquid sloshed over them, scorching their skin. I trained my gaze on the nearest vampire, capturing his eyes and sucking in his energy. Something else came as well, a tinge of cold energy. The necromancer. I felt the energy from him begin to flow into me, and I shied away from it. Evil as I was, I didn't want his taint and didn't know what it would do to me.

I didn't need to bother. As soon as I began draining the vampire, the necromancer released him. Good. I killed the vampire and turned back toward the necromancer. The circle of candles remained, but he was no longer inside them. I caught a glimpse of his white robes flapping behind him as he ran away down a tunnel. "Coward!" I yelled, pushing against a witch blocking my path. Something sharp pierced the skin of my leg and I screamed. The bottom of my jeans had been torn and a vampire latched onto my calf, teeth sunk in and leeching blood from my body. I'd lost my shield at some point and hadn't even noticed, drained of energy once more. I found the gaze of the nearest vampire and repeated the process, draining him until he was only dust. Another vampire had latched on my thigh, and yet another on my left arm. The pain was excruciating, but I was still keeping my concentration on the necromancer and his next attack. The lines on my chest pulsed, alerting me. I flung my shield up again, hoping it would last long enough this time. The vampires were thrown backward at the impact of my magic, and I sagged to the ground in relief. It was short-lived. The necromancer had found a safe place and had begun his personal attack once more. I clawed at the lines across my chest. Even with the shield in place, I was vulnerable. I needed to get rid of this mark, but I didn't know how. Not yet.

My energy leeched out at a steady pace. The longer I remained, the weaker I would become. This place was empty. I crawled. It was the only thing I could do. Pushing my shield ahead of me to clear the path, I crawled on hands and knees through the vampires and witches toward the tunnel I'd come from. Every few moments, I'd stop to catch the gaze of a vampire. Their energy filled me in a flash, and I was able to move forward. Briefly.

The wolves came then, rushing through the tunnels, howling. They attacked the vampires, tearing at their throats. I crawled past them, keeping my head down and my shield tight and small. The necromancer continued to attack, hammering at the mark he had left on my skin, pushing me down.

"Gia!" I glanced up at the familiar voice, then immediately back at the ground as Hunter and Steve ran toward me, guns out. Steve reached out to touch me and bounced backward, finding my shield instead. "Gia, lower your shield. Let me help you."

I shook my head and kept my head down. "I can't. If I do, he'll attack me again. I'm too weak here."

"Then let me help you get out of here."

I shook my head again and continued crawling. Steve didn't have time to argue as vampires swarmed toward him. He took aim, the gunshot loud so close to my ear. I shook off the ringing and moved forward as fast as I dared, wanting nothing more than to run. Arms closed around me and I gasped as my shield didn't bounce back, but absorbed the arms instead. The smell of mint, gun powder, and cedar enveloped me and I sighed in relief.

"I got you," Hunter said as he lifted me in his arms. I closed my eyes and tightened the shield as we moved out of the tunnel.

Steve's gunshots rang close behind us, but the necromancer's attacks didn't cease and it took every last ounce of energy I had leeched to keep him at bay.

"Hurry."

Hunter sped up at my insistence, then he was running. Steve's gunshots stopped, but I could hear him cursing occasionally beside me. Another wolf howled, echoing down the cave. I had gotten used to reading the landscape by sound, having to keep my head covered so much around people, but this was torture. With each passing moment, my energy drained away. I opened my eyes a crack, risking a glance down at my skin. Even in the darkness of the tunnels, I could see the fine sheen of green and black scales mottling my skin. I was losing the battle. If I didn't feed and replenish my energy, the shield around me would snap, and who knew what the necromancer would do next.

"Vamps!" Steve yelled.

"Put me down," I said, as calmly as possible. Hunter lowered me against a tunnel wall as he and Steve moved to take care of the vampires. There were enough for all of us. I shuffled along the tunnel, holding on and waiting. The first vampire broke past Steve, running toward me. He yelled my name, but I was ready for him. I held his gaze, draining him in seconds. Already, I breathed a little easier. Another vampire came at me, and I took him down, grabbing his face and holding it. Each time, the necromancer let go as soon as I took control of the vampire's gaze, but he wasn't fast enough to get away unscathed. I took out four vampires before Hunter and Steve moved back to my side, and each time I took a little bit of the necromancer's energy.

Hunter picked me up and ran again. He didn't stop until we were outside the cave, but we needed to go further. I felt for the energy in the earth, but there was nothing here. "Keep going," I said, my eyes tightly closed. "We need to get away from this place."

He didn't respond other than to begin his run again. After a few minutes, I felt the magic return. It was like breathing fresh air after a fire. I tapped him on the arm and he stopped, lowering me carefully to the ground. I ran my hands through the grass and pulled on the energy, strengthening my shield. It wouldn't replenish me completely. For that, I would need to feed again, in great quantities, but it was strengthening my magic.

"Are you alright?" I could hear Steve in the grass beside me, breathing loudly.

"There's something wrong with this place. It is as though there is no life. I can't sustain magic there. We're just outside it."

"What do we do?"

"Leave."

"We can't. The warlocks and witches are still there. They're fighting us."

"They're under the necromancer's control. Where's William?"

"Right where you left him. Practically foaming at the mouth to get out of that shield you put up."

I opened my mouth to respond when I felt a warmth of magic moving toward me. A shield enveloped me, strong and bright, shimmering with a blue light. "Gia," Maggie said between sobs. "Are you alright?"

"Your shield," I said, smiling and leaning back against a tree. "That's impressive. Can you hold it here, just like this?"

"Yes, I think so."

"How big is it? How many can you hold?"

"I have the four of us right now just fine. Probably another ten or fifteen could fit. Why?"

"I have an idea."

∆NCHOR

IT WAS EASY TO say I had an idea, and much more difficult to execute. For starters, I couldn't open my eyes for fear of killing everyone around me. I could almost hear the unspoken thoughts. It was dark, what did I have to fear? The moonlight couldn't possibly damage my eyes that easily, could it? I had no idea what Hunter and Steven had seen me do. I hoped they'd been too preoccupied killing vampires to notice what I'd done to those in my sight. Second, I was weak. Yes, I was finally out of the dark pool of nothingness, but that didn't replenish my strength. Pulling on the energy of the earth was only enough to help sustain a portion of my magic. My energy, what kept me walking and talking and looking human, was something else. Sure, I could eat a burger and feel better, just like an ordinary person. But, without my special kind of feeding, I would revert to my base nature, snakes and all.

They left me alone to gather my thoughts, for which I was thankful. I could feel them all close by as I moved behind a tree and knelt in the earth. I rubbed the dirt onto my skin. It wasn't anything magical; I was trying to hide the scales that flickered across my skin. They had dulled a bit and were no longer seeming to glow, but they were still there. I ran a hand through my hair, feeling around at the base of my skull. No snakes, thankfully. It had only happened to me once before, centuries earlier when Theda decided to punish me for some infraction I no longer remembered. She had locked me away with no one to feed off of for months. First, the scales had covered my skin. My hair grew longer and snakes began forming in their place. After the hair had become half snakes, my tongue split and elongated. My nails turned yellow and venom dripped from teeth that were as long as a vampire's fangs. When I was completely hideous and incapable of speech, she finally freed me, and fed me. I had definitely learned a lesson, but not the one she was trying to teach. She wanted me to cower down to her and obey her every word. Instead, I had learned to take care of number one. As soon as I'd regained my strength, I left her side and never went back. That was also when I'd learned to have a few statues for slow feeding. They helped keep the worst of my symptoms at bay. I felt along the lines of my energy, feeling for those statues now. One was missing, drained to death.

Becoming like Medusa was something I had been careful to avoid since that time with Theda. I didn't know a place such as this existed, that could drain my strength, weaken me, and suck my magic down so quickly and completely. I remembered the witches I'd seen, or rather felt, with their weak emptiness. It drained them too, so it was based in magic, but it hadn't affected the necromancer. Why? Because he was a vampire, and already dead? Maybe. The necromancer attacked again, and I winced at the pain in my chest igniting. Maggie's shield was working to protect the group, but it wasn't effective against his single-minded attacks. He had marked me magically, and I didn't have the means to figure out how to get myself unmarked. Not right now, in any event. I wanted William, strangely enough, but he was still back at the cave. I could attach to the shield around him again, and lead him here. It would take a lot of energy that I just didn't have. If I kept up like this much longer, I'd have snakes in my hair in no time. Then what would everyone think? What was worth the risk? I needed William.

The vampires were closing in. Their dark shapes darted between the trees, but they weren't attacking. I could only assume Maggie and Steve had also taken my potion, which was enough to keep the vampires away. I hadn't seen or heard the wolves for a good twenty minutes now. I didn't know how many there were, but one, at least, should have been here. I could only hope the werewolves were keeping enough vampires sidetracked.

Someone walked around the tree and knelt down beside me. "Gia, are you alright?" Steve asked, his voice soft and full of concern.

I kept my head down and nodded. "Yes, just very weak."

"You said you had a plan." It was a statement, but I could sense the question behind it. Did I know what I was doing?

"Any idea where the werewolves are?" I asked.

"No."

I sighed as another pair of feet moved into view, then another. They all moved around me, circling me where I knelt in the ground with my head down and my hair shielding my face. "The necromancer keeps attacking me."

"I know," Maggie said, her voice small and fearful. "I can feel it. He breaks through my shield like he's pushing it away and aims straight for you."

"He may not realize you're there," I mused. "When William and I fought him months ago he marked me with magic. I thought it was just an injury, but now I see it for what it is. They planned this, even then."

"Who?"

I ignored the question and pressed my hands to the ground, letting my fingers sink between the blades of grass. A light snow coated the ground, but it had melted within Maggie's shield. "I'm weak. That place, just beyond these trees, is... wrong. It is pure death. It is the absence of light, the opposite of life, and the complete depletion of energy of any kind. I think anyone who stayed there long would eventually whither away and die. I cannot face him from inside there."

"He knows that, doesn't he? So he'll just stay there, hunkered down," Hunter mused.

"Yes, I believe so. That place doesn't bother him."

"How do we get the witches he's controlling out of there? Can we?"

"I used some magic on the vampires, and each time I did, I could feel the magic rebound into him. He always let go, but he's not quite fast enough. I think if I had enough vampires, I might be able to attack him slowly, through the vampires."

"Could you do the same thing with the witches? You said he lets go of them, right? If you use the right magic, can you release them?" Steve asked.

I shrugged, wincing at the pain in my shoulder. "Maybe if I had my potions. Although, there were a bunch back in that cave."

"What about the spell you used on the vampires."

"That...magic... would kill them. I have no qualms about killing vampires, but I get the feeling you all might be angry if I just let loose and killed all the witches and warlocks too." I laughed, but no one joined me. "I need to get the vampires to me so I can take care of them while you take Maggie to free William."

"What? Me?" Maggie asked, her feet backing away from me. "Gia, I can't. I'm barely holding this shield up."

"Maggie, it's fine. I've been pulling William closer by the minute, but it's weakening me. I think if you can get him out of that place, he can break free from the necromancer. With William's help, we should be able to free everyone else."

"What will you be doing?" Steve asked. He knelt down beside me and I shied away, but his arm slid tenderly around my shoulders.

"I'll be draining the necromancer, and keeping him busy, by killing vampires."

"You can barely stand."

"I'll manage. It's more important that you take care of Maggie and get William back here. He's connected to his coven. Free, I'm sure he can release the rest."

"You think he'll be better back here?"

"No, but I think I can hurt the necromancer enough that he focuses all his energy on me. Enough that William can break free on his own, but William will be useless in that place too. He needs the earth and magic, just like the rest of us."

"And you're going to do this on your own, by killing vampires."

"Yes," I replied, rising to my feet and keeping my eyes tightly closed and my head down. "Hunter," I said softly.

He moved up beside me. "What?" he asked gruffly.

"My shoulder is dislocated."

He didn't respond, but pressed his hands to my injured shoulder, snapping it back into place without a word. I cried out at the jolt of pain, but at least I could move my arm again. "Better?"

I nodded and rolled my shoulders. "I'm strong enough right now. Maggie can keep you safe with her shield. I'll go this way, you head back for William." I pointed and began walking, feeling the darkness in front of me. I'd need to stay at the edge of the energy pit, toeing the line carefully. My senses were attuned from so many years pretending to be blind. "Don't follow me," I ordered. The footsteps ceased, and I continued on alone.

I walked until I could no longer hear the others, then I opened my eyes carefully and peered around me. The glow of Maggie's shield told me of their location, and I breathed a sign of relief. They wouldn't be able to see me from here. I took a breath and stepped over the threshold. Darkness descended, and I could feel myself sinking. I straightened my back and found my first vampire, racing to attack me. He met my gaze, shuddered, and became dust. I attacked as quickly as I could, concentrating on the quick retreat of the necromancer. There was a moment just before the vampire died when I could feel the magic of the necromancer, like a spiderweb of putrid decay holding the vampire in place. By the third vampire, I was barely standing upright, but I had a plan in place. As soon as I raised my gaze, I sent a spray of fire back toward the vampire. I felt it hit the vamp and follow up that spiderweb, just missing the necromancer. Damn! I tried again, retreating occasionally to regain my strength out of the darkness. It took six vampires before I managed to cast my spell back on the necromancer again. He screamed, and I pushed my energy back into him as I took deliberate steps backward. I fought to hold the necromancer in place even as I fought to stay upright and conscious. My foot crossed the invisible mark, and I felt a surge of energy flow into me. I stepped backward fully, pushing fire back at the necromancer. He burned. I felt it, then I heard the screams echoing through the tunnels just before I lost contact with him. Fire blossomed in the woods, beyond the caves. That's where he was. I stared down at the ground, debating the wisdom of crossing over the line again. Another vampire came running at me, rushing over the unmarked barrier to plow into me. I stared at him, feeling nothing but dying vampire. Another ran at me, and another. I backed up, taking them one after another, but each time the necromancer let loose well before they reached me. He was running away, and using the vampires as a distraction.

I cried out in frustration and killed one vampire after another, letting loose with my gaze, with my own magic, and filling myself with energy until I could burst. My wounds healed, my arm mended, the blood that had been dripping steadily down my legs ceased. Power filled me. Another sound of footsteps behind me and I spun, ready. No, not ready. I squeezed my eyes closed at the sight of five o'clock shadow and a concerned face. No, no, no, I cursed, keeping my eyes tightly closed. A hand touched my arm and I let out a sigh or relief. "Gia, are you alright?" Steve asked.

I fell into his arms, letting him hold me. I had almost done it. Almost killed him. I had been high on magic and energy and it had almost cost me this new life I'd been trying to build. More... it had almost cost Steve his actual life. Damn. I peeked through my hair and around his shoulder. Maggie and Hunter stood with William between them.

"I need you all to back away," I said as I gently pushed Steve back, my head lowered so my hair once again shielded my face. Their feet shuffled backward, but it wasn't enough.

Full of energy and able to pull on earth magic, I knew what I needed to do. I turned away from them, pulling William with me until we were away from the others. I didn't want to accidentally catch one of them in my gaze. I slowly lifted my face until I could just see William, and the shield that still held him. Taking a deep breath, I let myself into the shield, or rather, I expanded the shield and let it surround both of us. William attacked the moment I was inside the shield, but the necromancer was controlling him still, and he had learned to be cautious of me. This time when I built the fire spell, he was ready for it. I sent heat toward William, and the necromancer let go. William yelped in pain, but I quickly dropped the spell.

"What the hell?" he gasped, dropping to the ground.

I averted my gaze and knelt beside him. "No time to rest. Your coven is in there."

"He let me go? Why?"

"I found a way to attack him through anyone he's controlling. I can show you," I said slowly.

If I could have seen his gaze in that moment, I'm sure it would have been full of eagerness. His voice said enough. "Show me."

I nodded and stood up, yanking him to his feet. The others had closed in around us, but I didn't have time for them right now. I moved back to the edge of the darkness and waited for the attack. Sure enough, another vampire came at me. I used the fire magic again, weaving it as I had to free William, and sending it shooting back through the vampire. He let go before it hit him, but my intention had only been to show William how it was done.

"Got it," he said, stepping across the invisible line. He shuddered and took a step back. "Except..."

"Except when you cross the boundary, you lose access to magic. Yeah, that's a problem. Any ideas?"

"We need an anchor. Where's Ian?"

Shit. "He didn't make it," I said softly.

"Oh," he replied, his voice losing its edge. We stood in silence for several minutes before he suddenly cleared his throat. "Well, you'd make a shitty anchor. What about her?"

"Me?" Maggie gasped. "What about me?"

"She knows shields and basic energy shifts. That's about it," I replied.

"She feels strong enough. An anchor doesn't have to do anything except tether us to magic and supply energy. She stays here, pulling in earth magic, and we siphon that from her."

"We siphon energy through her?" I asked.

I wished I could see the look on his face. His voice grew smug, cocky. "Of course. It's a very basic spell. I'm surprised you don't know it. Coven magic, 101."

Why would I? I had no problem getting energy, and I usually worked alone. Until now. I shrugged and said, "Can she feed both of us enough energy so we can free your people?"

"Not for long, but if we can get a few of my people free, they can join her and help lighten the load."

It was a decent plan, but I wasn't a witch, and I still didn't have my sunglasses. I looked down at what was left of my jeans. They had been torn to shreds by vampires and stuck to my legs with dried blood. I grabbed a chunk of fabric and began tearing, trying to keep a straight line. It didn't work, tearing off short of what I needed. I tore off a second chunk, tied the two pieces together, then tied it over my eyes. Better than nothing, I supposed, although I could only imagine what I looked like. My legs had been gnawed on my vampires, and even with all my magical healing, I still sported deep gouges in my skin covered in dried blood. My left pant leg ended just below the knee, while my right was nothing but a series of torn strips barely covering my ankles. Holes, rips, tears, and blood covered me from head to toe, and to top it off, I now had a bloody scrap of fabric covering my eyes. Swell.

"Ready?" William asked and I nodded. Maggie squeaked behind me. "Maggie, is it? All you have to do is pull in the earth magic and hold it. We'll do the rest. If you feel yourself running out, pull in more. You'll want to snip your shield off though, so you don't have to maintain it. It won't be as strong, but it'll help your focus."

"Snip my shield off? What do you mean?"

He made a noise with his mouth and walked closer, brushing against my arm. "You taught her shields, but not how to separate them from herself?"

I shrugged. "Didn't really get far in the training."

"I don't have time for this. Fine, Maggie, you'll just have to do both. If you have to, drop the shield. You two, you're on guard duty. Keep her alive."

"I'm coming with you," Steve said.

"No, you're staying here and keeping this girl alive." I expected more argument after William's firm dismissal, but Steve didn't say another word. William's hand touched mine, and he led me to the edge of the darkness. "Reach out to Maggie before we cross. Feel her magic, feel her energy. She is a live wire of electricity, and as long as you are flying with her, you'll be fine. If you ground yourself out, you'll kill both you and Maggie. Let the energy flow. Reach for it, but don't grab it. Let it slide over and through you. Let it consume you. When you do, you'll feel the weightlessness. That's the moment you can reach out and use the energy. Once you have it, she'll feed you through it."

I nodded, opening myself up to Maggie's energy. We'd played with that energy ball a hundred times, but this time I let myself wash through her energy instead of grabbing hold. I breathed in and out, relaxing as her magic flowed back and forth, like waves on the beach. It consumed me, drowned me, and then we were one. Energy pulsed through me, feeding from Maggie, through the earth.

"Good. And on the first try." He sounded amused more than anything, but I felt him pulling on the magic from Maggie as well. It was different than an energy pull, like we do from the earth. It was more of a communication, a give and take. William still held my hand, and we joined our energies together. I had a moment of panic, wondering what he'd sense in me, but it was too late. We were one, filled with earth magic and ready to take on the world. Or at least the darkness. As one, we stepped forward.

Rescue

THE DARKNESS DRAINED ME as it had before, but I was able to pull energy through Maggie and keep my magic flowing. I'd worked in the darkness as a blind woman for centuries. I used my magic and the touch of magic through William to see. The bigger problem was the energy I needed to maintain myself, my food, started leeching out of me the moment we crossed that invisible threshold. I shouldn't have expected any less. They were two different types of energy. But I was full, so to speak. If we hurried, I'd be alright.

William didn't say anything as we hurried back toward the cave, but his magic spoke for him. He was very good, weaving spells with finesse, seeking out his lost flock of witches and warlocks. We found the first witch outside the cave, wandering around in a stupor. Together, William and I wove the same spell I'd used on him. He worked to wake up his witch, while I followed the trail back to the necromancer, hitting him with everything I could. It worked the first time, and I felt the necromancer recoil. The witch was in no state to help us, but we directed her back toward the others while we searched for the next victim.

After ten minutes, I felt a boost of magic pouring into me. The witch had made her way to the others and recovered enough to join Maggie. We found another witch, repeated the process, then another. After we'd freed three witches and two warlocks, the rest came to us on their own. The necromancer had tired of our attacks and was anticipating our next move. He abandoned them and fled.

I felt a weight lift off me when he moved on. It was good, since I couldn't walk around in that darkened place much longer. He took the coldness of death with him, and a sense of warmth filled the air. My energy reserves were draining, and if I didn't get back, or feed soon, I'd start getting scaly once more. William still held my hand, leading me through the woods, even as he greeted his coven. "William, let's get out of this place."

"Sure, we can lead everyone back to the clearing."

I sighed in relief and let him wrap his arm around my waist, pulling me close. My energy was waning, and I leaned on him more with each step. "You're exhausted," he said softly in my ear. "We're almost there."

We made it back out of the darkness and I would have dropped to the ground if William hadn't been so close, his arm holding me upright. Then Steve was there, pulling me away from him. "You're back. Are you alright? You're a little green looking."

Green? I rubbed my arm, but I didn't feel any scales. "I need to rest," I said. "The necromancer let go of everyone. I'm not sure where he went, but for now I think the threat is over."

"That's good to hear. I'd like to get out of this place," Steve responded.

"What about Mike?" Maggie's voice was soft, but it broke through the chatter. "The werewolves haven't returned."

I couldn't go back into the woods again. There might be a few vampires still wandering around, but I doubted it now that the necromancer had fled. "None of them?" I asked, turning toward Maggie's voice.

"No, and I haven't heard any howls in a long time."

"The last time I saw them, they were in the caves," Hunter said. "I wonder if they chased the necromancer off."

It was a thought I hadn't considered. "Perhaps. If I had the strength, I'd go back in there, look for them, and get my supplies. I just... I can't. Not today."

"I understand," Maggie said, her voice a breathy whisper.

"I'll go," Hunter said.

"Me too," Steve added.

"Wait," I said, standing back up before they took off. "Let me shield you two first."

Steve came back to my side. "You're barely standing as it is."

"I can do it," William stated.

"No, I can manage a shield, no matter what state I'm in. Just come here and take my hands," I said, reaching outward. Two sets of hands gripped mine, both calloused and strong, although one was larger than the other. The energy of the earth flowed up through the ground and into me. I pulled on it, channeling it to my will, forming two separate, distinct shields around the two detectives. Then I snipped them off, as William called it, keeping each man safe within his own shield. "Go, and hurry back."

We waited. William tended to his people, pairing them up so the weakest were with the strongest. I had suggested sending them back to town, to the hospital, but no one wanted to be separated. I didn't blame them. The necromancer was not only powerful, but crafty as well. Too many had already died at his hands.

It felt like an eternity, but was probably less than an hour, when Steve and Hunter returned. I had stationed myself against a tree, watching the darkness with my makeshift bandana lifted just above my eyes. No one bothered me as I sat and did my best to recharge. I needed to feed, badly, and was distracted when they returned, not noticing the dark shapes moving between the trees until someone behind me gasped. I quickly lowered the fabric, but could still make out eight large wolves and two men. Maggie sobbed behind me and ran forward, wrapping her arms around a large, gray shape.

It was done. Not only had Hunter and Steve returned with all the wolves, they also returned with all my books and a handful of potions that hadn't been broken. I tried to hide my excitement as we trekked out of the woods and back to the few drivable vehicles we had remaining. It took ten minutes to load everyone into the cars and trucks, filling the beds with people and wolves. Steve insisted I ride back with him, and William insisted he ride with me. So, the ride back I sat stiffly smashed between Steve and William, with a witch named Nancy on the other side crowding us closer together. No one wanted to sit in Steve's back seat, so I used it to stack my books carefully.

We drove in a convoy back to town. I wished I could see more than the small slit in the fabric allowed, because I'm sure it was quite a sight to see trucks loaded with werewolves as we all drove slowly back to town. The ice and fog were gone, leaving only the pieces of wreckage behind. We drove past those too, silently.

"I see you got your books back," William said after ten minutes of silence. I had almost dozed off, leaning my head on Steve's shoulder, his hand resting on my knee. William, on my other side, had his arm draped across the back of the seat while Nancy clung to him, sobbing into the remains of his shirt. "Yes, I think that's all of them."

"So... the necromancer was responsible for the break-ins?"

"I suppose," I hedged, not really knowing how to answer.

"Did he hire those women?"

"I don't know."

"Did he mention them?"

"We didn't talk much."

"Did you catch his name?"

"No." I sighed and sat up. "Why did he take you and your coven?"

"He didn't say," William responded quickly.

I didn't ask any more questions, and neither did William. We were both obviously lying, or at least avoiding the truth. What did he have to hide? I had plenty, and I supposed the head of a coven of witches probably did too. Nancy continued her sobbing, and Steve was uncharacteristically quiet. He wasn't brooding, but he was definitely deep in thought. We made it back to the hospital uneventfully. I stayed in the truck even as everyone else climbed out. "Gia?" Steve asked.

"I just want to go home, Steve."

"You need to get checked out."

"No, I don't. Take me home."

"Gia."

"Fuck it," I said, climbing out of the truck. Everyone began walking and limping into the hospital and I slowly followed behind. I wasn't planning on getting myself checked out though. I needed to feed, and a hospital full of sick people was just the answer.

William took the lead, getting his coven set up for treatment. The werewolves had run off now that we were in town, heading back to their homes, I assumed. Maggie waited with Hunter for a ride home as Steve escorted the worst of the group. They weren't watching me. I slipped away, relieved to be away from the emergency room. The main wing of the hospital was silent and empty at this time of night. I turned down the first empty corridor and spotted a man entering the bathroom. He was probably in his fifties, with a smattering of gray at the temples. He hit the bathroom door angrily and I followed, stepping in right behind him.

"Hey!" he said in surprise as I came up behind him.

"I'm afraid I'm lost," I said.

"Looks like you need the emergency room. It's back down the main corridor. Uh... can you see?"

"Oh, this," I said, pulling the fabric off my head. "Yes, I can see just fine." I turned my gaze toward his, capturing his eyes. Energy flowed into me and I kept pulling and pulling, sucking him dry until he was nothing but a pile of ash at my feet. I breathed a sigh of relief. That was much better. I looked down at the ash, feeling a moment of remorse that I quickly shoved away. I didn't have a choice, I reminded myself. Placing the fabric back over my eyes, I hurried out of the bathroom and back the way I'd come.

"There you are!" Steve called, running toward me as I turned down the last hall toward outside the emergency room. "Did you get stuck?"

"Stuck?" I murmured.

"Yeah, these halls lock down at night. You have to hit the buzzer to get back in."

"Oh, a buzzer. Of course. I was searching for a bathroom."

"Wrong door," he laughed, as he pulled me back to the emergency room and hit the buzzer. A moment later, the door swung open and we were back in the waiting area. He moved me toward the bathroom and I smiled weakly before going in. Maggie was in there, sobbing loudly.

"Gia, there you are," she said, wiping her eyes.

"Are you alright?"

"Yes, I think everything is just hitting me, you know."

"Sure," I said, moving to the sink to wash my hands.

"And I want to go home and check on Mike. He'll be shifting back."

"I'd like to hear what happened to the wolves, but it can wait," I said. "I'd like to get home too. Hospitals aren't my favorite place."

"I'll go tell Steve," she said cheerfully, wiping her eyes.

It took some convincing, but Steve finally relented and agreed to drive Maggie and me both home. Before we left, William pulled me aside. "You look better already," he mused.

"It helps being away from that place."

"I'd like to see you tomorrow, if that's alright. We have some things to discuss."

"Sure, how about lunch?"

"I'd prefer to be somewhere... private. Away from prying eyes and ears. Why don't I pick something up and bring it to your place?"

"Sure. That works."

"Great. I'll see you around noon," he added before reaching his arms around and pulling me toward him for a hug. His lips brushed against my cheek in a soft kiss before he let me go.

"Gia," Steve said, making me jump at the closeness. He moved up behind me, putting a hand at the small of my back and leading me outside.

We drove Maggie home first, and Steve made sure Mike was home, and human, before leaving her alone. He drove quickly back to my house. As soon as the truck stopped, I hopped out and began grabbing my books. Steve was there beside me in a flash, taking the books from my hands. I didn't argue as I walked to the house.

My wards were all still in place when we entered, for which I was thankful. It meant Theda and Amy weren't there, and I could maybe get a night of rest. Steve hurriedly dropped my books on a table before moving through the house to check for threats. I could have told him everything was fine, but I didn't bother. He still would have done it anyway. It was fine, since it gave me a chance to grab out an extra pair of glasses.

I desperately needed a shower and a moment to check on my statues. As drained as I'd become, I wouldn't be surprised if I'd lost more. I didn't have many left as it was. I hurried to the cellar, to my once hidden room, and looked alarmingly at the place my status had stood. Only two remained and I cursed silently as I kicked at the dust. The first wasn't a statue of my own, but the one that had been sent to me. The one who resembled the first man I'd ever loved. Of my own personal collection, only the hooded warlock remained. How, after all these years, was he the only one left? Perhaps it had to do with his own magic. I didn't have time to ponder further as I heard Steve calling my name.

Steve strode toward me as soon as I entered the living room, wrapping his arms around my waist and kissing my neck. I relaxed into his embrace, letting his kisses trail from my neck down to the swell of my breast. He held me tighter and I felt his hardness press against me. "I need a shower," I said softly.

"Hmm," he replied as he pulled my shirt off. "Same."

I laughed and let him lead me up the stairs as we left a trail of clothing behind us. Despite the hour, and our mutual exhaustion, we found we still both had reserves of energy enough for one thing. After I was sated, Steve held me, spooning me, his arms wrapped protectively around me in a tangle of sheets.

"Gia," he said softly, startling me as I had begun to doze off.

"Yes?"

"About William," he began, clearing his throat. "I don't like him."

"Well, he's a warlock," I shrugged.

"He's a little too... interested... in you."

"Is that jealousy I hear, Detective McNeill?"

"Maybe a little." He was quiet for a few minutes as he absentmindedly ran a hand across my stomach. "I don't trust him."

"Good, neither do I."

"You don't?" he sounded surprised. "I thought, maybe..."

"Maybe what?"

"You're having lunch with him tomorrow. Here. I heard you two talking. And you had his tie. Look, I know we've never really spoken about us, uh, our relationship. We never said we were exclusive, but..."

"No, we haven't," I said bluntly, and I felt him flinch, his hands stilling on my body. "I'm not interested in a relationship."

"Well, no, me either," he said quickly, a little too fast.

"Then we're in agreement?" He was silent and I knew I'd hurt him. "Steve, I just can't have a boyfriend, or whatever, right now."

"Not with me anyway," he mumbled, pushing off the covers and standing up.

I rolled out of bed and stood with my hands on my hips, staring at him as he hunted for his clothes. "It's not like that," I said.

He found his pants and pulled them on, grabbing his shoes and stalking out of the room. I followed him as he hurried down the stairs, grabbing his shirt from the bottom of the railing. "What is it like then, Gia? I thought things were going well. I really like you."

"I like you too."

"And William? Do you like him too?"

I didn't say anything, not sure how to react. There was a part of me that was attracted to William, but attraction didn't mean love, or even feelings. "I don't trust William," I hedged.

"Nice," he murmured as he pulled on his shoes. "I'm not the sharing type, Gia."

"What? I wasn't asking you to share. I'm not with anyone else. Just because I said I don't want a relationship doesn't mean I'm off screwing other guys."

His actions slowed as he finished tying his shoe and slowly stood up. "You haven't?"

"No!" I screamed, shoving him with one hand. "I don't want to be exclusive because it's not fair to you. You can't have a relationship with me, Steve. I'm no good for you, but I will gladly date you. I like you. I like the fun we have. I'll be here as long as you want me, but we will never get married and have kids. I just can't."

"That's a choice, Gia. Just like being exclusive with each other because we care about each other is a choice. I don't want anyone else." He sighed and stood up, putting his hands in his pockets.

"Do you want the whole family life some day, Steve? Is that your plan?"

"Of course it is. We have time, though. We're both young."

"I can't have kids."

He stared at me for a heartbeat before closing the distance and wrapping his arms around me. "Is that why? Oh, baby, it's alright. You don't have to push people away. Please, let me in. I... care about you. Please."

I closed my eyes and fought off the feelings. He was a great guy, and I was going to break him some day. I wrapped my arms around his waist and felt myself sinking into his embrace. "I'm sorry," I whispered, and I meant it.

"This whole William thing," he said slowly and I cut him off.

"Please, stop."

"What about us?"

"What?"

"I don't want to date anyone but you. Gia, I know it sounds corny, but will you be my girlfriend?"

"Steve..."

"I'm not talking marriage, or anything like that. Not right now, but I like the idea of you being just mine. And me being yours. Exclusive. Whatever you want to call it."

Fuck, what was I doing? I'd tried to let him know, to tell him that I couldn't be that person for him. For a time, I could. Where was the harm in it? I liked him too, more than I should. What was I doing? Despite my better judgement, I smiled and answered him. "Yes, I'll be your girlfriend."

Agreement

STEVE WAITED AROUND UNTIL lunchtime to leave. It had been a late night and we hadn't gotten much sleep, getting up just a little before 11am. I knew what he was doing, but chose not to comment on it. He was still feeling insecure about William, but I'd already stuck my foot in my mouth. It might be nice to have a real boyfriend. When was the last time I'd had someone that was for more than just sex? A couple hundred years, maybe? I tried not to think about it. That could be dangerous.

The gate alarm buzzed and I let William in. Steve glared at the door, waiting, it seemed. He turned suddenly toward me and pulled me into his arms. "Be careful with him," he said softly, his mouth grazing my ear. "I don't trust him, and not just because he keeps undressing you with his eyes."

I smiled and kissed him. "He can't hurt me. Don't worry."

"That's not what I worry about," he muttered, but I didn't respond, choosing to ignore his comment.

The knock at the door pulled us apart. Steve followed me as I let William inside. He held two bags of food that smelled heavenly, and a drink carrier with two hot drinks that smelled of spices. We hadn't had a chance to eat breakfast, and my stomach growled loudly. "Gia, I brought lunch. I hope you like seafood."

"Love it," I responded, letting him into the house.

William grinned at Steve as he walked purposely toward my table overlooking the ocean and began unpacking our lunch. As usual, he was dressed in a suit, but today he had foregone the jacket, choosing instead to wear just a vest over his white shirt. "Detective? I wasn't expecting you."

"I'm just leaving," Steve responded, a smile plastered to his lips. "You two have a good lunch."

"See you tonight?" I asked as Steve moved toward the door.

"You couldn't keep me away," he replied, stopping to pull me into another embrace. His hand trailed down my backside as he kissed me exuberantly. After too short a time, or maybe too long, I couldn't be sure, he walked away.

I closed the door behind him and headed toward the table, where William had already set out lunch of fish and chips, along with clam chowder and two cups. "Have you been to the little fish shack across the bay? It doesn't look like much, but it has the best fish and chips around."

I smiled and nodded. "I have, and couldn't agree more."

"I heard you like chai tea," he added, pushing the hot cup toward me.

"Where'd you hear that?"

"Steve," he said, grinning. That surprised me. I took the cup and breathed in the spicy sweet scent. It really was wonderful and it helped keep the chill away that seemed to linger on my skin. "And Maggie told me you liked the fish and chips."

I chuckled at that, and we ate heartily, passing the time with idle chatter and avoiding the topic at heart. When we'd finished, I leaned back, cupping the last of my tea. William picked at his fries, stirring them around in ketchup but not eating them. I was waiting for him to break the ice. Waiting for him to tell me why he wanted to meet, even though I had a pretty good idea.

"The necromancer," he began finally, pushing away his food.

"Yes, the necromancer," I replied.

"I think we have a common enemy."

I raised an eyebrow at that, but I wasn't sure if he could see it behind my glasses, even as slim as they were. "Common enemy? What makes you say that?"

"Well isn't it obvious? He had your belongings which indicates he works in collusion with those women who robbed you. He kidnaps my people. He took me to that place of anti-energy, and he lured you there."

"What makes you say he lured me?"

"You showed up, didn't you?" He smiled, or perhaps it was more of a grimace. "Ian didn't seek you out for help."

"How do you know about that?"

"I was linked to him when it happened. He was trying to help me, but was being sabotaged by the necromancer at the same time. I saw through his eyes. I was there when you arrived. At first, he was so excited that you'd arrived to help him that neither of us gave it much thought. When I lost link with him, a part of me knew he was gone. I also knew it was a trap, and not for me. Not for Ian, either. It was a trap for you, and it worked beautifully."

I drained the last of my tea and absorbed his words. All these traps just for me? Why go to such extremes? "Why did he capture you and all your witches then? What did he need them for?"

"A spell, of some kind, but for what I don't know. Let's just be thankful it didn't work."

I hoped he was right, and that we had thwarted his spell. "What good would your coven have done? That place was so devoid of energy, they couldn't do magic."

"I didn't say that they'd be doing the spell. I believe they, we, were the spell. Whatever he was doing, he needed to be in that location. Since there was no energy, he needed to bring some with him. Some human batteries."

"He's a necromancer. His magic doesn't work the same way yours does, or your coven. You saw that. That place didn't even have an effect on him."

"Yet he had your books, cauldron, and ingredients. He was doing magic, not necromancy. Or maybe it was some hybrid. I don't know, but it seems like something we should find out."

"We?"

"You know we barely stopped him, if that's even what we did. Stalled him, is more likely. If this is important, and I think it is, then he'll try again. My coven can't take another attack like this. As it is, most of the coven is moving into my home. It's safer that way."

"You must have a big place."

He shrugged, feigning an air of modesty that I didn't believe. "My home will suffice. Like I said, most of my coven is moving in. The rest are moving away. I can't force them to stay. They're afraid, and I don't blame them. They'll be safe with one of my brothers."

"Brothers?"

"Craft brothers, not biological. I am not alone."

His words sent a chill down my spine, and I wasn't sure why. Had his voice dropped a little at those last words, or had that been my imagination? "How many remain?" I asked.

"Not enough."

"Not enough for what?"

"To fight off a necromancer. To keep this town safe. My second-in-command is dead and half my coven is dead or fleeing. This is not a good time to be alone."

"Alone. Like me?"

His eyes flashed but he kept his face carefully neutral. "You, and your little witch-in-training. You're who this necromancer wants, and if I didn't like you so much, I might just hand you over."

"Except for the fact he killed and ran off half your coven."

He shrugged. "True. I can forgive a lot, but not that. So what do you say?"

"To what? Joining forces?" I laughed.

"Moving in with me."

I laughed harder at that. Oh, if Steve had been in the room to hear that, he probably would have torn William to pieces. "You want me to move in with you? Oh, but William, what about Steve? I don't think he'll be interested in threesomes."

"Very funny," he murmured, but a smile crossed his lips. "My home is quite large. You could have your own room, plus group protection." He leaned across the table, his fingers twitching toward mine. I lowered my hands into my lap.

"I don't need protection."

"Don't you?" He sat back and held up his fingers, counting off. "Let me see, you've been attacked by a necromancer once, twice now, your home and shop broken into by these mysterious women, but you don't need protection."

"No, I need to keep people away." I stood up, shoving my chair backward noisily.

"That necromancer isn't going away." William slowly stood up and walked away, but not toward the front door. Instead, he moved toward the stack of recovered books that were still sitting on the entryway counter where Steve had left them. "Have you looked in here for answers?" he asked, picking up one of my books.

"Haven't really had a chance," I retorted, snatching the book from his hands and slamming it back down on the counter.

"You should probably figure out why he's after you, before someone else decides to do their own digging."

"Someone like you?"

"Come on, Gia, did you really think I wasn't already looking into you?" I shook my head, and he smiled in response. "That's what I thought. No, I was referring to our illustrious police department. You've made them very curious. They haven't connected the dots about this last attack being all because of you... yet."

"I don't like games, William."

"This isn't a game. I just want to help you. Even if you don't want to move into my home, the offer still stands. I have a room for you. Come visit me, at least. Let me help you, and in turn, I hope you'll help me. This could be a great partnership."

"I'm not looking for a partner, and I don't need your help. Stay out of my business."

"You'll change your mind."

I sighed and moved toward the door. William took the hint and followed me, but he didn't give up. "Let me propose something else."

"What?"

"The truth is I need your help. It chagrins me to ask, but I let my people down. They look to me for guidance and protection." I didn't believe half of what he said, but this had the ring of truth. He didn't like being vulnerable any more than I did.

"I can help you ward your home, if that's what you need."

"I would appreciate your expertise, and thank you for the offer, but I need your personal assistance."

"With what?"

He rubbed his hand, where black lines still crisscrossed his skin jaggedly. I reached up to touch the necromancer's mark on my chest. It hadn't faded like last time and gleamed just as black and angry as the marks on William's hand. "We're sitting ducks," he said. "Both of us. As long as these marks remain. Some of my coven have them as well."

"Only some of them?"

"As far as I can tell, just the last ones he released have them. No one else."

"So he sent them back on purpose. Marked so he can trigger them, or us, and get inside our defenses."

"That's my thought."

"And let me guess, they're all living in your home?"

He winced as though I'd hurt him but he nodded, running a hand across his goatee. "They're in a separate wing, but yes." He had wings to his house? How big was this place?

"Fine, I'll look through my books and see what I can find on necromancers. We can work together to get rid of these marks. For now, I suggest a really strong shield, and some extra warding of your separate wing." I smiled and eyed his shield, which looked like a haze of green light to my eyes. "You'll need more than earth magic to fight him off."

"I don't do blood magic, if that's what you're suggesting."

Why did people always jump to that conclusion? Perhaps because it was easy and powerful. "No, I meant use the other elements. Earth is easy because it is with us always, but water is strong as well, and fairly easy to tap into. Wind can be tricky, but doable if you channel it properly. And fire, well, that's just dangerous. Earth and water should be enough."

He stared at me as though I'd just sprouted snakes for hair, and I felt the nervous desire to pat my head down. That was silly, though. "Use the other elements for a shield? You know how to do that?"

I shrugged. "Don't you? It's not just for doing locater spells, you know. They're more difficult, and I'll admit they can take prep work, but they have their uses. Such as a much stronger shield."

"I can't see your shield."

"Of course not. I don't want you to."

"Show me."

I shrugged and let my shield be visible. It was the same shield I always used, earth and water swirling together in perfect harmony. I just didn't let others see it. He stared at me for the blink of an eye before changing his shield. It glowed from green to a dark purple.

"Earth and fire?" I frowned, realizing he'd played me. He knew exactly how to use other elements.

"I don't usually let people see my true shield either. I like the earth and water mix, though. It's nice. I just prefer fire."

"That's volatile."

"Easier to return an attack that way." He frowned at me. "You don't like fire, do you?"

"Not particularly. I've seen the destruction it causes and it is difficult to contain. Especially around books."

He laughed and diminished his shield again, letting it appear to be nothing more than a simple shield. "I'll keep that in mind. Not many witches or warlocks know how to use anything other than one element at a time."

"You do."

"I'm not exactly a warlock," he said, and I frowned, feeling an echo of my own words. "Of course, you're not exactly a witch, either."

"What do you mean, you're not exactly a warlock?"

"You tell me and I'll tell you."

"Not happening," I replied, opening the door.

"I guess that's my cue to leave." He stepped into the doorway, but held still, one hand on the frame. "So, you'll come over?"

"I'm not staying, William."

"Fine, for now. How about 8 o'clock tonight? I don't want to be used as a necromancer puppet. We should move quickly on this."

"Not tonight, William."

"Some things should take priority over your dating life."

"I'm not blowing off my boyfriend to do research. Let's meet on Monday."

"Boyfriend? Wow, that is serious. Does that mean you're exclusive now?"

"I suppose so," I replied softly.

He cocked an eyebrow and leaned forward until our lips were inches away, his breath warm on my face. "Are you sure?" he breathed out, his eyes locked on my mouth. I held still as his lips brushed against mine, finding it difficult not to kiss him back. So much for self control. The kiss was soft and gentle, but it stole my breath away. I snaked my arm around his neck, pulling myself closer as the kiss deepened. It was over too quickly and I found myself gasping for breath. He leaned back and looked at me, his steely gray eyes shining with mirth and self-satisfaction,

"Monday night. I'll send you my address." He walked away before I could get in another word.

I closed the door and turned back to my stack of books, rifling through them quickly. They were all accounted for, but I had to make sure they were intact. I carried them in two trips to the couch and did a quick inventory of their contents. The last twenty pages were missing in one book. The rest were as they should be, but the missing pages angered me. It wasn't just the fact that they'd defiled my books, which was enough to have me seeing red, but that now I was missing potentially vital information. The book wasn't something I knew front and back. It was an old Gaelic book, written in an almost illegible hand on brittle paper. I pulled out a pen and paper, transposing the last page before the missing section into English. The text spoke of an ancient magic and a gathering. It cut off before saying what sort of gathering. A gathering of people, of ingredients, of magic? All of the above? At the edge of the binding at the back of the book were words written in English in a much different hand.

The eyes hold the power. Take the eyes and seize the power.

CONSULTANT

SEARCHING THROUGH MY STOLEN books didn't yield any more information. I needed the missing pages, which were either with the nameless necromancer or with Theda and Amy. Knowing Theda, they were with her. She wasn't very trusting to begin with. I decided to turn my search to the internet, but after two hours, that also yielded nothing. I was better at book research than people research. I used my last vial to perform a locater spell, but they were outside my map area. Now that I'd replenished more of my supplies, I could do advanced tracking spells that didn't require a map, but they did require a great deal of energy and time. And where would that get me? What was I going to do once I found them?

My phone rang and I picked it up without looking. "Hey, Gia, are we opening the store up tomorrow?"

"Oh, sorry Maggie, I should have called you earlier. It's been a crazy couple of days."

"That's alright. I spent a much needed day in with Mike."

"How is Mike? I was hoping to talk with him."

"They're out hunting now. Full moon and all, but they're fine. He said they chased the necromancer. Almost caught him, but he collapsed a tunnel on them. That's why they didn't return. They were trapped and trying to dig their way out. He said Detective Daniels found them and got them out."

My gate alarm chimed and I glanced at the police car on the monitor before opening it. "I'm glad they were all okay."

"Me too," she said softly. "So, about tomorrow?"

"Take the day off. Actually, I think I'm going to close up for the remainder of the week. There are some more pressing concerns right now."

"Yeah, I thought that might be the case. William Dervish stopped by here earlier. He invited me to join him."

I stopped flipping through the book in my hand and turned my full concentration on Maggie. "He came to your house?" I couldn't help but chuckle. "What, does he want you to move into his house too? That man is unreal."

"Um, he brought that up but said he couldn't invite a werewolf in and figured I'd say no. What I meant is, he invited me to join his coven."

I was silent for several moments, unsure what I thought of this announcement. I had never intended to train Maggie as a full witch, but that certainly seemed to be where this was going. "Oh."

"Should I?"

"Should you what?"

"Join his coven? He said he could set up more teachers to help me in my training. I could still work, and he'd send different tutors to come work with me. He even suggested coming to the shop personally to work on my training, if you allowed that, of course."

"What did Mike say?"

She laughed suddenly and I walked to the door as someone knocked. "He told me to ask your advice. He said if you trusted William, then he would too, but that his gut said there was something off about the guy."

I stopped with my hand on the doorknob. "Mike wanted my advice?"

"Yeah."

"Well, I mean, you do what's best for you, Maggie."

"I knew you'd say that." She laughed again and I opened the door, surprised to see Steve standing outside. I waved him in and walked back into the living room. "I already told him no. Mike's right. There's something off about the guy. I can't put my finger on it. Something with those weird gray eyes of his."

"Gray," I mused, running my hand over the torn book. "Gray, not blue?"

"No, definitely gray. Is it weird that I think his eyes look more gray now than they did a few days ago? Well, no matter what color his eyes are, they practically scream suspicion."

"I think you're right to trust your gut."

"Thanks, Gia. I hope this means you'll still work with me. Teach me, I mean."

"Of course," I replied, feeling the need to add more. "Please understand though, that I'm not a witch. You probably would learn more with William's coven, if that's what you wished."

"If you're willing to teach me, then I have no desire to go anywhere else." I smiled at her words, feeling a swelling of something... pride, perhaps. "Okay, I'll see you on Monday?"

"Yes, Monday sounds good."

"Great! Say hi to Steve. Bye!"

She hung up before I could question her remark. I turned toward Steve, who had stood silently in the entryway through my conversation with Maggie. Now, he looked far too serious. I moved into the living room I used as a library and sat down, waiting for the bad news. "Why do I get the feeling this isn't a social call?" I asked.

"I'm here on official police business," Steve said, pulling out a paper and holding it in front of himself. I felt my chest tighten as he stared down at the words on the paper. "We'd like to officially offer you a job as the County Witch."

"County Witch?" I asked, frowning. "What does that mean?"

Steve grinned and shrugged his shoulders. "Hunter said you'd hate that name."

"Well, for starters, I'm not a witch," I replied, folding my arms.

"The title can be changed," he said, crossing his arms and setting the paper down on the end table. "We can call you a magic-user if you like, or whatever you want. The title doesn't matter."

"This isn't a game, and I don't like that title either."

"Consultant?" he urged.

"Don't you already have William on your payroll?"

Steve's eyes darkened and he shook his head, moving to sit next to me. "No, not exactly. We've called him in the past because he's a local and has been around here for quite a few years. He's never had any official status with the department though."

I stopped, thinking about his words. "What exactly are you asking of me?"

"You know some of the big police departments already have witches or psychics on staff, but there's nothing in the area. Nothing for miles, actually. The chief is afraid."

"Afraid? Afraid of what?"

"That you'll join another department, move away, or..." Steve mumbled something unintelligible while taking my hands in his.

"That's not it," I said as I looked down at our hands. "He's afraid of me, isn't he?"

He shrugged, but kept his eyes down as he intertwined our fingers. "It's not like that. The chief doesn't like many people. This is big for him, and for this department."

"Steve, let's be honest here." I pressed.

"He wants you where we can keep an eye on you."

"Figured."

"But you get paid."

I didn't need the money, but I couldn't very well say that. "Paid well, I hope?" He nodded and handed me a check. Very well indeed. "That's for the most recent assistance. If you help bring down this necromancer, you'll be paid even better."

"Who's funding this?" I asked, setting the check on top of the paperwork. "Your department doesn't have this kind of money."

"When I said County Witch, I really mean multi-counties. This is a joint effort, among the local counties and cities."

"So if I agree to help, I'll be working with other cities potentially? Other cops?"

He shook his head. "Yes, and no. You'll work with other cops, but Hunter and I are your contacts. Everything funnels through us first. We bring you the cases, we organize interactions with other departments, stuff like that. You decide when and how you help."

"Your boss really wants to keep an eye on me," I murmured.

Steve sighed loudly and pulled my hands to his lips. "Please, think about this. It's a good thing, and the money will be great. And if you can't help us with something, that's fine. You just say no. All contract type work."

"You're guaranteeing a lot of money," I added, pursing my lips. "Where did this extra money come from, even if all the offices pool their money together?

"Anonymous donor who is a worried citizen asking us to squash the bad supernatural element."

"What's that supposed to mean?"

He shrugged. "That's all my chief said. Anonymous, but it's a well-funded grant, with a large budget guaranteed for a minimum of ten years."

"It's William Dervish, isn't it?"

"Anonymous," he repeated again. " I honestly don't know, but it doesn't matter where the funding came from, it continues no matter who is hired. You're just at the top of our list."

"I have a business."

"With an employee. Plus, this is freelance. And with this kind of money, you could always hire another employee to help run your business."

"Why do you want me so bad?"

Steve stiffened at my words and for the first time I realized Steve truly was just the messenger. Did he realize he was being used? "The boss is insistent, and our list currently consists of you and only you."

"I'll need to think about this more."

"Sure, just as long as you say yes. It's contract work. You come in when you can, help us with cases that you can, and go about your own business the rest of the time. It's a good deal." I looked at Steve, who just grinned. "It means we work together more often, and the department pays for you to make some more of that special protection potion."

"This check wouldn't even cover one batch," I said. "But, I'm sure we could work something out for emergencies."

"So, you'll do it?" he asked, his smile wide.

"How about a trial run?"

"Sound like a great idea," he said too quickly.

"No contract, Steve. I won't sign anything."

He hunkered slightly, but nodded his head. "Okay, we can work with that."

"Consultant," I said slowly. "And I say what I help with, and when. And if I need to, I bring in other help."

"Those details can be worked out later."

"Those details will be agreed upon, or I don't do anything." He sighed, but nodded his head. "Fine, we'll try this out."

"Yes!" Steve hugged me in excitement. "This will be great," he whispered in my ear between kisses.

"Sure," I replied, wondering what I'd just gotten myself into.

"Hey, don't be like that," Steve said, his hands wrapped tight around my waist.

I smiled and leaned into him. "I know, it's just..."

"You're worried. Hey, we all are. That necromancer is bad news, but we'll take care of him, and anything else that comes along. This will be good, I promise."

"We?"

"Yeah, we're a team."

A team. That word took on a new meaning in my life when I thought of who my team was. Of course it meant Steve, and now the rest of the police force, but it also meant Maggie. With Maggie came Mike, and the werewolves, who for some reason I couldn't fathom, trusted me. And there was William. In a way, we were part of a team too. Despite the dangers ahead, I felt a genuine smile come to my lips. I had a team of people, some of whom seemed to actually trust me.

"Hey, there's my girl," he said, kissing my cheek.

"Sure, it'll be good."

"Hey, it's not every day you get to go to work with your extremely sexy boyfriend."

I laughed, like he knew I would. "Boyfriend," I murmured.

"I'm all yours." He kissed me, but it was brief and chaste. "Well, let's go."

"Go? Where am I going?"

"Well, we sort of need your help with something."

"Already? Not the necromancer."

Steve shook his head and stood up, pulling me to my feet. "Missing persons case," he replied. "Several, in fact."

"Several? As in, you think they're related? Isn't that an FBI type of thing?"

"It's an unofficial stance." Steve blew out a breath, stepped away and straightened his back. The boyfriend was gone, replaced by the police detective in a matter of seconds. "I don't have a lot of details on the case. It's Hunter's thing."

"Locals?" I asked.

"A little girl," Steve said. "She's been missing about six months now. We thought it was the step-dad, but it's not looking that way anymore." "Why's that?" I asked.

"There's been another one. This time it's a little boy only about three years old. The story is exactly the same. They put him to bed and at midnight they heard a noise that woke them up. Mom went to check and found the bedroom door open, kid missing."

"And the little girl was the same?"

"Exactly," he said. "Same time, window open, and something was left behind."

"What?"

"A drop of blood in the middle of the window."

"The child's blood?"

He looked down at his shoes and shook his head. "It's unknown."

"Unknown? What do you mean?"

"The child's blood is there, for sure, but it's been contaminated. There are trace elements of something else in both cases. It's the only link between the cases."

"Why do I get the feeling there's more to this?"

"Like I said before, it's Hunter's case. He can explain more."

"Steve," I urged.

"There are more cases, potentially."

"Potentially? What does that mean?"

"There are some similarities to an old cold case."

"How old?"

"Ten years," he said, shrugging again, but he kept his eyes downcast.

"And?"

"Will you come along and help?"

"If you tell me what's going on, I might."

He looked up suddenly, a frown on his face. "There isn't enough information to really put the pieces together. It's too circumstantial and we don't have a lot of info on the older case. They chalked it up to corrupted labs. That's why we need you. Hunter thinks... well, it's just odd."

"What exactly does Hunter think?"

"He thinks it's something not human."

"Such as?"

"I don't know," he said, letting out a sigh.

"You don't agree."

"Hunter likes the supernatural a little too much. I think he's trying to make a case that isn't there. A drop of blood is just a drop of blood. It doesn't mean it was staged."

"Fine," I said, grabbing my purse from the counter.

"You'll check it out?""I said I'd agree to a trial run."

"It's probably nothing," he said.

"Children are missing. If I can help bring them home, then I will."

"The outcome—" he began, but I cut him off.

"No, please don't. I don't need statistics. I'll help, and I will find these children."

"Gia, you need to—"

"What? Prepare myself for the inevitable? We have to have hope for something in this world, or else what is the point? You can't give up."

I stalked out the door with Steve on my heels, slamming the doors closed behind me with a flick of my wrist. Steve raced to catch up, guiding me into the passenger seat of his car and leaning over to buckle my seatbelt for me. He stopped, staring at me as though he could see through my sunglasses. Without a word, he leaned forward and kissed me, this time taking extra time and effort to leave me gasping for breath. When he pulled away, both of us were flushed and breathing hard.

"What was that for?" I asked after he'd started the car and backed us out onto the road.

He grinned, his usual excitement returning. "I think it's just hitting me how great working with my super hot, sexy, and downright amazing girlfriend is going to be. I know this sounds corny, but you bring out the best in me. I think you're making me a better cop."

I plastered a smile on my face as he drove us to the police station, my heart heavy with dark thoughts.

To be continued in *Gorgon Kisses*, book two of the *Medusa Memoirs*.

Police consultant, on a trial basis. Gia isn't sure why she agreed to such a thing. It might have something to do with her sexy new boyfriend, Steve, the police detective who talked her into it. Or, it might have something to do with the missing children.

Two children abducted months apart, with nothing else to link them except a drop of blood and a couple of insistent detectives. Gia isn't a psychic, but she does possess magic and knowledge, something the police detectives are hoping will help. A quick visit to the homes of the missing children is all Gia needs to know this is out of her league.

Demons were not in the Gorgon handbook, but with the help of the local Warlock, William, they might have a chance to find answers. As an unnatural darkness covers the homes of the missing children, extending to the surrounding communities, the danger of the situation grows. Finding the missing children might be the key to stopping a demon invasion, or it might be an elaborate trap.

Magic and lies converge in the second installment of the *Medusa Memoirs* series.

www.laurahysell.com

For more updates, sneak peeks, and exclusives, subscribe to Laura Hysell's newsletter.

About the Author

Laura Hysell is a USA Today bestselling author. She writes dark urban fantasy and paranormal romance, with heavy doses of sarcastic humor throughout. She lives in the beautiful Pacific Northwest of Oregon, less than two hours from beach, mountain, desert, or city. It's been said that the key to her heart is coffee, but she's also easily won over by chocolate and books. When she's not reading or writing, she is frequently at the beach, camping at a lake, or otherwise enjoying the great outdoors.

To hear about her latest misadventures and other sarcastic ramblings, in addition to book updates and freebie short stories, be sure to join her newsletter at https://www.subscribepage.com/BB.

www.laurahysell.com.

Also by Laura Hysell

Medusa Memoirs Series

Gorgon Curses

Gorgon Kisses

Gorgon Darkness

Isabella Howerton Series:

Bloody Beginnings

Bloody Consequences

Bloody Defiance

Bloody Endings

Made in the USA
Las Vegas, NV
03 December 2021